# The Blue K.

# The Blue King

FG Laval

ISBN-13: 9798805311933

Cover by Adam Laval

# DEDICATION

for Mum and Dad

# PROLOGUE

## *The Wedding*

My mother used to say to me, 'Nerys… appearances can be deceiving, and that is the greatest tool a queen can have in her armoury.' Since arriving in Tordre, the truth of that statement will forever haunt my life.

Something was wrong at Castle Ryemont.

My skin prickled the moment I crossed the threshold, where I caught my first glimpse of the king, albeit briefly before his attendants hurried him along. He seemed taller than in the portrait mother had shown me, and much younger.

King Morra Dreiden looked up the moment I passed by and caught my eye. We shared a brief moment of mutual understanding as our gazes locked. His steely grey eyes made me catch my breath before he looked away. His silvery-fair hair was tied loosely back to reveal a slender, taut neck and alabaster skin.

Anxious thoughts stormed around my mind.

What if we don't get on? What if he doesn't like me?

We had locked eyes for only seconds yet silently appraised one another. The disappointment when he looked away surprised me. Then I remembered it was deemed unlucky for the king to see his future consort before the ceremony. Did he give as little thought to superstitions as me? Perhaps he too, was feeling apprehensive. He had only others' accounts of what the Carentan princess was like.

He was no doubt thinking, *what if we don't get on? What if she doesn't like me?*

The attention generated on my journey through the capital city of T'sar towards the castle was astounding. I had hoped to have a tour of the Kingdom of Tordre before the ceremony, but because of the travel arrangements, mother had thought it best to arrive fresh from the Carentan border, and then to accept a formal tour with the king another day.

But the people had come out in celebration to see me arrive. There were musicians and jugglers in the street, and everyone was dressed in bright clothes, waving flags with both the Tordre and Carentan standards flying alongside each other.

I realised the magnitude of this alliance and, despite my creeping unease, I could claw back some of the dignity and royal duty I had been raised to embrace. It was the beginning of a new era for our two nations.

Despite wanting to ride my pony, mother had insisted that I was carried in a litter, which they had opened upon arrival so I could wave and smile at the onlookers. It was all a bit regal and imperious for my liking, and I hoped the king would not see me arrive like that.

The people of Tordre were friendly and reverent. They spoke a mixture of languages, both their native Langan and Etanese; the common tongue of most southern countries in the Western Isles. Fortunately for me, my lessons in Langan before I arrived meant I could understand their words and phrases.

Touched by the display of regard from the Tordreans and their joyous enthusiasm, my spirits were lifted.

The maids fussed with my appearance as I sat in the royal chambers at King Morra's castle. I had spent the last few moons moping over the misplaced love of a deceitful boy and I was angry and embarrassed, but there was an emptiness gnawing away inside me. If only I had believed my sister, Alliane, when she first came running with news of his deceit. We had argued, and I accused her of being jealous and spiteful and trying to ruin my happiness. Alliane had accused me, quite rightly, of being stupid and gullible.

Now I felt so alone. Alone and stupid. I had wanted to bring Alliane with me to T'sar, but mother would not allow it. My family were to travel separately to attend the ceremony, so I was there alone, but for my attendants, to face my future as the Queen of Tordre.

I looked at my reflection in the mirror; the maids had done well. My dark hair curled down my back, intertwined with sparkling jewels that looked like the reflections of a million lights on the surface of a lake. I had a delicate nose and petite face that was framed by a few curls, giving me a more sophisticated look, and they had brushed my cheeks with pink blush. My gown was sky blue silk, encrusted with silvery sequins, which hugged my slim figure. A white lacy veil topped the outfit, to hide my face until the moment I was to be revealed to the king.

There was a loud rap on the chamber door, which made me jump. The attendant took a note from the messenger and returned to my side, unfolding the parchment.

'The Royal family of Andolin has arrived,' she said, in what I thought was probably her best spoken Etanese. 'They are settling now in the guest's quarters to prepare for the ceremony.'

'Thank you.' A little corner of my loneliness lifted. I stood up and drifted to the window, then looked out over a courtyard of frantic activity. There was something odd about the way people were moving to-and-fro, with a desperation that belied such a momentous occasion. Something was amiss. In a panic, I ran to the door and was face-to-face with a young maid I had not seen before.

'You're not one of my entourage,' I said.

'Your Highness,' she said with a curtsy. 'My name is Lana, and I have been assigned to you as your personal maid.'

'But… where is…? Oh never mind, what about my family,' I said, 'is everything all right? I was told they had arrived safely.'

'All is fine, your Highness. Please…' Lana gestured for me to sit back down. 'It is a minor issue with the supplies for the feast. Please do not concern yourself.' Lana had her head bowed down, but there was a flush of red spreading across her cheeks. It was the same giveaway that Alliane displayed when she was lying.

The ceremony was a lavish affair with gifts of gold and ermine presented to us. We took our vows outside, on the largest parapet in the castle, overlooking crowds of people from across the land, some of whom had travelled for days and camped outside the castle gates until being allowed into the sanctity of the inner keep to bear witness to this historic occasion.

I took centre stage in my long and flowing gown. My veil, now lifted, revealed a pure gold tiara, with jewels to match around my neck. The king wore a modest tunic of gold and blue, offset by an elaborate sash across his chest. I could just see a baldric of knives peering out from beneath the sash. It bothered me that the king might feel the need to wear weapons to his wedding, but he also had a sword strapped to his side, as was tradition with royalty. His hair was swept back, giving him a rather austere look, and he avoided eye contact throughout the repetition of our vows.

There was something different about him, but I couldn't quite identify what it was. Perhaps my nerves were playing tricks on me. Afterward, when he leant in to kiss me, it was with none of the promise that I had read in his gaze when we had accidentally crossed paths earlier.

Courtiers and castle dignitaries crowded the parapet, with my family accorded pride of place to watch the event. The crowds below in the courtyard went wild when the king made a big show of taking my hand and placing a golden ring on my finger, turning me after to face the people and wave whilst jugglers, acrobats and singers flitted amongst the crowd, adding to the festivities.

I felt strangely alone, standing up there next to this man who was cold and refused to meet my eye. As soon as it seemed appropriate, I looked around for some familiar faces, but everyone was chattering away in Langan. There was a flash of red, which I thought might be Alliane, but it disappeared into the crowd and an assertive hand turned me back towards the onlookers and I could do nothing more than follow the king's lead to wave, smile, and attempt to look content.

For the first time, I noticed an inordinate number of priests milling about in the crowd and rather thought they should have been part of the ceremony, but then dismissed the thought, remembering that Tordreans were not an ecclesiastical nation.

I tried to keep my head forward, but with surreptitious side glances at my new husband. He was looking ahead, into the crowds, eyes darting to-and-fro as though looking for something or tracking movement in the crowds. He sensed my scrutiny and turned, blasting me with an icy gaze.

'Perhaps your Majesty would like to be seated before the feast gets underway?' he said.

'Oh.' I would have to get used to that title. 'May I see my family first?'

The king smiled thinly. 'They too will sit at the royal table.' He placed a palm on the small of my back, applying enough pressure to encourage me off the parapet and towards the great hall.

My family was already sitting when we arrived, but at the opposite end of the table and I was spirited past them, given only enough time to acknowledge their presence with a quick curtsy to my mother and sisters.

My brother, Gereinte; the Crown Prince of Carentan was away on a journey and would not be present. Perhaps it was Gereinte's absence that made this whole affair seem so wrong, like something fundamental was missing.

I trailed a hand behind Alliane's chair and caught the touch of her fingertips, giving me a brief surge of warmth and confidence. I gave Alliane a nervous smile before being seated at the head of the table next to the king.

The feast was an indulgent spread, with several hog roasts that filled the room with the scent of crackling pork, dishes loaded with paprika spiced orange roots, and grain of every variety peppered with parsley and thyme. I couldn't believe there was ever a problem with the supplies. There were platters layered with little square glutinous sweet cakes that would normally have sent my taste buds into a spin, but somehow everything turned to ash in my mouth.

The celebrations wore on well into the night, before I was finally so exhausted that I could barely keep my eyes open. My mother and sisters had long since taken their leave and had to be up at some ungodly hour to begin their journey back to Carentan. I had begged Mother to stay longer, but the political unrest in Carentan could not afford to be ignored for even a day, much less the several days it had taken them to get here and return.

Most of the people had gone home, except a few drunken stragglers hanging about the courtyards who the castle guards duly ushered away. Some of the hardier courtiers were still drinking and dancing, which would likely go on until they either dropped where they stood or were carried away to their rooms by the castle staff.

Upon reaching the royal suites, the maids bustled me inside, undressed and re-dressed me in silk shifts, befit for a queen on her wedding night. I had almost forgotten the most important part of the ceremony; the consummation. Sitting on the edge of the large four-poster bed, my stomach griped and my heart hammered.

A bowl of incense sat on the dressing table, and emitted thin plumes of a bitter spiced scent unfamiliar to me, but somehow seemed to calm my nerves. I awaited my king and the inevitable liaison that was to be my duty as wife and queen.

# CHAPTER ONE

## *Six Moons Later*

I woke amid a feverish mind-fog, sat up and blinked away a film of sleep from my eyes. The castle was quiet, dark. The depth of night sat in contemplation of daylight hours, mocking my fitful dream-state. Despite the night chill, my shift was damp from the heat of my body, and clung to my skin like tendrils of seaweed.

For a moment I forgot where I was, but then the distant scent of salty sea air brought it all back to me.

Tordre.

I was in Tordre. Thousands of leagues south west from my family home of Castle Helmstedt in Carentan. Then the memory of what happened came crashing back to me. I choked back a sob, but it was a feeble attempt to stem the flow of tears.

It had started not long after the wedding. First the dreams, then the night-sweats, followed by cries piercing the still of night. In the early days the king would wake and try to console me, but after a while he gave me my own room, while my attendants slept in an adjoining chamber, ever attentive to their queen. I shed silent tears, not wanting to attract their attention, knowing that every day the king would expect their report.

I had to get myself together, it was my duty.

As a princess of Carentan, I had always dreamed of becoming a queen and leading a nation alongside my king. Now that I was here, why did it all feel so wrong?

The people of Tordre called him the Blue King. There was a deep-rooted sadness about him; a melancholy that must stem from a life devoted to his country. A life in which he was only ever destined to be king. That can be lonely. Goodness knows I understood that. But then I thought of my brother, Gereinte. He survived several assassination attempts, the death of our father and then our baby brother, yet still he made me smile.

Indeed, this king was blue, for my king had no face.

Such was the nightmare that had haunted my dreams from the day we'd wed. I'll admit, I was terrified. First night alone, to share the bed with a foreign man; a stranger. Who wouldn't be? I was only sixteen. Six moons on, that night still terrified me, so much so that I was minded to believe that I really had dreamt it all.

There I was, my insides twisted in angst, waiting for my newlywed husband to join the marital bed when I heard voices that appeared to come from the walls. Curiosity overcame my nerves, and I swung my legs over the side of the bed, parting the ridiculous layers of silken shifts that the ladies had dressed me in, and tiptoed onto the floor. The wooden boards hummed with a voice of their own, making my feet tingle.

It was dark outside, and the ceremony was long since over. Guests had returned to their rooms or to their own humble abodes. Moonlight cast enough of a hue for me to see the outline of the chamber walls. I was not usually given to impatience, but to be left waiting in such a state of uncertainty was too much to bear.

I pressed my hands to the gnarled stone surface of the wall, finding little crevices to rest my fingertips. The wall rumbled with its own tune, as though the voices I had heard were locked inside the very fabric of the castle.

With one ear to the wall, and fingertips tingling in anticipation, I heard a faint chanting. The repetition of words in a distinct language, muttered like a prayer to the many gods we celebrated in Carentan. Odd, as I understood the Tordreans were a secular race, not inclined towards reverence either to the priesthood or any higher authority, for that matter.

I had heard about castles in the south that had been reduced to rubble by rumblings of the earth. My imagination hooked its claws into my mind and the vision of being buried alive in that bedchamber sent me spiralling into a panic. I threw open the chamber door, crossing the antechamber to reach the corridor. One of my maids appeared bleary-eyed from the adjoining room.

'Your Majesty... my queen. You cannot leave...' her voice trailed off as though she could not find the correct words in Etanese to explain, and I sped off down the corridor without a care to wonder if she followed. It became clear within moments that she had alerted others. The pitter-patter of distant feet and a faint clash of armour carried down the corridor behind, as my attendants and guards hurried after me.

12

Driven by a claustrophobic panic, I hoped to dodge the castle guards who would only try to send me back to my room. It was as though the building was alive, the walls and floors groaning with the weight of its history, and yet no one was there to bear witness. Other than me. Perhaps I was the only one who felt it.

I rounded a corner and leapt back when I saw the guards patrolling. Perhaps there was another way around. I doubled back and found a small circular stairway with stone steps that led down. I hid for a moment, crouched down, hugging the cold stone balustrade as it hummed beneath my fingertips. The muttering voices of the guards grew louder and more guttural as they passed by, then faded into the distance.

I let out a slow breath and sat there long enough for it to become apparent that the castle was not about to fall into a pile of rubble. But going back would mean running into the guards and attendants following me. My irresistible curiosity made me follow the spiral staircase down towards the very source of the thing that had frightened me.

My slipper-shod feet skated over the steps as they narrowed towards an open door, from which cast a thick wedge of light onto the base of the stairway. A steady crescendo of chanting drew me towards the room beyond, where a figure stood in the middle of an ornate chapel at an altar adorned with a lattice-weave of laurel leaves that symbolised worship of the one god.

I knew before he turned it was Morra Dreiden, the Blue King. My Blue King.

What I wasn't prepared for was the absence of his face. A flat empty stretch of skin, which undulated where his face should have been, and glowed with a faint ripple of disquiet. I gasped and clasped my hands to my mouth. His head turned back to the altar, as though he realised his mistake. The chanting came to a sudden halt. His hands covered his face as though smoothing over a mask, then he turned back and stared at me through Morra Dreiden's eyes.

I screamed. I couldn't help myself. I turned and ran from the chapel. Climbing the steps two or three at a time, I didn't stop running until I found my way back to the sleep chamber, closely followed by the clatter of my attendants as they finally caught up with me.

My maid was flapping around me, speaking too fast for my mind to catch up with her words, so I pushed past her and slammed the chamber door shut behind me. I gasped at the exertion and scrambled into the bed, before burying myself as deeply as possible beneath the covers, hoping beyond reason I would wake up from a dream.

Later that night, the door creaked open and the soft pad of bare feet roused me from a fitful sleep. The king lay beside me, and uncurled the blankets enough to reveal my face. I must have looked like a frightened rabbit staring into the eyes of a fox as I lay there looking back at his beautiful pale face in the light of the moon. He smiled and kept a respectful distance.

'I heard you scream,' he said, brow knitted with concern. 'Was it a bad dream?' I stared back at him, wondering not for the first time if I had in fact dreamt the entire episode in the chapel. I decided to play safe. It would not do for a rumour to escape about the mad Queen of Tordre.

'I… sometimes have nightmares.'

'It has been a difficult time for you, I know. But the past is now behind you, and we can move on together.' He reached out, and I flinched away from his touch. 'Shhh… you are safe now.' He stroked a long pale finger in a line from my temple to my cheek. My body shivered in response and, to my unconscionable relief, he left me to my night fears. Our marriage was unconsummated.

That was my first night as the Queen of Tordre. That night, and every night since, my Blue King had sought me out, laying soft hands across my brow as though seeking to draw an illness from my body, but never lying beside me. In time, but always in the light of day, I tried to find my way back to the chapel. Just to see. When I looked for the spiral staircase, all I found was a flat grey floor covered in rushes. As I sat there in the deep of night, six moons on, I clung to a strange combination of fear and comfort.

# CHAPTER TWO

## *The Coastal Road*

'Nerys.'

I swung around, turning away from the window and the sight of gloomy skies hovering above Castle Ryemont. I don't know what shocked me more, that the king had addressed me by my given name or the familiar tone of voice he used. Amusement crinkled the lines in the corners of his eyes.

Lana had dressed me in a long woollen gown, threaded with pale blue beads that off-set the light grey of the wool. My hair ran in a long dark stream down my back, held away from my face by a beaded net that matched the gown. The king's eyes travelled up and down with silent appraisal, then came to rest on my eyes. I was flattered, in an uncomfortable way.

Meeting the king's eyes made my skin itch, so I had become accustomed to looking at his nose. It meant that I could appear to look him in the eye without having to meet that piercing grey gaze. He had a regal nose, if such a thing existed.

The Tordreans, being independently minded and egalitarian, had developed some unusual rules in relation to succession. Direct descendants of the current ruling monarch would not automatically be crowned, but would undergo a series of votes and acclamations alongside a pool of eligible aristocrats.

In some ways I should be thankful, as this relieved me of some of the urgency to reproduce, though the Tordreans were clamouring for a royal baby. I wasn't so sure about the king himself. As he stood there looking at me down his patrician's nose, he certainly showed no interest in producing an heir.

'Your Majesty,' I said with a deep curtsy that enabled me to break away from his searching gaze and stare at the floor.

'Lana tells me you have had several good nights in a row,' he said, putting his fingertips under my chin and lifting my face. I swallowed the lump in my throat and focused on the bridge of his nose. 'And you can stop all that "your majesty" nonsense. We are alone here, and we are man and wife.' He paused and peered at me. 'Do I scare you that much that you can't meet my eyes?'

A warm flush crept over my cheeks.

He tilted his head to one side and raised an eyebrow, as though my reaction affirmed his suspicion. 'Well then, we shall have to do something about that.'

Before I contemplated what that might mean, Morra Dreiden took my cheeks between his long pale fingers and raised my face to his. His eyes swam with a combination of desire and confusion. 'See, look. Nothing to fear here. What has it been now... six moons?' He moved his hands to my belly. 'And people are noticing how thin you look.'

My body went rigid at his touch. It was as though his words and tone blamed me for the lack of a child. 'Six moons isn't long, but we may not be able to play this out for much longer. I should tell you, I am about to turn around the current constitution to make my blood line the sole ascendants to the throne of Tordre.'

*What? Where did that come from?* I knew perfectly well what that would mean for a queen who did not produce heirs. I also knew what that would mean for the people of Tordre.

'That, amongst other things,' he said, leaving the 'other things' hanging in the air between us. Now I had an even bigger reason to speak to my family.

I tried the semblance of a smile; a weak attempt to warm him to my next request. He raised an eyebrow, as though he had already guessed what I had in mind.

'I would feel so much better if I could have a brief visit home to see my family.' I tried my sweetest smile. The one that had always worked on the Carentan boys; sons of lords who would eat from the palm of my hand like little baby birds, pecking hopefully at crumbs. I watched my words sink in and his eyes cloud over. He released my face with a disgusted push.

'We've had this conversation a hundred times.'

I shrank back. If I kept trying, perhaps one day he would soften and let me go.

'I miss them terribly. That is why I can't sleep at night; why I am so tired every day. I need to see my family.'

'No. It is not safe at the moment. There is a civil war brewing in Tordre, which will only worsen over time with the constitutional changes.'

And there it was, hanging in the air like rancid breath.

16

Civil war.

The whole point of this marriage was to avert war and unite two nations, and now it looked like Morra Dreiden was intent on starting one on home ground. Sometimes I wished I had spent more time with my sister, who I had always teased for playing at fighting games with the boys. I wished I had a modicum of her tactical combat skills.

The king turned away from me. His body was tense, and anger rippled beneath his skin. Give him his dues, he controlled it well, and when he turned back to look at me his expression was serene and calm. I think it was his unpredictability that scared me most. Sometimes when he looked away, then turned his head back, I braced myself for the man with no face. But that man had never again appeared since my first night in the castle.

He reached out and held my hands. His touch was gentle, but didn't feel real. 'Take a walk through the grounds. There is a superb view on the coastal road, and I am sure that I can find some of the king's guard to accompany you.'

'Thank you.' I smiled as reassuring a smile as I could manage. A walk through the grounds was better than nothing, even if the guards were to accompany me. Maybe that would be my strategy from then on. Ask for the entire Western Isles, and I might get a little piece of Tordre.

'In the meantime, write a letter home and I will ensure they deliver it post-haste.' His smile was a bit too disingenuous.

I had written letters before. Letters of angst and longing, letters beseeching my family to come and visit, and I believed either they did not get delivered at all, or someone rewrote them to describe a completely different experience I was having in Tordre. So I held no confidence in the king's assurance that they would receive my letters. My family would surely have responded.

The king left and Lana fussed around me, trying to persuade me to change into more appropriate attire for walking, but I couldn't summon the enthusiasm.

'Just bring me a shawl and I will be fine,' I said, sitting at the looking glass.

Lana stood behind me and coiled a woollen wrap around my shoulders. 'At least let me pin your hair up, your Majesty. The wind will ruin it otherwise,' she said. Her Etanese had become quite accomplished recently since the two of us had spent time poring over each other's language in an attempt to better communicate. Despite careful tutoring as a young girl, fluency in Langan only really came to me once immersed in the language and culture of Tordre.

I let her coil my hair into a ball and pin it up into a headdress. She had a point. It would not do to come back from my walk looking like a scarecrow queen. My eyes already had permanent dark shadows beneath them, making my face feel heavy and drained.

'Thank you,' I said, and Lana smiled back at me, giving a small curtsy. I wondered how much she really told the king in her daily reports.

In the early days after the wedding, I had tried to persuade the king and whoever would listen to let me keep my personal maid from Carentan, but she had been packed off soon after with the promise I could keep one or two of my attendants. One by one, they too had been summarily dismissed, and each time, a little piece of home went with them. I had no choice now but to rely on Lana.

I tried as much as I could to pretend that I was out on my own for a relaxed and private walk through the castle grounds. The two heavily armoured guards who trailed along behind me, however, were a constant reminder of the invisible shackles that tied me to my king.

'Take the coastal road,' he had said. And so, we left the castle grounds at the outer gate on the western side, and took a narrow path that before long opened out onto a wide track.

The track wound in an upward trajectory towards the black cliffs, which overlooked the western sea, with a sheer drop to it for anyone foolish enough to venture too close. From the sea, the cliffs looked monstrous, and loomed over the pebbled beaches like the eye of a storm. But they protected us from the devastating gales that lashed the western coast.

I shivered and pulled my shawl tighter around my shoulders, thankful that we were on the right side of those forbidding boulders. The salt air was refreshing to breathe, but made my skin and hair feel gritty and unclean.

I glanced back at the guards and doubted they had the same problem beneath their unforgiving metal plating. They bore the light blue and gold standard of Tordre on their chests and carried pikes that flew the king's standard high into the air for any unsuspecting travellers who didn't notice the import of their garb.

The fresh air and the wind were invigorating, and I was grateful at least for that. We veered away from the coast in order to take a lesser-trodden path back towards the castle grounds and were about to venture south alongside the estuary that led towards the capital city when a travelling man on horseback appeared on the path ahead of us, cantering in our direction. For the first time, I felt relieved to have the company of the guards at my back.

The man slowed his horse to a trot, and then a walk, acknowledging our presence. I kept myself tight to the left side of the path and the guards appeared to my right, acting as a barrier to any passing traffic. The rider sat in an upright position with his eyes focused ahead.

As we grew closer to a passing point in the track, he turned his gaze towards me, and there was nothing welcoming in the look on his face. We were almost side-by-side, so close I could see his dark eyes flit from the guards to me and back again. He was of middle age, a little grey at the roots of his mid-length dark hair, with a thin face and a calculating look about him. His garb was the robes of a priest of the one god, layers of grey linen tunic and leggings, belted at the waist by a long piece of frayed rope, peering out from beneath a long brown hooded cloak.

The air shimmered around him like ripples of heat, and sent a prescient tingle across my skin. Perhaps that was to put the fear of the one god into any who crossed his path. A strange way to convert followers, and completely at odds with the traditional worship of the many gods in Tordre and Carentan. An image of the Blue King in his chapel flashed across my mind, head turned with a cold, faceless stare. I gasped and the travelling priest turned his attention once again to me.

'My Lady,' he said, and reined in his horse to look down on me.

The guard nearest to his side lifted his pike to raise the king's standard and then slammed it into the ground between the man and me. The man started and inched his horse towards the guards to match the unspoken threat. A small smile twitched at the corners of his mouth.

'I beg your pardon, your Majesty,' he said, with a tiny bow of the head. 'I did not recognise you in such plain attire, and out for a walk indeed. Not what I would have expected to find on a windy Tordrean morning. Good day to you.' He tapped the flank of his horse with a heel and trotted off.

I pulled my shawl closer around my shoulders and looked at his departing figure. A few paces down the track and he turned to look over his shoulder at me.

'Yes, well. I thank you,' I said in a quiet voice that not even the guards would have heard. The man nudged his horse into a trot and disappeared up the track. His words had been courteous enough, but his manner left a sour taste in my mouth.

On my journey back to the outer circle of the castle grounds, I noticed a milestone marker, made of stone, and wondered if this was once a well-used route into T'sar. Bramble bushes lined the path and overflowed with fruit, making it difficult to pass without getting covered in berry juice. Wild pheasants strayed into the open spaces of green grass, which were interspersed between copses of short flat trees with huge long leaves.

Wooden fencing penned off sections of green space, which I supposed must belong to a local farm, though there was little evidence of such activity this far out, other than a hay-like animal scent in the wind.

I stopped in my tracks, the two guards a few seconds behind me. There was a stile at the end of the path. Oh Lord, how was I going to get over that in my skirts? A young man sat atop the stile, winding a piece of string around a small flat metal object.

# CHAPTER THREE

## *A Travelling Minstrel*

He had shoulder-length fair hair, swept back into a single plait, and a well-travelled look to him. A long flowing shirt with open cuffs revealed a string of beads around his wrist, and what looked like a leather plaited bracelet. His shirt was half-tucked in and half hanging out of his cropped trousers and ankle boots. A wine-red jerkin topped the outfit. I couldn't help shivering on his behalf, though the wind appeared not to bother him in the slightest.

He sat atop the stile winding a piece of string around a circular object, which had slivers of alternating red and blue stripes painted on its surface. He looked up and smiled at me and released the object from his hand in a flourish. The metal disk shot out of his hand and spun towards the ground. The colours moved so fast that they appeared to melt into a singular purple haze. Before the object hit the ground, it reversed its journey and spun back up its string to meet the man's waiting grasp. He looked up and raised an eyebrow as though waiting for applause.

'Da'ashtange Drei'ha!' he called, upon realisation that I was not about to give him a standing ovation.

The two guards dropped into a ready stance, moving forward to flank me on either side. The man looked over his shoulder to contemplate his escape route, then back at me with a worried expression.

'Good morning to you too,' I said in Etanese.

'Ah,' he looked me up and down with open scrutiny. 'You must be the queen.'

'Indeed,' I said. He had a cheeky glint in his eye that I warmed to but instantly distrusted. I once made the mistake of falling for a strange young man who nearly ruined my family's reputation, and I wasn't about to fall into the same trap twice. 'A little chilly to be sitting out today, is it not?' I looked up at the roiling clouds above and hugged my shawl tight around my shoulders.

The young man followed my gaze. 'Your very radiance will bring the sun to shine on us all.'

Whether he intended it to sound disingenuous I didn't know, but it was the kind of statement that held no weight and stank like the obsequious pandering I expected from a Carentan lordling, which I'd had a plethora of in my time. I stepped closer, and the guards made to follow, but I waved them back. They settled back and looked disgruntled, but they would get over it.

'Do I look like I care whether the sun shines? I am not some kind of goddess, just an ordinary girl in an ordinary dress, going for a walk on a blustery day.'

'I beg to differ on the ordinary front,' he said, with a casual tilt of his head. He had a saddlebag that looked as though it ought to belong to a horse, but I saw no such animal in sight. Propped up against his bag was a small lute with a carry strap.

'You seem well-spoken for a travelling man,' I said.

'I have travelled the length and breadth of the Western Isles, learnt the languages of many people, and tasted the bounty of many a table. Here,' he lifted his wrist, 'this is a bracelet made by a craftswoman in Dern and this,' he jangled the beads like charms, 'is made from gemstones mined in the foothills of the great Helm.' He waited for a reaction, and when he received none, continued to roll out his spiralling plaything, throwing and catching it in a hypnotic rhythm.

'So why are you sitting on a stile, miles from anywhere in Tordre?' I said. 'Because I would have thought that the city would be a far more interesting place to be; lots of people and taverns and markets, teeming with life. Why sit in a dull spot on a dull day with nothing to entertain you other than passing walkers on the coastal path?'

He stopped spinning his toy and stared at me with his mouth open. He clamped his lips around whatever words he wanted to say and gave me a calculated look.

'The city is lively indeed, but I come here to find the space to think and to retrace my steps.'

'To where?'

He frowned, and a look of vague confusion flitted across his face before disappearing into a hearty smile.

'Why, to the history and consequence of this great nation, of course. There is speculation aplenty in the city of T'sar about the new Queen of Tordre,' he said, as though that explained everything. 'And it is fortuitous that you have fallen across my path today, my brave queen.'

'Brave?' *Where did that come from?*

'Is it not brave to have travelled from a foreign land to marry a man you don't know, and be surrounded by foreign sounds, smells and sights?' he said, reading my thoughts.

I flinched and narrowed my eyes at him.

'You presume much for a travelling man. Why fortuitous?'

'Because,' he reached for his lute, 'I have composed a new song about the brave Queen of Tordre. Inspired by the stories crisscrossing every tavern in T'sar.' He settled his instrument against his chest as though cradling a babe in arms, then flicked the back of his fingernails across the strings in a lazy strum.

'Stories about me?' I couldn't hide the child-like curiosity in my voice, and he looked up with a measured gaze.

The lute was carved of wood and gleamed with a soft rosy polish. Its bowl tucked neatly against the young man's breastbone as he plucked the strings and fiddled with the tuning keys, then lifted his head to one side and dropped his ear to the instrument with concentrated focus. The sound was soft, yet hollow, as the notes were lost in the wind. He looked back at me and smiled a little nervously before plucking a series of notes. His voice resonated in short waves before disappearing into the air. He stopped, looked up at the clouds, and frowned, then, holding the lute by its neck, he swung it back and forth.

'It's no use in this weather. Maybe next time you are in town, you can find me at the Tower Tavern. I sometimes play, if the crowds will part with their coin for a poor travelling minstrel.'

'Maybe,' I said. Disappointment crushed my curiosity. He watched me as I turned to make my way back to the castle, guards in tow.

'Well, all right then,' I heard him say. 'But it doesn't sound as good out here. You don't get the same effect. As long as you understand that.'

A warm joy made my cheeks glow. 'Give the man some coin,' I said to the guards, who looked blankly at me. 'Dansche?' They rummaged around in their belt purses and, producing a single coin, tossed it at the young man's feet. *Oh well. Better than nothing, I suppose.*

'All songs are for you, my queen. No payment necessary.' He left the coin on the ground where it lay, and the guards made no move to reclaim it.

I shooed the guards back and sat down on the grass in anticipation. The young man hopped off the stile and sat opposite me. He warmed up his instrument with a few strums, and plucked his fingers in and out of the strings.

It always fascinated me to watch the court musicians and the intricate patterns they made with their instruments, body, and soul; behind the magic they weaved with music. It hadn't occurred to me until then how it was odd that Castle Ryemont had so few court musicians. Perhaps the king had no penchant for music.

At first, the plink plink of the strings and his sonorous voice transported me. The music eased my longing for home. His eyes closed, and his fingers flitted across the strings like they were born to make music. I lifted my face to the sky to feel the warmth of the sun on my skin, before the meaning of his words, sung so eloquently in Etanese, sobered me.

She sailed away with no sails at all
A whip sharp wind at her back
Service to a nation to seal a deal
Duty-bound and sold to bidders high.

Sunshine on a blustery day
Black clouds on the horizon
The Blue King in his mysterious shroud
Hides Tordre's queen, the peoples' prize.

Lucky number seven, a milestone of regret
Blood of your life, blood of the berry
Drab brown feather down blends to the tune
Bold and brave she must be to survive.

Brave princess of Carentan
Where are you now in duty bound?
Your people call your name like mantra
You hide away and they rue the day.

When he opened his eyes, he must have realised too late that I had understood his meaning, as my face must have reflected the dark black cloud that hung over my head. My throat constricted, and the wind felt oppressive. I took a deep breath through my nose and let out a long exhale through my mouth.

'Who do you think... how?' I jumped up and grabbed my shawl. The guards stood to attention.

'My queen, it is just a story; idle speculation by the people. They have hardly seen you since the wedding. They hunger for their queen and they yearn for an heir to the throne.' The young man's face looked stricken, and he cast a worried glance towards my guards as though they might at any moment seize him and lock him up for a traitor.

'But that's not how it works here. I thought the people chose your monarchy?' I said.

He gave me a smug look as though I were a small child being told that fairies don't exist.

'Well, that's true enough in theory. The Dreiden line has sat on the throne for centuries. The people are not likely to choose otherwise.'

'Oh.' I looked down, my shoulders rounded forwards over my deflated sense of self. I rested my palm on my stomach, as if through will alone I could conceive a child without ever having to touch the king.

'The Blue King is a direct descendant of the original Tordrean warrior class that settled in the Western peninsula. There have been many pretenders to the throne, though none have come close enough to the hearts of the people.'

I gazed at him and wondered what it might be like to escape responsibility and lead a simple life like that of a travelling minstrel. 'The song has no ending, it continues with the chorus refrain. What happens in the end?'

He stood up, dusted himself down, and slung the lute over his back by its strap. 'That is not for me to determine, my queen.' He pocketed his colourful play wheel and leapt back up onto the stile. 'Is it not your story? Surely, you are the one to determine how it ends.'

I watched him for a moment as he settled himself back into a comfortable position, then pulled out his wheel and begun the repetitive motion of throwing it out on its string only to draw it back up into his hand.

'May I know your name?'

He looked up at me. 'Tristan. Tristan Bacha.'

'Well, Tristan. Thank you for the song. Perhaps it is as well that you sing it in Etanese. I wouldn't want folk around here to believe in stories.' I turned to leave. 'Perhaps one day, I may return with the last verse for you.'

'I will be waiting,' he said, as though he had no intention of ever moving from that spot atop the stile.

I had gone but a few paces when a thought occurred to me, and I turned to address Tristan again. 'Could you tell me who that man who rode past here was?'

He looked at me blankly.

'Older man with dark hair, thin face and priest's robes?' I said.

'No such man passed this way,' Tristan said.

'But he must have,' I said. 'This is the only route he could have taken.'

'Perhaps you are mistaken.'

I stared at him for a moment, trying to work out if I was going mad or if he was the one who was mistaken. I turned to the guards for confirmation, but their gaze was blank and non-committal.

'Yes, I suppose I must be,' I said, and turned back to my journey home.

# CHAPTER FOUR

## *Food and Fables*

The mystery surrounding the dark priest deepened as we walked back through the inner circle of the castle. I caught sight of a stable boy brushing down a large, mottled-grey horse that stamped and snorted with impatience. It looked remarkably like the horse that the priest had been riding.

The guards escorted me back to my rooms, then took up their customary vigil outside the door. Ever since I can remember, it was my dream to marry a distinguished lord or a prince to seal a deal for my country and my family. I imagined my life to be one of a revered and celebrated partner in a political alliance. To be showered with gifts and sought after for my wisdom and knowledge of the culture of Carentan and its people. It didn't bother me too much that it was an arranged marriage. Love would have time to grow and flourish, especially with the inevitable children that would follow.

How wrong could I be?

I paced up and down in front of the window and stared at the grey skies. Should I run away? Run back to Carentan and tell them about the faceless king. But, what if they didn't believe me? And what would mother say? I imagined her face; the stalwart look in her eye, and the disappointment behind her gentle smile. No, I couldn't do it. Couldn't let her down. Let Carentan down. I imagined what my sister would say:

'It was what you always wanted. You always reprimanded me for wanting a different life. Well, you got what you wanted. Now the diplomatic seal of the country rests on your shoulders. Where are those little princes and princesses you always insisted you were going to have?'

The thought of Alliane's "told you so" sing-song voice made me quiver with indignation. I stopped my pacing and bunched a fistful of skirt in my hands until I realised I was making myself look a state.

Children. I never thought for a moment that it might not happen. If only I could get over my fear; banish the image of the faceless Blue King to the far recess of my mind and get on with what they expected of me, producing the next Dreiden heir to the throne.

But then, it wasn't just my fear of the king. Despite his attempts to console me, consummation of our marriage was the furthest thought from his mind. I had always thought my looks to be an asset; so many young courtiers in Carentan had shown me that. Yet now I questioned that assumption, and my confidence plummeted.

The king did not find me attractive.

I let Lana help me into a fresh robe and tidy my hair, before I set off for a wander around the castle. Damned if I was going to spend the whole day cooped up in my chambers. Besides, I had worked up quite an appetite; perhaps the cook would rustle up a snack for me. I left the room and one of the guards settled into step behind me, while the other stayed put outside my door.

I hadn't yet seen them, but I was sure the castle had spies like the network in Carentan run by the seneschal of Castle Helmstedt. I'm sure the Blue King would not want any evidence sent back home of my unhappy childless state. My brother, Gereinte, would be the first to charge into Tordre with an army of Forest Rangers at his back. Although my mother would be quick to quash his impulsive nature in the interests of diplomacy. Darkness take diplomacy.

Then it hit me. I stopped in my tracks, and the guard screeched to a halt just shy of walking into the back of me. The castle spies. Ways and means of getting messages home.

First stop, the kitchens. I headed down the western staircase and heard the clang of pots and pans with muttered curses and the reprimanding voice of Ailsa, the head cook. It was the one thing that reminded me of home, the one familiar constant in my life.

When we were growing up, Gereinte used to drag me along to the kitchens to pilfer snacks. 'Wherever you go, Nerys, make friends with the cook. Then you will always be well looked after,' he always used to say.

The gnawing emptiness of missing home rose up and threatened to consume me, so I stood for a moment and listened to the banter in Langan between the cook and one of her apprentices. The scent of onions, meat, and broth wafted up the stairwell, and I took a deep long breath, and smiled to myself when I heard Ailsa cussing in Etanese with a few words I had taught her.

I sat on the steps for a moment. Most unbecoming for the queen, I know, but at that point I didn't care. The guard glanced at me with a worried look, but didn't relinquish his immediate duty of care. When finally I had chased away the ghosts of homesickness, I stood up with resolve and wandered into the kitchen.

The kitchen was a long, oblong-shaped room that ran the length of the southern side of the inner keep. A line of cooks, assistants, and apprentices sat at tables or stood in front of fires chopping, stirring, and skinning. It was a familiar sight and made me again ache for home.

Ailsa's face lit up at the sight of me, and I basked in the warmth of her greeting.

'Child, look at you… all skin and bones. Queen or no, you need to eat, yes?' Then she ladled a portion of broth into a wooden bowl, and set it on the table in front of me, fussing and coaxing me to sit. It was comforting and made me smile; so few things did these days.

Ailsa was big and rosy and wore her hair in a loose bun on top of her head, covered with a white lacy net. She turned to her apprentice, a young man about the age of Tristan or myself, who looked at me with wide eyes. I gave him my best princess smile, hoping to ease his tension. Ailsa rattled off a few clipped words in Langan, and the young man snapped back to attention and moved to his pots and pans on the far side of the kitchen.

I lifted the bowl to my lips and savoured the sweet spices and the scent of cinnamon that filled my nose. Ailsa knew how to warm the belly as well as the heart.

'Most of them won't talk to me, you know,' I said, looking at the apprentice.

'Well now, you mustn't blame the staff. Most of them have been told not to, but I'm too old to pay attention to them that thinks they are above us lowly kitchen folk. Present company excluded, of course. Never known the castle to be so crawling with those priestly beasts. Besides, them who knows what's good for them know to leave me be. It can be a long day without lunch.' Ailsa doubled over with a snort of laughter.

'Tell me more about the king,' I said. Ailsa was the only willing source of information about Morra Dreiden I had found since being there, though even she sometimes took a while to answer my questions, as though something held her back. She opened her mouth to speak and then, when no words came out, frowned and looked around the room at some unseen ghost.

'Well now,' she said, her voice croaky and unsure at first. 'He was such a cheerful, cheeky little boy. That was before the old king and queen died. It was then he started to change. Not straight away, mind, it happened over a period of time. The entire country was in mourning, and there was a hiatus when the people had to decide if they wanted to accept his ascension to the throne. That was a difficult time.'

And so, she veered off the topic of the king himself, as usual, and started to talk about politics. 'The old king and queen were quite traditional, you know. The people were their subjects and given their rules, which they should obey without question… you know the kind of thing. And here's where our young king would come into his own. Not unlike your own king in Carentan.' She smiled and drummed her cheeks with her fingertips. 'See… not just a rosy face, eh? Know my history too.'

I admit, I was puzzled. Was she talking about my father, King Reiner? It was as though she was talking of a past era. For sure, he brought peace and stability to Carentan, that much I knew. When I thought about how much Gereinte had to live up to, it made me shudder. But then, was I not in such a position myself? Maybe I once thought I would be, hoped I would be, but now? Now that I knew the reality of my situation, I was as far from being able to influence the future of Tordre as I was from eloping to the Green Isle with a farm boy. The irony was gut-wrenching. I concentrated my attention on Ailsa's words.

'But has he always been like this?' I said, interrupting the historical monologue.

'Like what?' Ailsa said.

'Odd, distant… blue.' I stopped at the word faceless. It would be too terrifying to discover that there was some truth in my nightmarish visions.

She stared at me.

'You said that he started to change.'

30

'Did I? Now why would I say that I wonder?' She looked confused, as though I had thrown her off her train of thought. 'I mean, yes, he changed all right, but for the better. I mean, the people loved him. He became the voice of the people. The voice for parity that had been missing from the previous king and queen.'

Now when people talked about the Blue King, they referred to a melancholy and pious individual, not the cheeky cheerful boy that Ailsa seemed to remember. I sipped my broth and watched Ailsa look upwards, following the breadcrumb trail of her thoughts back to where we started.

'Have you ever heard of a young man called Tristan? Tristan Bacha,' I said.

She looked back at me and frowned, as though noticing me for the first time. 'No... I don't believe I have. No, wait. There used to be a family called Bacha. Now that is a strong family name. Comes from good stock, does Bacha. Going back some two hundred years, yes... Bacha. Strong Tordrean name.'

I started, 'Oh... what happened to them?'

'Far as I know, the line died out. But could be wrong... yes, there was a family called Bacha...'

'Tristan?'

'Oh, I don't know no given names. None that come to mind, anyhow.' Ailsa shook her head from side to side, as though to dislodge an uncomfortable thought, then turned and went back to the stove to fuss around the apprentice. I finished my broth and slipped out of the kitchen with a meek 'Thank you' in Langan.

I walked back through the castle corridors, up and down staircases, and along the outer walkway in sight of the castle lookouts, with my one personal guard, who trailed along behind like a ghostly apparition. Staff bowed politely to me, but that was as far as any conversation went.

Exhausted though I was, I thought long and hard about my circumstances. I had resolved nothing that day, but meeting Tristan had opened my eyes to a world beyond the castle. A country where the people had thoughts, voices, and opinions that until then I had never known existed. I had almost forgotten the joyous abandon of the celebrations on my wedding day.

What I feared sat in the back of my mind; the images from my dreams, the dreadful revelation of my husband's second face. It was all there, but it was like a veil had been lifted from my eyes. The smokescreen surrounding my existence thinned.

It was strange, but I had never thought much before about the presence of the priesthood. I had assumed they had always been part of castle life, part of the Tordrean tradition. What had Ailsa called them? Priestly beasts. I had never really noticed them before, but then one passed me along the walkway and inclined his head with a pious smile, dressed in a grey tunic and trousers topped with a brown hooded robe, similar to the dark priest on the road,. And there was another, going down the western staircase as I made my way along the outer wall.

I looked out over the parapet and into the distance, where I could see the coastal road I had walked earlier, and the city rooftops of T'sar. I looked back at the guard, who wore a bored expression, then back out towards the city and the hilltop where Tristan had sat. The wind whipped around the castle walls despite the buffer of the cliffs, and my hair and attire were most likely ruined and left in a most un-queen-like way, but I didn't care.

I had always been the sensible, realistic one out of my siblings. My sister was always the impetuous one, off gallivanting in the forest. It was I who was schooled to be the princess and taught to fulfil her royal duty. There I stood atop the parapet of Castle Ryemont, scarecrow hair, clothes all over the place, with deep dark circles beneath my eyes, wondering if I was going crazy.

My father had taught me nothing if not to make the best out of a bad situation. How could I usefully serve the people of Tordre and the castle staff? I wasn't sure what they would allow me to get involved with, but I knew a man who would. The seneschal of House Dreiden: Milo Dorsa.

It was time to take some control of my time and my life.

# CHAPTER FIVE

## *The Seneschal*

Milo Dorsa was a grey-haired man with hollowed cheeks who bared a grim smile as though he knew what the world was all about and was waiting for the worst to happen.

'Your Majesty,' he said with an obsequious smile, 'the former queen felt no need to interfere with household matters. I have been managing the castle finances and administration for years quite adequately.'

Deep breath. 'Seneschal Dorsa, I have no compulsion to interfere. I merely wish to make myself useful.'

He looked taken aback. Perhaps the idea of a royal being useful was unheard of in his time. Milo Dorsa's apprentice, Bax, sat behind a wood-carved desk, with an ink quill hovering above a sheet of parchment. He was about twelve years old, and stared at me with his mouth open, as though he had never been in the company of a young woman before. A drop of ink plopped onto the sheet and Milo Dorsa looked at him with a weary expression.

'Bax, mind your manners and go collect some refreshments for her Majesty.' The boy jumped up, oblivious to the ink patterns plotting a course across his sheet of sums. He bashed his knee on the desk leg, untangled himself and scurried out of the door. Dorsa peered over at his work and frowned. 'Perhaps I might need your help after all. Do you have a steady hand?'

'Handwriting was my best lesson at Helmstedt,' I said, and plonked myself down at the desk. At last, something to take my mind away from more unsavoury matters.

I picked up the quill, gave it a quick dunk, and poised over the parchment. Bax had appalling handwriting, and Dorsa was quick to snatch the parchment away, but not before I had deciphered the name, Abiel Morda, scrawled beside a not inconsiderable sum of money. A shiver of recognition steeled through me. What was the Archbishop up to in Tordre?

Dorsa opened a drawer in the desk and pulled out a fresh piece of parchment. He pushed on the drawer, but it didn't quite swing back into position, leaving it partially open and revealing a pile of papers and a few scattered letters, half sealed with the king's waxy emblem. Dorsa gave me an insincere smile.

'Let's start again, shall we? I think Bax has well and truly butchered this quarter's account statement.'

I smiled and glanced with curiosity at the semi-open drawer. Dorsa dictated a list of castle goods, which I itemised under kitchen essentials, and I spent the next few hours pleasantly distracted by the work that Bax should have really been doing.

The boy returned, of course, with castle assistants in tow and prepared a table of refreshments, then seated himself at the edge of the room to watch in fascination as the queen took over his duties in the interim. After a while my hand cramped, and Dorsa called an end to our quiet distraction. Bax was quick to take my place and looked a bit uncomfortable when he glanced at the work I had done.

'Perhaps you could see to it that Bax has some further schooling in his letters,' I said, then took a seat at the refreshment table. Dorsa looked as though he wanted to retort, then thought better of it. 'He might like to run along and find a tutor who could give him this kind of practice,' I said.

Dorsa opened his mouth to say something, then noticed my stern expression. He turned back to Bax and said, 'Bax, you know where to find the Meisters. Please do as your queen bids.'

Bax's eyes darted to the semi-open drawer. Quick as a ferret, his fingers flicked out, prised open the drawer, and concealed a small square of folded parchment, then he jumped up and stumbled out of the door. The hulking shadow of the guard outside shifted, then settled back upon the realisation that it was merely the apprentice, not I, who had left the room.

'Plenty of time to see to the accounts. No need to rush, I am sure,' Dorsa said with mild irritation, as he surreptitiously leaned against the drawer. It shut with a muffled thud.

I sliced a piece of fruit and offered some to Dorsa, who popped a piece of orange into his mouth. I followed suit and was rewarded with a burst of sweet citrus filling my mouth, which made me smile.

'We ship them in from Southern Arrontierre,' Dorsa said.

'That must be quite costly,' I said.

'The king likes them,' he said. 'And what the king likes, the king gets.'

'In Carentan, the crown prince is looking to introduce a citizen's charter. Even royalty has to answer to somebody,' I said.

Dorsa popped another piece of fruit into his mouth and chewed thoughtfully. 'Ah yes. The crown prince. Your brother. He came here and tried to influence the Blue King to adopt a similar system. I have to say, it nearly worked. But then…'

I remembered those couple of days when Gereinte had visited during his grand tour. It seemed such an age ago now. I never had the chance to talk to him alone or to admit how lonely and fearful I had become. It had been a brave face I put on for him. Now I wished I had pushed for a private moment.

'But then, we are not in Carentan, your Majesty.'

'No. Quite.'

We looked at one another. I was quietly appraising the seneschal, and he was trying to show polite deference, but failing miserably. I took some bread and cheese and ate while I waited for him to elaborate. He sensed I was not there just for a writing lesson or to help with the accounts, but he was not making it easy for me to get the information I wanted. 'In Carentan, the seneschal has… how shall I say this? Networks.'

Dorsa smiled thinly, and if I had caught him off guard, he revealed nothing in his expression. 'Why are you really here, your Majesty?' he said.

'I have sent many letters home…' my throat constricted, and the words died on my tongue. I took a cup of ale, trying to still the shaking of my hand. Dorsa's eyes followed my movement with dispassionate interest. I took a deep breath and composed myself. 'Did you work for the old king and queen?'

Dorsa's eyes widened a little. 'I did, your Majesty,' he said with a frown.

Good. He was confused now. 'So, what changed when their son ascended to the throne?'

Dorsa thought about it for a while before answering. 'Morra Dreiden brought stability back to Tordre. The old king and queen were very set in their ways. The people were growing restless. He sensed this and offered a solution.'

'Through a people's charter?'

Dorsa had a guarded expression. 'Yes… and no. It was clear that it would not work. He needed to take back control. The old king and queen gave too much freedom to the people. He is also reclaiming his right to rule through bloodlines and not through public acclamation.'

'Such a reversal of public rights will surely result in civil unrest, perhaps even conflict.'

'You have a curious imagination, my dear.'

'Don't patronise me, Seneschal. I am your queen.'

He bowed his head in acquiescence, though I realised I would not get much more from him. Seneschal Dorsa was the Blue King's man, no doubt about that. He was probably even responsible for re-writing my letters for me. That gave me an idea, and I leapt up from the bench.

'Thank you, Seneschal. It has been a most interesting and informative morning with you. And the refreshments were appreciated,' I said in my most polite tone, then bolted out of the door with my guard lumbering after me.

I thought if I found Bax, I might persuade him to tell me what was so secret about the contents of that drawer, so, I made my way down through the stony corridors and out into the courtyard of the inner keep, thinking all the while what good reason I might have to visit the tutoring rooms.

As I crossed the yard, a stable boy brought out that large grey horse I had seen earlier. It was a beautiful steed, no doubt about that, and I stopped to stare and admire his mottled coat. The stable boy dropped into a low bow the minute he saw me, and I waved him up.

'Please carry on. Don't stop on account of me,' I said, and offered the horse my hand to snuffle. Its nose was cold, and its hot breath tickled my fingers. The stable boy kept his head down, but handed me an apple with which to feed the horse. The horse munched it in two bites, then continued to snuffle and rub his nose against my hand, looking for more.

A shadow crept across our light, and I looked up to see the priest watching me. He moved into my space, and I took an involuntary step back. Without taking his gaze from me he waved two fingers in the air, and the stable boy jumped into action to adjust the horse's bridle and stirrups.

The priest smiled.

Perhaps it was meant to be a friendly smile, reassuring even, but all it did was make my skin crawl.

'The king tells me you are still not with child,' he said.

I stared back at him and willed my legs to stand firm. I remembered how I used to tease the Carentan boys with my arrogant princess face, so I lifted my chin and looked down my nose to recreate it. I wasn't sure if it quite had the intended effect, as due to him being somewhat taller than the boys back home, I was looking up in a downward kind of way.

He opened his mouth to say something, then hesitated. He wasn't expecting such a response. But I was the queen, and he was my subject. I presumed. I could do that. Being presumptuous was something I was good at. I was well practised, as it used to drive my sister to distraction.

A ghost of a smile, then a small shake of the head. 'My queen,' he said, mocking me with his tone.

Then he did a strange thing. He waved his fingers in the air, in repeat of what he did with the stable boy. The air shimmered like the heat on a summer's day, but it was cold out there. So cold, the horse was blowing misty breath. I looked around for my guard, but he was no longer there. 'Don't worry. He will be back.'

*Oh.* 'The king will be cross,' I said. 'They are not supposed to leave my side.' His hand swished this way and that in front of my face, and I followed it with my eyes, transfixed by the movement of his fingers.

'The king will be fine. Don't you worry yourself about that, my dear.'

*My dear?* 'Excuse me?' I said in the haughtiest voice I could muster. 'I am your queen.'

The priest's hands moved furiously now. He looked quite ridiculous, waving his hands about like a madman. His eyebrows were knitted together in the most intensive frown, meeting in the middle of his forehead as though he had one long eyebrow. I looked round at the stable boy, who stared at the priest with wide eyes, rooted to the spot.

In exasperation, the priest dropped his hands. The stable boy went back to his duties, released from the grip of a waking dream, and my guard appeared from a door behind the armoury.

'What business is it of the priesthood that I am not yet with child?' I was playing haughty queen, though my blood raced inside me. My cheeks reddened despite the cold. He looked taken aback.

'As the king's closest personal adviser, I am merely looking after the interests of the people,' he said with insincerity. The king had plenty of advisers, so why did he need to take counsel from the priesthood?

I gave his horse one last ruffle behind the ears, sympathising with the poor beast on having such a disagreeable master, then stepped back. 'What is your name?' I said, with a mind to report this unusual behaviour to the king. But he merely shook his head and walked his steed towards the stables, without so much as a "by your leave". *What a rude, unpleasant man.*

I turned and marched onward towards the tutoring rooms, the guard following in my wake. As I reached the oaken door, it swung open and Bax shot out of the door and slammed into my shoulder.

# CHAPTER SIX

## *Letters and Lies*

*Ooof.* I lost my balance and fell onto my backside, sprawled across the cobbles like a drunken minstrel. A spear of pain shot up my back, then settled into a dull throb around my waist. The look of horror on Bax's face was almost worth the undignified scene. I looked over my shoulder, but the priest had gone. Fortunately.

'Your Majesty.' Bax dropped to his knees and bowed his head, not daring to offer me a hand. The guard appeared by my side and, with one iron-fisted hand, lifted me to my feet. The next thing I knew, he had swept me into his thick-muscled arms with a care that belied his strength and demeanour.

'Let me down.' I thumped his breastplate and was rewarded by a resounding thud. *Ouch.* I shook my hand as it tingled with pain. 'I'm perfectly fine. It was just a tumble.'

'Your Majesty, I will take you to the medic,' the guard said, his words muffled somewhat by his headpiece.

'No medic, please. I'm fine, put me down.'

To his credit, he did as he was told and returned me to the ground. Bax stood and sneaked a glance at me with a mixture of fear and relief in his eyes.

'In. In!' I shooed him back into the tutoring halls. 'Find us a small corner. I need to speak to you in private.'

Bax looked startled but complied with my wishes, and found us a small cove with velvet covered bench cushions and a desk with writing materials. The hall was half-full of children of varying ages, who sat and worked at similar desks, as two or three tutors dressed in long flowing robes strode around, glancing at their work and offering nuggets of guidance at opportune moments.

It was calm, except for the moment I entered the hall, at which the entire populous stopped and bowed, with murmurs of Your Majesty under quiet breath, before they resumed work. The room had the musty scent of old books.

Bax sat and looked at me from across the desk. I wasn't sure how to ask him what I needed to know, so I ran my hand across the desk, which had an uneven feel to it where past pupils had etched grooves into the wood. Bax watched me with a faint smile.

'Sometimes they give us metal quills,' he said.

I smiled to myself. I knew how boring it could be to go over and over your letters. Someone had tried to scrape and varnish the marks, but the desk had clearly accommodated plenty of distracted pupils over its lifespan. Maybe it was the naughty desk, stuck in the corner.

'I finished all my letters like you said, your Majesty.' He had a worried expression.

'That's not what I wanted to check.'

Bax dropped his eyes and I think he knew what it was I wanted to know. He took a folded piece of parchment out of his pocket, placed it on the desk in front of him, looked up, and then, with a sheepish gesture, pushed it across the desk to my side. I looked at it for a moment, then reached out and flipped it over. My own handwriting adorned the outside with the names of my family, and I glanced up at Bax, who wouldn't meet my eye. I unfolded it and scanned across the writing inside.

'Did you do this?' I said.

He looked away, looked back at me, then nodded. 'Am I in trouble? Will you tell the seneschal?'

I shook my head. 'Wasn't it the seneschal who asked you to do this?'

He looked away. A deep blush crept up his neck and across his cheeks. 'Please don't tell, your Majesty... he sends money home to my family. I didn't mean no harm.' Bax looked spooked, as though he had only just realised the import of what he had done.

I studied the script. It looked enough like my handwriting to fool anyone but those who had studied the curves of my letters. Unfortunately, my childhood tutors were most likely the only ones with deep knowledge of my script. This was good enough to fool even my mother, and it was a happy picture Bax had painted for her of my life at Castle Ryemont. His own handwriting may leave a lot to be desired, but Bax had an uncanny talent for mimicry that was wasted on a weasel like Milo Dorsa. This explained a lot. I folded the parchment and tucked it inside my bodice.

40

'Don't worry. I'll tell him I stole it from you, and if he gives you any trouble, I know a most amenable seneschal in Carentan who could make good use of your talents.'

Bax bowed his head in acquiescence. My skin itched with irritation, but Dorsa and his little spy were without doubt doing someone else's bidding. I needed to find the courage somehow to confront the Blue King with this newfound evidence. But first, I had to get a message home to Gereinte.

'Can you please get me a quill and some parchment?' Bax looked a little nonplussed at first, but, under the watchful eye of the tutors, jumped up and disappeared into a corner of the room. One grey-haired and bearded meister with a friendly smile bowed his head in my direction. Perhaps they thought I was helping Bax with his letters. *Well, good. Let them think that.*

Whatever I wrote would undoubtedly be open to scrutiny before it left the castle grounds, but my brother and I had devised a system of communication when we were children, shared only with my other siblings, to evade prying adult eyes. We took The Pygmies Tale, one of our favourite stories, and translated words and sentences into common phrases and messages we wanted to tell each other.

It might be tough to pass on the detail of civil war brewing in Tordre, civil unrest not being something that our childhood imaginations might have thought to need in the future, but the least I could do was alert him to the fact that there was something wrong in Castle Ryemont.

Bax returned and placed the parchment and quill on the desk alongside a pot of ink. This is what I wrote:

My Dearest Gereinte,

… he would know something was amiss for a start, as I always called him Ger…

I write with a heart full of thanks for the life I have been granted as Queen of Tordre. The people at Castle Ryemont are looking after me well, and filling me with hope for a continued and peaceful relationship with Carentan. Soon, when I fall with child, I will recite to them one of our favourite childhood stories. Do you remember the Pygmies Tale? One could almost liken my king to Hercules in his reign, whilst Anateus is, as always, surrounded by pygmies. Poor Anateus. Given my new status in Tordre, I empathise with his predicament. Sometimes I feel like I am surrounded by pygmies. I miss Nana's telling of the tale. Things are infinitely more interesting in real life, with one constant being that change will always drive stories. In my telling, our trusted cleric makes a cameo appearance. Perhaps the pygmies may unseat him too. I wait impatiently for news from Carentan.

Forever your dearest sister, Nerys.

Gereinte would get it, but to anyone else, I hoped it made no sense. With neat precision I blotted my words, folded the parchment, and handed it to Bax.

'Post-haste, please.' I knew full well that there was every likelihood that it might end up back in Dorsa's top drawer for scrutiny, but one can hope.

I stood up, and Bax flinched. He followed suit, before tucking the letter away. I swept from the room and sensed the guard drop into step behind me. What would it take to get some privacy around here?

I knew where the king would be. It was his afternoon adjournment to deal with all matters constitutional. No doubt he was plotting the assured longevity of the Dreiden line on the throne. I made my way to his workrooms and was about to knock on the outer door when I heard voices raised within. I looked to the guard, who appeared not to have noticed anything amiss, and waved him away. The guard settled back with another, who was waiting outside the door. They glanced at one another with a shadow of unease as I stood with my hand raised.

'… don't care about your personal proclivities… matter of national…'

'… your Holiness, I understand, but…'

'… enhance the…'

The door flung inward, and I was stood face-to-face with the priest from the courtyard, whose face was burning red with ire. Behind him sat the Blue King behind a long oval desk, surrounded by parchment and quills. He looked up in surprise and narrowed his eyes at me. I stood there a moment, dumbfounded, my hand raised as though to knock on the door, then dropped my arm and stepped into the room.

'Good afternoon, my queen. And to what do I owe the unexpected pleasure of your company?' He waved an impatient hand, and the priest barged past me and slammed the door on his way out.

I looked over my shoulder at the closed door and back at the king. 'What was…? He is a most disagreeable man,' I said. The king shook his head but refused to comment.

Emboldened by my discovery, I pulled the first letter I had retrieved from Bax out of my bodice, unfolded it, and placed it on the desk in front of him. He frowned and looked down at it, before looking back up at me. It took all the courage I could muster to not shrink away from his scrutiny.

He dipped a quill in the inkpot, shook it once on the blotter, then turned his attention back to whatever it was he was writing. After a few moments and without taking his eyes from his task, he said, 'I trust you had a pleasant walk this morning?'

His casual dismissal added fuel to the flames of my anger.

'I know about the letters,' I said. He looked up at me with a blank expression. 'You had that weasel, Dorsa, and his pet monkey re-write them for you.' I shook with a mixture of fear and anger.

'My dear, I have no idea what you are talking about.' His eyes softened.

For a moment, I was unsure. Had I got it wrong? Maybe it wasn't the king who was behind this. What possible motive could Milo Dorsa have for such deception?

'Where did you get this?' he said.

'I… acquired it. I've spent some productive time with the seneschal today and I saw this letter, recognised my own script, and wondered why it had not been sent. I can only assume…'

A cloud passed across the king's face and I faltered. Had I stepped too far over the mark? His eyes moved down and ran across the parchment, flicking left and right. He looked up at me with a measured expression.

'Well, at least you appear to be having a wonderful time here,' he said with a sardonic lilt. Doubt stalled my thoughts and for a moment I could well have believed he had not been at all responsible. 'Right.' He stood up, his chair scraping the floor, and placed his own work to one side. 'Let us put all this nonsense to rest. You shall have your visit home and I shall accompany you.'

I stood there with my mouth open. The blood rushed around my body and I was overcome by sudden dizziness. It was too much to believe that he might mean it; I had been asking for so long. I stumbled back a pace and the king scooted out from behind his desk and lent me an arm to lean on. Grateful for his solid support, I looked up at him with new eyes.

'Are you all right, my dear?' He snapped his fingers, and the attendants rushed off and returned moments later with a jug of watered wine, some bread, and a cushion. The king laid the cushion on a bench and lowered me down to sit.

I winced, at first, at my bruised backside, but the cushion was soft and springy, and the wine warm and relaxing, so my beating heart slowed to a reasonable rate, and I looked up to smile at my Blue King with genuine gratitude. His expression was concerned but guarded. He patted the back of my hand like a kindly uncle, then returned to his seat and his paperwork.

'Your Majesty...?' I wanted to ask him why the sudden change of heart and felt that I needed to apologise for my accusations about his interference in my letters, but my voice was a faint warble, and I couldn't get my words out.

'Shh... don't worry.' He retrieved his quill and set it to the parchment with deliberate strokes. 'We will get to the bottom of this mystery of the letters.' He paused. 'And I would be most interested to hear what you learnt today from our trusted seneschal.' The latter he delivered with measured irony. So, all was not as it seemed with internal relations at Castle Ryemont.

I sat and watched the king for a good while, and every so often he would cast his gaze up to me, then look back down with a faint smile on his lips. I chewed softly on the crusty bread, savoured its yeasty comfort, then washed it down with small sips of wine. My nerves may have returned to normal, but the wine made me feel sleepy.

Eventually, the king put his quill to one side and looked earnestly at me, his hands folded on the desk in front of him. He stood up. The scent of wine and baked bread enticed him to break from his work and take a light lunch with me. He sat opposite me. It was the first time that we had found an easy silence in each other's company.

'Your Majesty,' I said.

'Yes.'

Did I have two husbands: the Blue King and the faceless king?

'What business does Abiel Morda have in Tordre?' I said it before I could stop myself. The king's face could have been carved from stone for all his thoughts he gave away in his expression.

Abiel Morda was the Archbishop of the Church of the one god, and was busy spreading his unique brand of worship across the Western Isles. My late father, King Reiner, and now my brother Gereinte had been chasing him out of Carentan for as long as I could remember. I knew he was a troublemaker.

# CHAPTER SEVEN

## *Homeward Bound*

The wind had lifted by the time we rode out from Castle Ryemont the next day. I rode my mare, and the king took a beautiful chestnut stallion from his stables. He was an accomplished rider, but the horse seemed a bit skittish as we made our way from the keep through its grey stone archway to the outer circle, which radiated in a circular vista of green land towards T'sar.

A retinue of the king's guard, two advisers, plus Lana, my handmaid, trailed behind us, followed by a string of packhorses carrying provisions and tents for our journey. For the first time since I had arrived in Tordre, my heart raced in anticipation. We were going home. Heading north east, towards Carentan. The king had sent a messenger ahead to inform my mother, the Queen Regent, and the Crown Prince.

I didn't mention Abiel Morda again, as it was apparent that the king would not entertain a conversation about the cleric's involvement in Tordrean politics, or indeed why he was taking sums of money from the royal coffers. Morra Dreiden had simply brushed aside my concerns. It bothered me that a country like Tordre, with such an affinity to Carentan in religious matters, would have succumbed to the dubious antics of Archbishop Morda: an ambitious politician and fanatical demagogue, whose power was growing fast. Even as I left Carentan, people flocked to his churches to hear how their eternal souls could be saved if they truly believed, perform the sacred rites and, naturally, make a generous contribution to the church's finances. I shuddered at the memory of a sermon I once overheard in Canrac.

'Godlessness has come to reign in Carentan,' he had screeched. 'We must return to the old ways. The Scriptures tell us that heresy must be rooted out, or the one god will forsake us.' Morda's so called 'sinners' were submitted to barbaric questioning by the church's inquisitors, and those who survived certainly seemed to lose the desire to sin, alongside most other desires. It was widely believed that my mother had given Morda too much scope for mischief, so it was not surprising that he now looked to Tordre to extend his powerbase. The thought that soon I could tell them face-to-face about my worries reassured me. Though I would say nothing about my faceless king.

I held back from the king's retinue and walked my mare alongside one of his advisers, a rotund and cheery spirited man named Arvind. The king looked over his shoulder at me and I flinched. His face looked normal enough, and I doubted he would reveal his other side amongst so many people. Or maybe they all knew? I shuddered, despite the fair weather. The king gave his adviser a steady stare, then turned back to the track ahead.

Arvind gave me a curious glance. 'You look startled. What is it you see, your Majesty?' He leaned in his saddle and searched the thorny undergrowth either side of the track.

'Oh, errr... nothing. It must have been a wild animal.' I recovered my composure and pressed my knees into the mare's flank to edge her ahead. But Arvind easily matched my pace and drew up alongside me again.

'Your Majesty... would you mind if I accompanied you?' He looked flustered over such a small burst of activity.

*Yes, I would mind.* I wanted to be left alone to think about things, but I said, 'No, of course not.' Had I detected a flicker of ire in the king's expression earlier? Perhaps he needed his advisers to monitor me. Or perhaps he needed someone close enough to distract my attention.

We rode in silence for a while. Arvind stole glances at me every so often, but mostly kept his gaze ahead. The air was fresh with a light breeze that brought with it the scent of bracken, though the rancid scent of wild foxes was still present, and I wrinkled my nose at it as we rode through a copse of trees. The trees bowed over the track, enclosing us in a tunnel of overlapping canopies where the sun peeked through at random intervals, spiking the ground with slivers of light.

As we moved farther north from T'sar towards Carentan the trees became dense, like those of the Forest of Dreams that lay on the border between Carentan and Tordre. It was at this junction we intended to take the trail towards the river Caren, where we would pick up a boat to take us the rest of the way to Canrac and Castle Helmstedt. The gentle clop of hooves on ground matted with leaves and the singsong of birds in the trees had a hypnotic effect on me. I swayed in my saddle and struggled to keep my eyes open.

'This whole adventure is most unusual.' Arvind broke the silence. I opened my eyes and sat up straight.

'In what way?' I said.

'The king rarely makes trips. I don't think I have ever seen him outside the border of Tordre.'

'Well, it will be an adventure for us all then.'

'Yes, indeed.' Arvind sounded doubtful.

We walked our horses alongside each other, and I looked up toward the king, who rode at the head of our entourage.

'Why is that, then? I mean… surely, as one of his advisers, you would advise him to make connections with foreign dignitaries and build alliances.' I remembered the lessons we had on diplomacy. At the time, I thought they were mainly for the benefit of Gereinte but was now realising that my mother's insistence that we all attend was not just to keep my brother company.

'Well, he does in other ways.' Arvind fidgeted in his saddle. 'We act as his envoys.'

I stared at him. 'I don't recall ever seeing you in Carentan.'

'Details, details,' he waved a hand in dismissal. 'You would have been too young.'

*Enough,* I thought. Enough of being mollycoddled and lied to. I was a queen and I should be up front riding with my king. I nudged my mare ahead with a squeeze of my knees, and in moments had overtaken Arvind and two of the king's guard to edge my horse next to his. His eyes widened, then his shoulders relaxed, and he let out a long breath.

'I thought you might be more comfortable riding to the rear,' he said.

'Why? I get only slightly better conversation from Arvind than the packhorses and the stable hand.'

He tried to cover the amusement that danced in his eyes at my comment. It was a brief moment of connection, which quickly passed.

The king had tried to persuade me to be carried in a litter, but I had insisted on riding. It was a small comfort I gained from the modicum of control I had over my situation. Enough to keep me sane for a little while longer.

'You can't be too careful these days,' the king said. 'There are brigands and rebels alike hiding in these parts.'

I glanced at him again, and his face remained impassive as he stared ahead. No secrets were forthcoming today from my Blue King. I wasn't so worried about brigands – as soon as we crossed the border between Tordre and Carentan, the forest rangers would find us and accompany us to Canrac. I was more concerned about him. He looked pale and his face was beaded with tiny droplets of perspiration.

It was some time before I realised that the rest of the entourage trailed further behind us. The dull thud of hooves faded, and the clatter of provisions on packhorses and murmur of light conversation had all but stopped. I looked over my shoulder and saw that there were a good hundred paces between us and the rest of the travellers, though the king's guard flanked us with customary determination.

'Your Majesty,' I said, and he turned. For a fraction of a second he looked like a different man. His face was rounder, and cheeks less sculpted. His expression, face twisted in pain, as though he held the burden of every war upon his shoulders, startled me. I turned toward the sound of racing hooves to see a single horseman appear around a corner and canter towards us. The trailing entourage stood, as though entranced, and as the rider drew to a stop in front of us, I knew at once who it was.

'I must advise most fervently against this course of action,' the priest said, and made an impressive circular motion with his hand, which left the guards in a similar state to the rest of the party. The king pulled his reins to the side, walked around the priest, and urged his horse forward.

'You cannot and will not continue with this façade of control,' the king said. His face and stature returned to its regal state, and a sense of pride washed over me. I brought my mare up close beside him to reinforce his defiance of the priest. 'This is a matter of State, and we are on a royal visit. I don't need an envoy. Return home, priest.' The king had a dangerous look in his eye.

The priest was startled and settled his gaze on me as though I was responsible for the king's behaviour.

'He is your king. It behoves you to obey his wishes.' I spoke with confidence, despite the rush of nerves in my body. I swallowed my fear of the priest and the king himself, more determined than ever to get across that border and into Carentan.

'This is not what we agreed,' the priest said. He turned his horse back towards T'sar and galloped off. The king inched his stallion forwards while the rest of the entourage stared around them, as though lost in a dream.

'Quick,' he said, 'I won't be able to hold it back much longer and there is something I need you to see.' The king's expression was strained, yet he pushed his horse forwards. His entourage stood immobile, as though stuck in time. The king launched into a canter as I urged my mare into action, only just keeping level with his stallion.

'Perhaps when we get to the border, you will see,' he said. 'Not far now, then you may judge for yourself.'

*Judge. Judge what?* I had thought we were on a diplomatic trip to Carentan, but clearly the king had something else on his mind. As we rode further and further ahead of the rest of the party, I cast a longing gaze back at the immobilised entourage. Where was Lana now? I was alone with him. No one was in sight, either ahead or behind. An oppressive air hung over us as we raced for the border, as though being chased out of Tordre by some demon from folklore. This was a side to my king I had never witnessed. The cool exterior had been replaced by a driven and torn man, desperate to make some kind of stand.

We rode hard for the border, our party now lost to us. The horses were damp with sweat, the king's face pinched and drawn, his head down and determined. My legs ached from trying to stay in the saddle. At some point, I must have lost my hair net, as my dark locks swam around my head, covering my face like a veil. Trees, bushes, and hedgerows rushed past us at speed, and the twittering of birds melted into a continuous hum of song above the thundering hooves of our mounts.

I didn't understand what we were doing or why, but it was a break in the continuation of normal weirdness that had become my life. At least we were heading in the right direction; the direction of home. There was sanctuary for both my strange king and me as soon as we crossed that invisible border.

Invisible was the appropriate word to describe it, as when we burst through a clearing in the trees and the king slowed his horse, all I could see was a vast stretch of land leading to dense woodland that I presumed to be the outskirts of the Forest of Dreams. He walked his horse right up to that invisible barrier, dismounted, then collapsed to his knees. He covered his face with his hands and let out a strangled cry. When he looked up and over his shoulder, the faceless man looked blindly towards me.

# CHAPTER EIGHT

### *The Faceless King*

My breath caught. Chest tightened. Throat constricted.

The king looked away, covering his face with his hands once more. I found the courage to slide from my saddle and approach him.

'Is there… can I… help in any way?'

When he turned back to look at me, it was through the eyes of a different man, hazel eyes a little closer together, and a face rounded and plump with less definition. His hair was matted and sweaty, a dirty brown like the silt that pooled on the riverbanks. He looked like one of the priests that scuttled about the castle in increasing numbers.

I recoiled, took a step back, and he reached for me like I was the last living thing in this world. Upon realisation that he had lost hope, he dissolved into a weeping heap on the ground. I wondered then what I had feared. Perhaps the unknown? That somehow this faceless man had some power over me. Well, that may well be true as the King of Tordre, but what I saw before me was neither king nor enemy. Just a broken man.

I knelt and touched his shoulder, pulling my hand away when he jerked around to look at me. 'We have to go,' I said, with a gesture towards the forest and the border between our nations.

He shook his head. 'I can't. We can't.'

'I don't understand. Why can't we just go? There is help beyond those trees. Here,' I stood and took his hand, 'walk with me a while and you'll see. You'll feel better once we're over the border. I promise.'

But he resisted my attempts to get him to his feet, and trembled like a kicked puppy. Abiel Morda had a lot to answer for, but until I could get my evidence over the border and into the care of my family, I had no proof, drive, or reason for such an unexpected return. I could imagine my mother's indignation: 'Don't be ridiculous, Nerys. Go home and start behaving like a queen.'

'But my country folk can help. Once we are over the border the rangers will take us to Canrac and Castle Helmstedt. There we will find help. Solace. Asylum. Whatever it is you need.'

'You don't know what I need.'

I flinched and drew back. His anger was like a slap in the face. Whatever he had been, this was not the same man I thought I had married. There was no way I was going to get him over the border by force, and if I couldn't persuade him, then the only option left was to get him back to Castle Ryemont.

'What could possibly happen to you if we cross the border?'

He gave me a look that would make anyone question their state of mind.

'What if I go alone?' I said.

He ignored my questions and stared at the ground like a sullen child. I resigned myself to this taking some time and sat down beside him.

We sat in silence for a while, and I listened to the sounds of distant birds in the forest canopy and the occasional rustle of wildlife in the undergrowth.

'I saw you.'

He looked up sharply.

'That first night after our wedding. In the chapel,' I said.

He looked back down at the ground. What was it, shame? Remorse? 'I know,' he said. 'I told them, but they wouldn't listen. Said that they would deal with it. But every day, your resistance grew stronger. I knew it was only a matter of time.'

'Who are they?'

He looked at me and shook his head as though he knew he shouldn't be disclosing information to me.

'The priesthood. Abiel Morda.'

'And who are you?'

He covered his face with his hands again and I sat patiently, waiting for him to fill me in. We were not going anywhere, that much was evident, so I figured I would let him speak and answer my questions at his leisure. I waited.

Perhaps it was fear, fear of being thrown into a foreign jail. Fear of what my family might do to him if they found out. Fear of whatever hold Abiel Morda had on him. Regardless, I knew then that getting him over that border was the least likely of options.

'I'm a priest. I thought… if the illusion held, it would do us both good to visit your family. I could have established myself as the king, and you could have replenished your wellbeing and banished some of that homesickness that has plagued you since you arrived. It was a good plan. But it is not to be.'

'So, what happens now?' I said. 'Do we return and hope we don't meet your objectionable brethren along the way?' He looked up at me upon mention of his objectionable brethren. 'And what about our people, waiting somewhere behind us for you to appear and give them direction?'

He exhaled a long-drawn-out breath. 'They will still be there, waiting.'

I raised an enquiring eyebrow.

'They won't remember. They only see what they expect to see. Like you. You expected to see the Blue King, and that is what you saw. Only now you see different.'

'What is that… some kind of magic?'

'Don't say that. Never say that. The Priesthood has burnt people caught dabbling in witchcraft. It is faith, nothing more. Just faith. The one god will protect those who believe.' He put his head down, clasped his hands together, fingers interlaced, then muttered some kind of chant to himself under his breath.

I decided to leave him to his faith, got up and brushed myself off, resigned to the fact that we were returning to Castle Ryemont. Gathering my mare's reins, I mounted, then nudged the horse around and walked her back the way we had come. I looked over my shoulder, hoping to see the Blue King, but he was still a dusty brown priest with a different face, muttering away to himself like a madman.

The trees came back to enshroud me as I re-negotiated my path back to the forest from which we had come; back toward our party and whatever lay ahead. I hoped beyond reason Bax had favoured me enough to send that letter back home, as it was now my only hope of navigating myself out of this mess.

The birds twittered in the treetops. Were they ensnared too? If Abiel Morda thought I was a threat to his deception, what would he do with me? For now, I would lie low and pretend. Pretend that I knew nothing, and all was well. At least until I could come up with some plan of action.

At some point, the priest-king must have noticed that I had gone, because he finally cantered up alongside me and reined in his steed to slow his pace.

'What do you plan to do?' he said.

I gave him a scathing look. At least I didn't have to pretend with him anymore. We walked our horses in silence. The sappy forest air acted like a tonic to revive my soul. 'I suppose we shall carry on as before, for appearance's sake.'

He glanced up at me. *Yes, he had better look shamefaced.*

'It won't be much longer before questions are asked,' he said. 'About the non-existent heir to the throne.'

It would work wonderfully for the priesthood to bandy about that Tordre had a barren queen. That there would be no Andolin heir. 'How would that work in your newly worked constitution?'

'I would appoint an heir,' he said.

*Oh. They had that one worked out well, leaving the priesthood free to appoint whomsoever they please,* I supposed.

The well-trodden path widened, and the forest canopy opened out as the trees became less densely packed. I could detect fresh tracks in the ground and milestones we had passed on our journey out there. Within moments, the peaceful chatter of wildlife was underwritten by a soft murmur of voices.

We walked into the clearing, and it was as though we had never left. Arvind fussed around the entourage, giving instructions on erecting a large tent. Lana unloaded one packhorse with blankets, clothes, and what looked like the compressed contents of my chamber dresser. The stable boy had lined up all the horses and tied them to a tree, and was busy fixing nosebags and filling a thick wooden pale with water. No one seemed in the least bit surprised when we trotted into the clearing.

'Your Majesty,' Arvind came over, and bowed before the priest-king. I glanced at him and saw him sit a bit straighter in the saddle. His demeanour shifted to regal, but his face looked the same to me.

'Why can't they see you for what you are?' I said.

'My dear, you see what the one god wants you to see,' he said. Well if that was the case, then the one god had truly forsaken me. I could make no sense of what I saw.

55

'We make camp, your Majesty,' Arvind said, 'and in the morning we move on.'

'Change of plan,' the priest-king said. 'In the morning, we break camp and make our way back to Castle Ryemont.' Arvind didn't look too surprised, as though this was the behaviour he expected from his king.

'As you wish, your Majesty.' He glanced at me as though seeking confirmation, and I bowed in acquiescence. Arvind scurried away to inform staff and amend arrangements.

I dismounted with a little stumble as my feet hit the ground, shaky from the unfolding reality. I craved a little time to myself, and the opportunity to ask a few questions of my handmaid, Lana.

A spray of live chickens darted around and pecked hopefully at the ground, while one of the cook's apprentices prepared a fire. A young servant peeled potatoes, onions, and carrots, and plopped them one-by-one into a large earthenware pot. My stomach grumbled in response.

Thankfully, the first tent up was mine, and I felt no compunction or guilt for staking my claim to the space. I was the queen, after all. *And he...* I looked back over my shoulder at the brown-haired rugged priest... *he was just that. A priest.*

I left the party to their own arrangements and followed Lana inside the spacious canvas-enshrouded haven, then secured the flap so that no one could disturb us without first making themselves known. Lana laid down a pallet for me, and arranged my things on a makeshift dresser, which was really an upside-down basket with a cloth draped over it. There were cushions scattered around and a couple of wicker chairs. It was a home-from-home. Of sorts. Lana cast me an enquiring look.

'It is fine, Lana. More than fine, in fact. Given our sparse resources, you have done a good job,' I said. She looked both relieved and proud in equal measure. She urged me to make use of the privy, a simple hole in the ground out back, and bathing facilities, which were a large tin pot of lukewarm water with some cloths. Adequately refreshed, I sat, and Lana took a large brush from the dresser.

'All this travel by horseback doesn't become your Majesty,' she said as she ran the brush through my tangled hair.

*You really don't know*, I thought. 'Yes. Somewhere along the route, I lost my hairnet.'

'No matter, I have spares,' she said, and, like magic, pulled a net from a basket full of many sparkly things.

'You are good, Lana. What would I do without you?'

She busied herself with my hair, face turned down, and tried to hide her rosy blush. I let her continue for a while in peaceful silence, brushing and plaiting and curling my hair into neat little loops. She had delicate hands, yet a firm and dextrous touch. I had many questions, but knew enough about the delicacies of diplomacy to skirt around the edges of what I really had to say.

'Lana, how long have you worked in the Royal castle?' I tried to sound casual, like I was passing the time while she made me presentable for supper. She paused for a moment before pinning the net in place. She was not much older than me, so probably had not served long enough to remember the old king and queen, but enough to be susceptible to Abiel Morda's influence.

'Nine moons, your Majesty. They trained me especially for you.'

*Oh.* That was interesting.

'May I ask who was responsible for your training?'

'Am I doing something wrong, your Majesty?' Lana let her hands drop and a mixture of fear and shame wavered across her face.

'No, no. Absolutely not,' I said, and her relief was palpable. Driven perhaps by a fear of the priesthood? I shuddered to think what the church's inquisitors did to servants who stepped out of line. She settled back into the rhythm of her task.

'I so much enjoy looking after you, your Majesty,' she said. Yes. That I didn't doubt. 'Will you join the king for your supper?' My stomach dropped.

'I feel quite tired. Perhaps you could arrange for me to eat here in my own space?'

Without batting an eyelid, Lana patted the net in place and said, 'As you wish, your Majesty,' then left the tent. It didn't pass my notice that she had not answered my question about her training. However, the bigger question on my mind, although I didn't have the courage to voice it, was that if this strange priest posed as the King of Tordre, where was the real Blue King?

# CHAPTER NINE

## *The Devil's Breath*

'It would be better, for appearance's sake, if you joined the party for supper,' the priest-king said as he slipped into my tent. He looked refreshed and alert, and his comment confirmed my suspicions about Lana, that at every opportunity she would go scurrying off to carry reports to the king about his queen's state of mind.

'It is hardly different from taking my meals alone in my rooms at Castle Ryemont,' something I often did after excusing myself because of ill health. The truth was, I could not bear the company of my strange Blue King. This priest in front of me didn't quite have the same effect, though he left me just as confused.

'True, but you are supposed to be happy to be on a visit to Carentan.'

I gave him a blank stare. 'We are not going to Carentan.'

'I know that, but they... the staff think we have been on a trip,' he said. I didn't think it was what his entourage thought that worried him. More likely what might come from the priesthood seeing he could no longer control his queen. Would they then replace him with another priest?

'So... you told the staff we have been to Carentan?'

'Not quite, but they believe the trip was successful, and that it has restored the queen to her health. For appearance's sake, it would be better if you joined me for supper.'

I gave the priest-king an appraising look. 'What are you hoping to achieve?'

'I serve the one god. For now, let's get back to Castle Ryemont. It is not open to negotiation.' He looked away, then turned back with a question in his eyes.

'Am I your prisoner?' I said.

He shook his head, then looked away guardedly. 'No... no. That is not what this is supposed to be. What will you do now?'

I honestly didn't know. But I would not let him know the thoughts that raged inside my mind.

'I am a queen, and I'm going to behave like a queen.'

That is what I told myself, but the nagging thought in my mind was that I was not a queen. I had not married a king; I had married a priest posing as a king. And now I was going to go along with the deception... for what? For want of anything better to do. To save myself from the embarrassment of running back to my family screaming about Blue Kings, faceless men, and priests with wagging fingers. Who would believe that Abiel Morda was dabbling in magical dark arts?

Gereinte would believe.

I clung to the hope that my letter would find him, and he would mount an operation to rescue me. I shuddered to think what my mother would do if she knew the truth of what she had married me into. Wars had been started for less.

I joined the priest-king in his tent for supper. He sat on a makeshift throne, with his advisers on either side, looking regal and not the least bit apologetic for it either. It rankled, but I kept face. Pretending was something I was good at.

As children, Alliane and I would play at being queens. She would get bored and go off to play at fighting with the boys, but I would continue the game with the young squires, approximating my mother's tone, and watch them squirm with obsequiousness.

This was no different. I lamented all the time I had wasted being afraid; afraid and homesick when home was but a fantasy away. I was at home playing this game, and I suddenly realised that I had status above everyone around me.

They had created a smaller throne-seat next to the priest-king. I sat, and looked down my nose at the assembled court with imperious curiosity. A servant handed me a bowl and spoon, and the thick scent of stewed chicken and vegetables pushed all thought aside. The carrots were soft enough to melt in my mouth, and the broth was heavy with onions and herbs. I closed my eyes, grateful for the simple luxury of food.

Conversation was minimal, and I kept my expression focused when Arvind tried to engage my attention. 'The trip was a success,' he said.

I looked at him and raised an eyebrow. 'Yes, apparently.'

'You are not feeling better, your Majesty?'

I had to be careful not to destroy the façade. It might cause a kind of chaos that I was ill-prepared to deal with at that point in time. 'Yes… Yes, of course. But I shall be happier to return home, now that I am reassured.'

Arvind gave an exaggerated bow, and made all the right noises for someone who believed in something that never happened. How Morda and his band of renegade priests had managed it, I didn't know, but you had to hand it to him, he had done a good job of casting a credible story across a large swathe of the population of Tordre. I wondered how far it stretched. Did it matter, as long as he held the king and the castle?

'What do you remember of our visit to Carentan?' I said, teasing at the edges of Arvind's reality.

He thought about it for a moment. 'Well now. There was the river Caren, which is an endless river, and beautiful trees. Lots of trees. And Helmstedt, of course. You couldn't forget the great Helm in the distance, the way it leered over the castle like a predatory bird, all sharp beaks and edges, and you never quite know when it might swoop down and take you.'

I had never quite heard it described like that before. It sounded like a picture from a storybook. I wondered how that memory had planted itself into his consciousness.

'Did you meet anyone interesting?'

'Yes, of course, your Majesty. Why, you were there yourself. We met the new Queen Regent, and lots of courtiers wearing strange garments. I would get a chill without my fur-lined cloak.' Arvind shivered, as though to make the point.

'Well, it is rather warmer in Carentan. We don't have the westerly wind there that batters the shoreline in Tordre. We are somewhat protected from the weather by the Helm mountains.'

'Yes. Yes, quite.' Arvind frowned to himself as though he thought there ought to be more but was finding it difficult to dredge up the memory. That would be because the memory didn't exist.

After supper I made my excuses: tiredness after such a busy day travelling, and no one needed to be convinced of that minor detail. I popped out of the king's tent and made my way two or three paces towards the adjacent tent with Lana trailing behind me, then stopped and lifted my head to the sounds of the forest nightlife. The birds were quiet, but the wildlife scurried around, restless to have the night to themselves in its envelope of silence.

All accompanied by the sensation of being watched.

The campfire lit up the immediate area, but stopped at the perimeter of the clearing, like it hit a wall of darkness. My skin prickled on the back of my neck and I knew, without knowing how or why, that someone was out there staring back at me. Could it be that obnoxious priest we had run into earlier? Perhaps he had come back to plant the false stories in the minds of our people and was checking to make sure the job was done.

Lana all but barrelled into the back of me and we held on to each other, then stumbled in semi-darkness into my tent.

'Your Majesty, forgive me,' she said, and blushed under the torch-lit entrance to our tent.

'Nonsense, Lana. It was my fault.'

She looked up at me with innocent eyes that spoke volumes about the mistreatment of her memories, not to mention her integrity. I smiled, and we clung onto each other as we tumbled through the tent flap and prepared ourselves for the night. Lana had partitioned off a section of the tent within easy reach of my pallet, should I need attendance in the night. I was glad, at least, for that, as the thought of prying eyes in the forest and potential unwelcome visitors made me still uneasy.

'Can we put something against the entrance, Lana?'

'Your Majesty?'

'To keep the foxes out,' I said.

'Oh. Yes, of course.' Lana pushed a basket full of robes in front of the tent flap, and knotted the ties on either side. 'There, that should do it, your Majesty,' she said.

Lana settled herself back down behind her partition. Anyone trying to sneak in during the night would, at the very least, trip over the basket and alert us to their presence. I lay my head back, secure enough in my surroundings, and exhausted enough by the day to let sleep take me.

It wasn't the noise that woke me. The intruder was either most athletic and very adept at untying the knots on our tent flaps, or they had sneaked in whilst we were having supper. It was the scent that woke me: a pungent, lemon balm, twisted with valerian root.

The Devil's Breath.

I had smelt it once in the Royal Apothecary. What was it doing in my tent? As the thought hit my mind, a hand clamped down on my face, and the stench of long-discarded lemons engulfed my nostrils. Without thinking, I rolled my body to the side and held my breath. I let out a squeal and rammed an elbow up and back, which connected with something soft. There was a muffled grunt from my assailant.

A dark, shrouded figure bent double behind me, and clutched a hand to their face. The distraction was enough for me to roll out of my pallet with an un-queen-like thump to the ground, which would likely result in bruised knees. That was the least of my worries as I shuffled on all fours over to Lana's section of the tent. I pulled back the partition and stared down at my sleeping handmaid. It was dark, but my eyes had adjusted, and I could make out the rise and fall of her chest. She let out a contented breath and rolled her head to one side. A light snore escaped into a wad of cloth drenched in the stench of the Devil's Breath. Lana would not wake for a good number of hours, and would not remember what happened here tonight.

I had to escape, had to get out of there or I would also end up in a sweet dreamless slumber, vulnerable to whatever ulterior motives drove the dark stranger in my tent. I leapt for the entrance, and promptly fell over the trap intended to stop intruders. The basket of robes spilled out over the rushes on the floor as I fumbled with the knots tied so deftly by Lana.

The shrouded figure had regained some composure and came for me again, swiping aside the deluge of silk, lace, and woollens that littered my path to the exit. They had a fistful of cloth that dripped with the Devil's Breath. I burst out into the silence of the night.

The camp was dark now that all torches were extinguished, with the only light coming from the faint embers of the cook's fire. The figure came up from behind. I darted towards the fire, but my pursuer was faster, and wrapped two arms around my thighs, tackling me to the ground. They groped for purchase on me, and I whipped my head around from side to side to avoid that damn cloth reaching my face. I kicked my feet any which way, with no actual skill but a fervent hope that I would connect with a vital point. I felt a crack and a heard faint groan from the figure. Their hold on me loosened enough for me to wriggle forward on my elbows and knees towards the fire, where I spied something handy to use as a weapon.

'Damn it, stay still,' a thick voice growled from beneath the heavy cowl that shrouded their face. 'It's for your own good.'

I had a mind to argue that if it was indeed for my own good, then why did my pursuer feel the need to knock me out cold, and then use violent behaviour when that plan didn't work? Did no-one practice negotiation in Tordre?

My breath came heavy and fast, and I was in no mood to discuss. My only thought was to get away as fast and far as possible. It seemed to be taking an age to inch my way forward towards the fire, and as I struggled, a hand grabbed my ankle and wrenched, sending me flat on my face and moving me back to my starting point.

I had enough foresight to reach out and grab the nearest pan, which happened to be a nice iron-bottomed skillet that would do the job I had in mind. I stopped, knelt up and used all the leverage I could muster to swing the skillet in a neat arc to where I calculated the stranger to be.

It connected, all right. There was a sickening crunch, followed by a faint moan and a thump, as the body hit the ground and lay facedown in an ungainly heap.

# CHAPTER TEN

## *Into the Forest*

I was stunned. For a brief moment, I stood and looked at the pile of dark robes that covered the body I had whacked with a skillet. I looked at the offending utensil, still clutched in my hand, then looked at the body. Never before had I hurt someone enough to knock them out like that.

I shuddered at what I was capable of. Although tempted to peep beneath the stranger's mask, I knew that if I didn't move fast there would be more wrongdoers appearing, backing up the first when they realised their accomplice had not returned with their target.

No one sent one person to steal a queen.

The thought spurred me into action and I dropped the skillet and fled into the relative safety of the forest. They had cut the horses from their tethers and the animals were out of sight, so I ran with only the thought of escaping whoever meant me harm.

Would it be safer to go back and rouse the priest-king and the royal entourage to come to my rescue? Perhaps. But how was I to know they were not the very people who sought to silence me? I was carrying a very grave secret about the King of Tordre and his so-called royal household. Somebody wanted me silenced. It also seemed strange to me that there was no one on lookout duty in the camp. Where were our royal guards, who were our shadows in times like these? Another good reason not to rouse the entourage.

Outside the camp, I realised with growing dread why no-one had come to my aid. The bodies of our guards lay littered like dead soldiers on a battlefield, dragged into the bushes and dumped. I nudged one with my toe and the useless mound of armour grumbled and muttered in deep sleep. If someone had the foresight to knock out the guards and my handmaid, they would be determined enough to come back for me.

So, I ran.

In my royal night-time shift, I gathered bramble scratches and tears in my skirts, despite hitching them up to ease my route through the trees. The direction didn't matter to me, I ran to get away. Away from the apparent danger and away from the horror of what I had done.

I was a respectable young princess who didn't go around hitting people over the head. I was nothing like my sister, who thought nothing untoward about gallivanting through forests with rangers and playing at sword fighting.

As I stumbled through the undergrowth, I thought about Alliane. Right then, I wanted nothing more than to be by her side; to see her sarcastic grimace at my disapproval of her behaviour. I wanted to cry… 'look, look, I can play at rangers too.' But this was no longer play. I was running for my life.

Some distance ahead, I heard voices arguing. Perhaps they had realised too late the stupidity of sending only one man to bring back the queen. Or perhaps they underestimated the resourcefulness of that queen. I slipped behind a large oak and listened as a group of five wandered into a clearing.

'We have little time,' a female voice said. 'The sleeping draft is only effective for a short stint, and those men required double strength to send them down.'

I peered around the trunk. Her face was visible beneath a burgundy hood that attached to a figure-hugging cloak. I could see she was older than myself by ten years or more. The others, all men, at first glance seemed to follow her, except for one who I presumed was young by the jaunty way he held his body. Confident, commanding. Not like the other three, who carried themselves with subservience.

'Kerrin, don't make assumptions. He'll return soon enough. It doesn't take the six of us to contain one young girl.'

Yes, definitely too confident. It already rankled. And who was the one making assumptions here? Not the woman called Kerrin, an unusual name for these parts. Perhaps they meant to replace the queen as well as the king?

'We have to wait,' Kerrin said. 'We don't have enough of the draft for the entire camp, and we can't afford to rouse the sleeping staff with our presence.'

'One last turn of the camp and then I'm going in,' the young man said.

Well, that was it. I couldn't go back now. Before long, they would realise that their accomplice was not coming out and provide backup. So, my only thought was that of escape. To where, I did not know, but anywhere was safer than near that camp. I hung behind the tree, and waited for the strangers to pass on their round before I darted off in the opposite direction.

Running was not my strength. Inevitably, in a short time, my breath ran ragged, my progress slowed, and I found myself utterly lost. Not to mention exhausted. My flimsy slippers were caked in mud, my arms and legs scratched and sore, and my hair probably looked more like a bird's nest than a style befitting a queen.

I noticed soon that it was hard to tell which direction you were moving in, as every path appeared to be the same in the forest. Every tree looked somehow familiar, and after a while I was certain I had passed the same tree several times over.

I lowered myself to the ground beneath the domed canopy of a beech tree. Exhausted and hungry, I raked my fingers through the carpet of fallen leaves at the foot of the trunk, picking up a few stray beechnuts that the squirrels had missed. I peeled one, then sat and chewed, allowing the nutty flavour to still my aching stomach. Food was the least of my worries. I didn't know where I was, how far from the border I had run, or where I should go next. Plus, I needed to find a freshwater stream to slake my thirst before I shrivelled up like a raisin.

The dark was fading, and the sun was rising. I guessed by now that the strangers had found their accomplice, and either extracted them from the camp or left them to the wrath of the priest-king when he awoke. I leaned my head back against the tree bark and took some slow breaths. Perhaps I could afford to take a quick rest. I must have run far enough to have lost the strangers, and had now lost my own sense of direction, with no idea whether I was still in Tordre, had crossed the border, or had been running around in circles.

I closed my eyes for a moment to contain my breath. The noises of waking woodland creatures crept around me, amplified by the fact I had my eyes closed. The sappy scent of wood calmed my nerves, and when I opened my eyes to a rustling in the undergrowth, though I almost leapt back in surprise, I held my ground in front of the curious predator that peered at me through green eyes.

A wild cat; eyeing me up as prey. This one was too small to want to eat me, I hoped. It had mottled tabby fur, which blended into the bark of the trees. If you looked from a distance, all you might see were its two green eyes staring at you. The illusion was broken when it crouched into the undergrowth, its two triangular ears flicking to the side and back, scanning the area for sounds. The ears had two little tufts of fur at the tips, giving it an owl-like appearance. I had seen the mountain cats of the Helm once before and knew what that crouch meant.

I sat still.

With its ears flattened, and backside quivering, the cat prepared to pounce.

'Please,' I whispered. 'I really don't taste too good. For a cat, anyway.' What kind of fool was I, sitting there in semi-darkness, bedraggled and wretched, munching on beechnuts and talking to a wildcat?

It sprang, and for one painstaking heartbeat I held my breath, waiting for the claws to dig into me. I had instinctively closed my eyes, preparing for the worst, but, when nothing came, I opened them again just as the cat sunk its claws into the tree above me and scampered up, disappearing into the canopy. I let out my breath. That cat was a lot bigger up close than I had originally thought, though closer to a medium-sized dog than a mountain cat.

I heard a strangled cry from the tree above me that sounded more human than a cat. As I scrambled to my feet, two things happened simultaneously. A body shot out of the tree to the ground, with a loud 'oomph' when it hit the carpet of fern around the tree, and the undergrowth burst into life as four robed individuals launched themselves at me.

I was held fast by two, while the third held a doused cloth over my face, the pungent scent of Devil's Breath filling my nostrils. I held my breath for as long as possible and watched the fourth robed stranger check out his friend, who screamed and held his lacerated face whilst drops of blood oozed from between his fingers.

Barely had I counted to twenty before expelling my breath, unable to last any longer. I had no choice but to inhale. By the third breath, a dark curtain descended inside my head, and I slipped into a deep sleep.

# CHAPTER ELEVEN

### *A Tavern in T'sar*

My head thrummed, and my nose and throat felt like someone had stuffed me with cotton wool. I groaned, and wondered why I had let the king persuade me to drink more wine. I turned my head to the side and opened one eye, expecting to see the tent flap and the cloth partition between mine and Lana's pallets. Instead, I saw a face peering back at me.

I gasped and tried to sit up, but a wave of nausea washed over me, and darkness crept around the edges of my vision. Taking a deep rattling breath, I dropped my head back onto a soft feather-down pillow, and closed my eyes until the dizziness receded, and I could trust myself to open them without losing the contents of my stomach.

'I'm sorry. It's not pleasant, but the effects will wear off quickly.'

I rolled my head to one side and stared at the face that looked at me with concerned eyes. He looked familiar, but I couldn't quite place him. Then I remembered.

'You?'

'Da'ashtange,' he said in a soft voice, with none of his previous mocking confidence. His greeting sounded like an apology. His fair hair was un-plaited and a tangled mess, and his tunic looked like it had been dragged through a hedgerow backwards, but his blue eyes sparkled with keen intellect.

'No.' My voice croaked through the mist of the sleep drug. 'Not well met. Where am I?' I looked around at the room for the first time: a comfortable chamber by any standards, with a hearth fire and a suite of chairs. A gaudy tapestry hung on the wall, and the heavy drapes attempted to cut out any natural light, though a sliver of sunshine peeped through gaps in the fabric.

'We are in T'sar,' he said.

'How is that possible?' T'sar was at least a day's ride away from our campsite. 'Was that you in the forest, with that red-haired woman and the cloaked men?'

He nodded, quick and curt, and had the decency to look sheepish. If I had the strength and wasn't feeling the ill-effects of the Devil's Breath, I might have slapped him there and then.

'Here.' He pulled over a tray that held a cup of steaming liquid and a platter of bread, with assorted cheese and meats. My stomach roiled at the sight of it. 'Let me help you sit up. After what you did to poor Idris we couldn't take any chances, and I'm afraid Kerrin gave you a dose big enough to knock out an elephant. You've been out for more than a day, you must be feeling pretty groggy.'

He lent me his arm, and I wriggled myself back enough to sit up against the soft pillow. *Groggy? I could smack this young man. What was his name?*

'What did you say your name was?'

'Tristan. Tristan Bacha.'

Yes. That was it. Now I remember. It was then that I noticed I was no longer wearing my nightgown, and was dressed in a long woollen robe. My hands and feet had been cleaned and were no longer caked in the mud of my midnight tramp through the forest. Soft silk slippers now covered my feet instead. I blushed from my chest up to my cheeks and let out a strangled gasp.

He raised his hands up in defence. 'Not me. Gods, no. Kerrin cleaned you up and changed you.' I was relieved, but insulted that the thought of seeing my body so repulsed him.

'How dare you steal the queen!'

He opened his mouth as though to argue, then thought better of it, and instead took out that strange round toy that I had seen him spin out from his hand on our last encounter. He played a little with the string, then launched it to the floor, the disc whirling down and then up, its colours swirling into a blur of muddy purple.

'Why do you keep playing with that thing?'

'It's called a banda, and it helps me to think.' He whirled it out on its string. 'Here, take it.' He caught the round disc in his palm after its string magically rewound and held it out to me. I took it, and turned it over in my palm, then slipped my finger through the loop at the end of the string, mimicking what I had seen Tristan do. I leaned over the bed and let go. It hit the floor with a "thunk", and stubbornly remained there.

69

He laughed, and poured out a cup of something hot, handing me the drink in exchange for the banda. I cradled the hot cup and inhaled the spices and sharpness of mulled wine as he wound the string back around his banda with studied devotion. I took a sip of the wine, which trickled down my throat and warmed my insides. The feeling of being stuffed full of cotton started to dissipate.

'Are you going to tell me, then?' I said.

'What?' He looked up.

'Why you felt the need to steal me away from right under the nose of our king?'

He smirked to himself and shook his head. 'No king of mine,' he muttered. 'Do you realise you nearly killed Idris?'

Events of the previous evening filtered back into my memory, along with the hopeless realisation that I had married a false king.

'He attacked me.'

'Besides... you're not really the Queen of Tordre.' He said it so matter-of-factly while staring me directly in the eye. I opened my mouth to speak, but instead took a large gulp of wine. My clarity of thought had returned, but if I drank much more it was likely to disappear again just as fast. I put the cup down and broke some bread, nibbling at it before swallowing. The dry blandness of it helped to ease the nausea in my stomach.

Tristan watched me, waiting for a reaction. When none was forthcoming, he spun out his banda and made looping shapes, narrowly missing the jug of wine.

'Who are you? Some kind of travelling entertainer with your lute and your strange... banda-thing? What do you care about the lives of kings and queens?'

He released the banda, and it went spinning off to clatter to a stop in a corner. He stood and reached for my shoulders. At first I thought he was going to shake me or hit me and, without thinking, I lifted my arms to deflect his grip, using my palms to shove him away. He toppled over backwards and landed with a thump on his backside.

*Oh gods, what am I doing? First his friend Idris, and now Tristan.* 'Are you okay?' I said, shocked at my behaviour. He merely looked surprised.

'Where did you learn to do that?'

I swung my legs over the side of the bed and stood far too quickly, making the blood rush to my head. I crouched down, and the dizziness dissipated, allowing me to creep over to where Tristan sat on the floor and look at him.

'Sorry, I didn't think, just reacted. My brother taught me a few things. It helped to keep at bay any unwanted attention from courtiers.'

'Hmmn.' He didn't look convinced. Frowning, he said, 'Your brother... you mean the future King of Carentan?'

Gereinte was on his grand tour, and I sometimes forgot he was the future king. They had not allowed me to visit for so long; all that time I had been kept a prisoner in that dreary castle by a false king when I should've been with my family.

'That bastard priest-king.' I slapped my hand on the wooden floor, and it made a satisfying crack.

Tristan flinched and held his palms up. 'Okay, okay. I'm not going to argue with you.'

'Don't touch me when I'm angry,' I said.

'I get it. I get it. I was only going to help you, but you got up too quickly, now look at you.'

'Now look at us,' I said. We both sat in the middle of the floor when there were two perfectly good seats near the window. 'How do you know about the priest-king?'

'Ah, well, I have my sources.'

'And who are you, anyway?'

'Well, that bit you may find harder to believe.'

I narrowed my eyes. 'Try me.'

'I'm the true King of Tordre.'

I looked at Tristan Bacha in his tattered and travel-worn tunic with his cheeky grin, and he reminded me of that boy who nearly destroyed my life. True king? So, I ran away from what I thought was true love for a peasant boy, only to be married off to a priest when, really, I should have married... a peasant boy? I erupted into a crazed, yet weirdly euphoric laughter.

'Oh, that's... rich,' I said. My sides ached, and tears leaked from the corners of my eyes. He looked at me with a somewhat bemused expression. He wasn't laughing. In fact, he looked a little hurt by my reaction.

'Sorry.' My laughter trailed off.

'I realise it must be hard for you to believe,' he said.

71

'No, it's not that.' I wanted to explain, but it was all too complicated. I wasn't in the mood to open up my barely healed wounds.

'Right, then.' He stood and dusted down his tunic, spreading more of the dust around. 'We have a false king to catch, and you need to be ready to return to Castle Ryemont by daybreak.' And with that, Tristan Bacha stood up and walked away.

'Wait. Wait a moment. I can't go back to the castle. He knows I know. My life will be forfeited. Would you really do that? Can't you help me get back to my family?' He swung open the door. 'They will be here before too long, you know. I sent a message.' He turned to look at me and grimaced as though I were an irritating fly. 'My brother will come and get me. Whoever you are or claim to be, I'm still a princess of Carentan.'

He turned back to me, and pulled a square piece of parchment from his pocket. 'You mean this message?'

I staggered to my feet and moved towards Tristan, my eyes on that familiar script on the outside of the letter. It was my letter. The one I had re-written and asked Bax to send home to my family.

Tristan watched me carefully but was not quick enough to stop me snatching it out of his hand and opening it. The seal had been broken and the parchment was crumpled, as though several prying eyes had already had their fill.

'How…?'

'Bax is my inside ally. About the only one I have until now.' He looked me up and down, probably reassessing that last assumption. 'What are pygmies anyway, and who is Anateus?'

'No… I mean, how dare you?'

He looked dumbfounded.

'That was a personal message to my brother, and if you think I'm going to explain it you are very much mistaken. Please get out of this room, and don't assume that I intend to cooperate with your crazy plan to send me back to Castle Ryemont, unless you can give me a better reason.'

'What better reason than to obey your true king?' He looked smug.

Never mind whether he was a true king, I was about ready to slap his regal face. He sensed my volatile mood and stepped back out of the door, well out of my reach. I stepped up as

72

though to follow, placed my palm on the door handle, smiled sweetly, and slammed the door in his face. I stood still for a moment, waiting to see if he would do anything, but all I heard was a loud groan of exasperation, followed by feet shuffling away.

# CHAPTER TWELVE

## *Music and Memories*

I stared at the door for a good few minutes, then stepped back into the room. My skin itched with frustration, and I remembered the sensation of helplessness as I recalled the last time I had been played for a fool. Well, that would not happen again.

I had to get out of there and return to my family. But what would I say to them? That I married a usurper who is really a priest with the ability to change his face at will, and that the real King of Tordre was a travelling minstrel with the cheek of a court jester, who wanted to send me back to Castle Ryemont to be his spy? They would never believe me. Darkness be damned if I was going to go from one puppet master to another, to do their bidding as though I were some fool of a girl who would fall in love at the drop of a pebble.

I was a princess of Carentan, and if I was going to get out of this mess I could damned-well do it all by myself, without being beholden to any Tordrean political antics. Once I had proof of what was going on, I would find a way back to Carentan and present it to my mother, the Queen Regent. The only place I knew where to look for proof was Castle Ryemont. So yes, I would go back to the castle and present myself to the false king, but it would be on my own terms.

I looked around the room to see if I could find any provisions to take with me. Tristan's group had snatched me from the forest with only a nightgown on my back, so all I had were the clothes they had put me in, and the food left on the trestle. I used a tablecloth to create a knapsack by tying two ends around my neck. I folded the remaining bread, cheese, and meats into the cloth, alongside a stoppered jug of watery wine, and tied the remaining ends together around my waist. It would do. At least it would keep me alive until I could find my way back to the castle.

I pressed my ear to the door. There were no immediate sounds on the landing outside, but my ear vibrated with a distant hum of music, which carried through the thin walls. It was pure, yet melancholic, and mirrored my mood. I inched open the door with silent deliberation and stepped out onto the landing. The music drifted up the winding spiral staircase along with the mingled scent of ale and mutton pie. My stomach grumbled, but I hugged my makeshift lunch sack tighter to my middle and pushed on past the entrance to the common room, past the kitchens, and towards the outside door.

'Hey, you shouldn't be down here. Does the Innkeeper know? This area is not for public use.' The man had come out of the kitchen carrying two steaming bowls. He had a towel draped over one arm, and his apron was stained and threadbare. Sweat beaded his brow.

'Of course, so sorry. I thought this way would be quicker. Please... let me help.' I moved to the man's side and offered to take one of the bowls. He turned away from me and snarled under his breath.

'Away with you. I won't tell him this time. Be sure to use the front entrance in the future.'

'Oh, yes, of course. Thank you.' I turned back to the hall and the door at the end that beckoned my freedom. The man trudged off towards the common room with his precariously balanced bowls of stew. A swing door opened, and the melodious tune of the lute and a soft vocal harmony stopped me for a moment.

The hairs on the back of my neck stood up as I recognised that voice. I looked back at the doors at the end of the corridor and could make out the hooded figures of two people outside. *Great.* Someone guarded the back door.

The door that the barkeep had gone through swung back, and the music muffled and dispersed into the background noises. I crept forward, unable to stop my curiosity, and nudged the door forward to reveal a crack of a view into the common room. Tristan sat at a table with the red-haired woman, Kerrin. She waved at someone, then she turned her attention to Tristan, but he was oblivious to her. His eyes were closed, and his lips moved with the sound and rhythm of the music. His fingers skimmed across his lute, as though it were part of his body.

How would a king find the time to play like that?

Angry though I was, something about him invited familiarity. Perhaps it was the music. Perhaps the nature of his talent was to make all of his audience feel that way; as though they had known him forever. The music held me in the grip of an illusion far stronger than that of the priest-king. So much so that I almost forgot why I was there, until the crash of a door caught my attention.

The two figures that had stood outside had left their guard post. I slipped inside the common room, hid behind the bar, and sat on a keg of ale, listening to footsteps clatter up and down the stairs on the other side of the door.

The music stopped, and another man appeared at the table, dropping into a seat beside Tristan and Kerrin. Tristan lowered the lute and turned his attention to the newcomer. The man's face had a couple of bruises and a swollen lip, which gave him a thuggish look despite his aristocratic attire.

With the music now stopped, it was possible to hear the indistinct murmur of voices in the room. I crept to the end of the bar and found a neat little hidey-hole where I could see through a crack in the bar and make out what they were saying.

'Your Majesty,' the newcomer said.

'Don't-' Tristan raised his hands as if to ward off evil spirits, then let his hands drop in defeat. Kerrin poured him a cup of wine. He took a long draft of the wine, and his facial expression relaxed. 'I can't get used to this. It still feels as though I am pretending. It feels like I am the usurper, not that... priest.' He took out the banda and idly spun it up and down beside him.

The newcomer watched the spinning object with an obsessive fascination. Kerrin squeezed the man's upper arm, and the newcomer looked blankly at Kerrin before he smiled, forgetting whatever had captured his attention.

'It's going to take time,' Kerrin said. 'If it is this hard for you, think how it must be for the average household. How did it go with our captive?'

Tristan caught the banda, rewound the string, and dropped it on the table. 'She's utterly insufferable. I don't know what else you expected from a Carentan princess.'

I took a sharp intake of breath, and covered my mouth with my hand to stop myself from squeaking with indignation.

'She can be as insufferable as she likes as long as she cooperates,' Kerrin said.

'Ah. Well, that might be a problem.'

Kerrin folded her arms. 'What did you do?'

'She didn't like the fact that we intercepted her letter.'

'Why did you tell her that?'

Tristan looked sheepish. 'I thought I could use it as a bargaining point. She clearly wants to return to her family after all.'

'We need her on our side if you want to take back your rightful place,' Kerrin said.

So he really was the true king? I found that difficult to believe.

Tristan picked up the banda and rolled it into his palm. 'Are you sure about this? About us?' Kerrin gave him a sideways look. 'As long as I never have to marry her, that's all. I want to choose my own queen.'

The dirty little weasel... it was an arrangement between our nations. My mother would lose her presence of mind if she could hear this.

'You are the true king,' the other man said, lisping through his swollen lip.

*Oh my word.* Through the crack in the bar, I saw he had a large purple bruise on his forehead and one eye squinted shut. I flushed with guilt, realising that it must be his friend, Idris, the one I had clobbered.

'You can marry whomsoever you wish. It is in the constitution.' Idris looked satisfied, as though being beaten over the head with a skillet by his queen was a fading memory.

'Well, if we don't do something soon, the usurper will change the constitution and we're all screwed,' Kerrin said.

'Okay,' Tristan said with resignation, 'what do I need to do?'

'Men... honestly. Would it hurt to get to know her a bit better?'

He glared at Kerrin. 'I tried that and she slammed the door in my face. Oh, not before pushing me over when I was only trying to help. Can't you talk to her?'

'It has to be you, you're the king. You're the one she was meant to marry.'

Tristan pocketed his banda and reached for the lute that was propped up against his chair. He plucked a few strings, put his ear to the instrument and twiddled with the pegs. 'Well, I think she needs some time to think. Pressing the issue now will not help. She's angry at being drugged and dragged out of the forest.

Can't say I blame her.' He looked up at Idris, who rolled his eyes and made "pffft" noise through his lips. 'Idris... you need to talk to her.'

Idris put his hands up. 'No, no, no, that won't help. Besides, I'm not sure I could remain impartial.' He rubbed the back of his head and ran a wet tongue over his bruised mouth.

I winced to myself from my hidey-hole, and felt an overwhelming sense of guilt. Echoing my thoughts, Tristan said, 'but she seems to feel guilty about what happened. Especially when she realised you nearly died.'

'I didn't nearly die,' Idris said.

*Okay, so maybe I don't feel so guilty.*

'So I exaggerated a bit, but still... she thinks you nearly died, and you do look a bit of a state.'

'So would you if someone had whacked you around the head with a skillet, your Majesty.'

'Stop calling me that-'

'Boys, can we agree on a way forward?' Kerrin looked as though she were about to bang their heads together. Tristan plucked a few notes and adjusted the strings on his lute. 'Evidently, we need to do some more work on your memories,' she said.

'My memory is fine, it's him you need to work on,' Idris said.

Tristan plucked a few strings and let the notes sing true across the tavern. A few heads looked up to search for the source. 'Remind me again, who is the King of Tordre?' he said.

'It is you, your Majesty,' Idris said, with a glance at Kerrin.

Tristan's fingers formed patterns on the frets of his lute, the skill so ingrained in his muscle memory that it needed no thought at all. 'Yes. So it is.' He looked up and gave Idris a pointed stare.

Idris raised his hands in submission. 'Okay, okay, I'll try. But don't blame me if it makes things worse.'

# CHAPTER THIRTEEN

## *Trapdoors and Secrets*

Idris stood and left. I knew that as soon as he reached the room where I was supposed to be, he would discover me gone and alert Tristan. I cursed my damned curiosity and propensity to eavesdrop, and uncurled myself from my hiding position.

Tristan played the lute, drawing the attention of the common room, but there was a movement on the other side of the door. Had the barkeep returned, or was Idris climbing the stairs? Indecision paralysed me.

I crept back to the door and peered through the crack. There were two figures on guard at the outside door. I heard a hurried crash of footsteps coming down the stairs at double speed.

The music petered out into a few single notes, then a strum, then nothing, as an agitated mutter of people replaced the music. Idris strode back to the table and whispered in Tristan's ear, who looked up with mild surprise. Tristan's expression turned dark. Then the pair of them took off at speed, closely followed by Kerrin, who didn't look surprised at all.

If I stayed there, one of two things was likely to happen: the barkeep would come back and discover me, or Tristan and his accomplices would find me as they scoured the building. I crouched down on all fours, my heart hammering inside my chest. The surrounding chaos escalated, and I realised now was my only chance to escape. If I could wedge myself under the bar, I could stay there until it were dark and the commotion had died down, and then sneak out. I had food, and I had drink.

Looking down I saw the outline of a trapdoor on the floor, and remembered when, as a child, my siblings and I had explored the kitchens and pantries in Castle Helmstedt after dark. Trapdoor meant cellar. Cellars often had skylights, an exit to the outside. It was somewhere they may not look.

I crept to the trapdoor and inched my fingers around the edge, looking for a catch, and found an iron ring pull. I looped my finger through it and lifted. Gods it was heavy. I had to wedge my arm underneath, and roll myself into the opening to make sure it shut above me. I was not dressed for this kind of thing. It was so dark that I missed a step and slipped down the stairs, saved only by the bundle of goods wrapped around my middle. I bounced off the staircase with a loud crack and landed in a heap on the floor.

A seeping river of liquid ran down my front, soaking my dress and trickling down my legs. The sweet, musky scent of wine filled my nose. *Great. Well, at least if I made it out onto the street, I could pretend to be a homeless peasant and most people would shy away from the stink of me.*

I unwrapped the bundle around my waist and picked out the shards of the broken jug as my eyes adjusted to the dark. It was indeed a cellar, and there was a crack of light from outside which illuminated a viable exit.

There was indeed a cellar skylight with two wooden doors, and a plank of wood leading down into the room where the stacks of kegs on the floor were kept. Must lead to the outside, where the inn takes their supplies. Despite being soaking wet and stinking like a commoner, I felt a spark of hope. There was no point in carrying around a sack full of soggy bread and food, so I sat and nursed my bruises and munched my way through wine-soaked bread and cheese. I would need the energy to get out of there before someone found me.

It wasn't safe to go out yet. The stomp of footsteps and barrage of angry voices descended through the cracks in the floorboards above my head. Maybe if they were so busy searching the tavern, they wouldn't notice me sneak out of the cellar. I crept a little closer to the doors, but the figure of someone standing outside obscured the light and plunged the room into darkness.

I sat still, barely taking a breath and thinking all the time where I could hide. An empty barrel, perhaps? I would end up smelling so much of wine and ale that I could easily pass for a drunk on the streets. The thought made me smile to myself.

I took a sharp intake of breath and my heart leapt upon hearing the sound of a boot kicking the door.

'Anyone checked the cellar?' A gruff voice barked outside.

'Don't be daft,' another voice replied. 'She was last seen at the back door. Dara saw her. C'mon, she can't have got far. Everyone knows who she is.'

I wondered how many of them were haring off into town to look for me. They had a good point, everyone did know who I was. After the wedding, there were portraits of the supposed happy couple circulated to every baronial residence, as was customary. How did I think I could walk into town and not expect a commotion around me? It was all very well sticking to back roads and forest paths, but we were in the middle of T'sar.

The figure shifted, and light seeped back into the cellar as a pair of boots stomped away. I slumped back with a gasp. My best hope was to wait until nightfall, then slip out by the outside doors. I looked around the dank room and positioned myself beside a stack of empty barrels, then finished the rest of the food.

I dozed in and out of a wine-induced sleep, waking to complete darkness and a raging thirst.

My first thought was, *where the hell am I?* Then, upon remembering, I sat up too fast, causing my head to spin and nausea roil in my stomach. *Okay. So, take it easy now.* I had to get out as quickly as I could whilst the darkness of night could still mask my exit.

My dress was crusty with wine stains, giving me an idea. I found the grubbiest corner of the cellar and rolled around on the floor. I would have laughed if I hadn't been so scared that someone might come in at any moment. For good measure, I rubbed some dirt across my face and hands, then sniffed myself. *Phew.* I stank well enough to put off the most well-meaning stranger.

I folded the cloth used to wrap my provisions into a triangle and tied it around my head, like the peasant women who worked in the fields. No one would ever believe I was the queen.

I creaked the doors open a crack and put all my meagre weight behind them, hoping that my feet wouldn't crash through the thin, warped plank that held me up. They opened outward, so I had to swing them, and they crashed to the stony ground of the outside yard, making me wince and hold my breath for a few moments.

The noise echoed around the yard, but the night was silent. No running footsteps. No one came. I hoped that Tristan and his merry band had rushed off after me, and were at a sufficient distance outside the town to not notice my creeping retreat.

I hauled myself out of the cellar and made my way quickly and quietly towards the town through the darkness, hoping most people were tucked up inside their beds and wouldn't notice the strange beggar woman out on her own. In the distance, Castle Ryemont loomed over T'sar, the black cliffs over the western seas serving as a forbidding backdrop. The town walls circled in the distance and the irony of how easily I had escaped at night hit me. The city gates would be locked. There was little hope of getting beyond the walls before sunrise.

# CHAPTER FOURTEEN

### *Hiding in Plain Sight*

I kept as much to the shadows as possible, and shuffled around the edges of the buildings. There were others out there, sleeping in doorways, covered in rags, and they looked up in curiosity as I stumbled past. I didn't even have to affect a limp, as the fall down the cellar steps had bruised my leg enough to make it painful when I walked. The street-peasants didn't seem at all suspicious at my passing.

I went around the outside of the Town Hall, weaving in and out of the empty barrows, which would be heaving with goods and surrounded by people in the morning. Most of the street people lived in the central part of town nearest to the markets, which offered the detritus of richer folk's leftovers for a scrap to eat. I knew people lived like this, but I had never seen it, and never walked amongst them. A lump rose in my throat. The gown on my back may have been filthy and stained, but at least it was still in one piece.

An old woman with gnarled hands and a sackcloth for a dress reached out and touched the hem of my gown with a dazed kind of reverence. Her expression changed as a spark of an idea lit up her rheumy eyes. I had to get out of there, and quick. The woman sprang forward, and I realised too late that she wasn't as old as she looked. Life on the street had taken its toll on her appearance, but she was lithe and strong enough to catch me.

I fell to the ground and bashed my already injured knee, sending pain shooting up my leg. Her hands grabbed me from behind, wrapping around my neck, and the weight of her bony body sat on me. This woman meant to rip the very fabric from my back.

*Think.*

This was a favourite of the bigger pageboys; get their prey to the ground and then sit on them. I lifted my backside into the air and bucked like a horse. The woman clung on with an iron grip around my neck, which tightened the higher I tried to lift.

I coughed and choked for breath, but those gnarly hands gripped tighter, mocking the weakness of their appearance. My energy flailed, but unless I could release her grip, I was going to be strangled to death right there on the street.

All for a dress. It made no sense. I had a flashback to the forest, and the fortuitous proximity of that skillet, although perhaps not so fortuitous for Tristan's friend Idris. My arms were free, but there was nothing within my reach, and even if I had a weapon, I was facedown, with no leverage to swing a saucepan.

I jabbed an elbow behind me in desperation. It hit thin air and only tightened the grip on my throat. The edges of my vision blurred, and emptiness buzzed around my head. *Any moment now it will all be over.*

I sent the other elbow up and back.

It connected with a crunch, and the woman whimpered. The grip loosened enough to give me traction, and I tried again to buck her off me. This time, she wobbled and wavered before toppling off.

I rolled to my side and coughed for breath, then scrambled away from the woman. The shadows around the street moved towards me as more street people came out of hiding, eager to share in the rich pickings of this strange traveller that had appeared in their midst.

*Oh Gods. I might be able to handle one half-starved woman, but three… five, six?*

I was surrounded. No place to run, and now, no place to hide. They knew it too, as they advanced on me with the greedy lust of people who have gone without for far too long. Out of the bundles of rags, stick-like arms reached out for me. I shrank back, only to find a sea of arms hovering behind me. With a snake-like speed, one of them snatched at my headscarf. A second attempt freed it from my head, and my hair tumbled down around my shoulders.

I closed my eyes, breath rattling and weak.

Let it be quick.

When nothing happened, I opened one eye to see a bunch of interested faces peering at me.

'It's her,' one of them said.

I blinked, and returned their curious gaze. Another of them, a woman older than the one who attacked me, had my headscarf tied haphazardly around her head, and inspected the ends as though expecting them to tie themselves. The mob parted to let a younger man step forward. He was dishevelled, like the rest of them. He had a grubby face, and wore tatters for clothes beneath a long, mud-spattered coat. He had a certain air about him, a deep-rooted confidence that marked him apart from the rest.

'You're the one they've been looking for all day,' he said. I rubbed my neck where bruises had formed.

'Who...' my voice came out strained and gravelly, like the pipe-smokers who sat outside taverns puffing all day.

'Who hasn't been looking?' the woman who attacked me said. 'First it was that lot from the castle, then this other lot today... who are you then?'

The young man rolled his eyes and gave the woman a little shove. 'Lyza, when are you going to pay attention to what's going on around you? It's the queen.' The entire group perked up, as a collective moment of realisation settled on them.

'Nah...' Lyza moved into my personal space and looked me up and down. She sniffed me and recoiled. I flinched and scrabbled backward, only to hit my back against the wall of the Town Hall. I wished for the ground to swallow me up. No such luck. 'What's she doing out? You people don't go nowhere without them guards. She's covered in wine and dirt.' She looked at me but addressed the rest of the group, who looked blankly at one another.

'Long story.' I said.

'Well,' the young man said, 'we like stories, so you can come with us and keep warm for the rest of the night, or stay out here and get caught by whichever group finds you first. That being if the scavengers don't rip you to pieces before morning.'

Other than the starving peasants, I wasn't quite sure which scavengers he referred to, but I kept my own counsel and allowed them to lead me through the narrow, cobbled streets to a large awning that covered the back entrance to the Town Hall. There, several makeshift pallets dotted the area, created from what looked like straw-filled blankets, crudely pinned at either end by some form of twine.

Waif-like people with soulful eyes looked up at me with passing curiosity, before resuming their attempts to sleep. Someone threw a blanket at me, which landed on my shoulder, and I pulled it down and around myself in defence.

'Respect for your queen,' the young man said. A few people looked up at me, then lay back down and dismissed the idea that I could be a queen. You could hardly blame them. I wouldn't have believed I was a queen.

Had I reached the bottom of the pit of desperation? Dressed in wine-stained rags, covered in grime with nowhere to go and no one to trust. What to do now, but hide? Hide in plain sight.

With weary resignation I sat down on an empty pallet, and shifted my weight to find a comfortable seat.

'What's your name?' I said. The young man appraised me with a knowing look in his eye. He sat opposite me, and produced a waterskin from the depths of his coat.

'My name is Dorshan. Dorshan Kharism. I once worked at the castle, you know. Until recent events, then all that opposed the new king's regime were ousted and named outlaws.'

'Recent events?' Had I been asleep all this time, while my false king plotted and schemed his way into power? And what of the true king? Dorshan read the look on my face.

'Ah. I see. That was a necessary evil, to keep you in the dark, keep you distracted. Tell me something. Since you left the castle, do you think more clearly?'

I must have flinched, because Dorshan looked pleased with his perception of the situation. 'It's a common phenomenon for those in the service of the Blue King.'

Dorshan was not like the others. He spoke like someone who had lived a life of privilege; someone trained to speak to kings and queens. 'I was the court scribe,' he said, as though reading my thoughts. 'I wrote all the accounts of the life and times of the Dreiden kings and queens.'

My fatigue abruptly lifted, and I sat up straight.

'You knew the true king?'

He looked me up and down with renewed curiosity. 'It hasn't taken you like the others, then.'

Of course, that was why the priest-king had kept me so tightly ensconced, with only ever the promise of visiting my family. Despite the ridiculous charade of travelling out to the border, he had no intention of letting me go. But he didn't realise how much clearer I could think once out of the fog of Castle Ryemont. If it hadn't been for Tristan Bacha and his dubious associates, I would have been back in that fog of despair. The idea of going back to the castle was not such a clever one after all.

'How does it work?'

'They thieve your thoughts is how,' Lyza shuffled into our space, having relieved someone of my headscarf. She held it towards me, and the tremor in her hand made it quiver. I shook my head.

'You keep it,' I said. She probably had more need of it than me. Lyza looked confused for a moment, before she wrapped the cloth around her head and neck. A gift was a rare thing in her world.

'They can compel you with the power of faith. The priests rise at the darkest hour of night to perform a ritual before the one god, usually in a holy place out of sight of others. The ritual spreads the faith across all people in proximity. I believe there are priests dotted all around Tordre at every temple and every place of worship. Their coup was swift and unrepentant. They captured those who showed any resistance, who either were sent to work in camps, ended up in one of the mass graves at Journey's End, or were swept out into the sea at the end of the Western Peninsular.'

I gasped at the memory of that night in the chapel, when I saw the priest-king at the altar of the one god. 'His face,' I said.

'You've seen it, then. You've seen him change?'

I stared at him, not trusting myself to say the words. Yes, I had seen the king change. His face, his demeanour. First in the chapel, when he appeared to have no face at all, then out at the border, when he became someone completely different.

'I lived in fear for a long time, and thought I was going mad. But now that I see him for what he is, I feel oddly liberated.'

'Fear is their secret. As long as you are afraid, they can take you. All those who dare to stand up to them end up in a death camp or on the streets. There are not enough of us here to stand up for a nation gripped in such torment.'

'Why can't we get a message out to Carentan, or anywhere… to get help from other nations?'

'No one has got beyond the borders. The priests have set up walls to intercept anyone who tries. Every carrier bird nationwide has been destroyed.'

'What about visitors? Surely they can't have stopped everyone coming and going in and out of T'sar? It is one of the largest trading centres for metalworks across the Western Isles.' How many lectures had I sat through with gritted teeth about the geopolitical advantages of Tordre? It had been part of my preparation to become a queen, to then be quashed and forgotten amid my post-marital nightmare. Out of the fog, the memories returned.

'Sure, we have visitors,' Dorshan said. 'But they too are conditioned by the concept of the one god. To the outside world, we are a nation that is fighting to better our living conditions and our wealth. That is often seen as an advantage.'

I needed to know what Bax had been writing in my letters in exchange for my own words of desperation to my family. Maybe there was a way to send a message if I could get back into the castle. But Tristan Bacha employed Bax. He had my letter. My skin prickled with heat at the thought of them poking through my personal messages.

'I have to get back to the castle.' I stood up.

'Whoa… wait.' Dorshan grabbed my arm and pulled me back down. 'It's not safe right now. Let's think this through. If you run straight back to the priests, all they'll do is lock you up for good in the castle, and what can you do there?'

I reluctantly sat back. He had a point. 'If I might get Bax to send my letter…'

'Bax. He's still in the king's employ?'

'Yes, but he works undercover for Tristan Bacha and his resistance. They had my letter. They are supposed to be working against the Blue King, but they stopped my letter being sent. Why would they do that?'

'Tristan Bacha, the true king?' Dorshan said, 'that's who the others were, the ones in black robes who were looking for you. Now, what does he hope to gain?'

'You're a storyteller-'

'-scribe.'

'Okay, scribe. But you tell stories - how would you play this one out?'

'For a start,' Dorshan said, 'a scribe differs from a storyteller. Storytellers make things up. I write the truth.'

'The truth as you see it,' I said.

88

He leaned his head in towards me. 'What other truth is there?'

'Show me.'

'I don't have any records here.' Dorshan looked around at the squalor they lived in. 'All the manuscripts are in the castle.'

'You're a scribe, you can't help but write, it's what you do. How else will you pass on the genuine history of what has happened here?'

He looked at me and captured my gaze for a moment, before he pulled out a battered old manuscript from an inside pocket of his coat.

# CHAPTER FIFTEEN

## *Truth, Stories and Lies*

I turned the pages of vellum, the double-stitched spine resisting my curiosity. This may have looked like a battered old book on the outside, but it made me realise that Dorshan was a master of his art. Without access to a stock of material, he had fashioned this book to record the passing of time in this most extraordinary era. His script flowed with care and resolve. A calling to capture the truth of this story for future generations.

My fingers skipped over the pages, my eyes lingering for brief moments on sections where I caught my name.

'Huh. That's not what happened,' I said. Dorshan leaned forward to see what I was reading.

'Well, then. You must tell me the truth of it, so that I can write a full and honourable account,' he said.

I read on, making small noises of appreciation, followed by disgruntled exclamations when the words didn't quite match my memory. Although I have to say that once in possession of the truth, it was hard for me to gauge what really happened as opposed to what I had imagined in my feverish state.

The only solace I gained was the knowledge that I had not made up this whole sorry state of affairs. I was not the crazy foreign queen that the court physicians and ladies-in-waiting would have had me believe. It must have been convenient for the priest-king to keep me in such a state of confusion and ignorance for so long.

'What now?' I said, handing the book back to Dorshan. He tucked it away, and patted the front of his coat for good measure.

'If I were a storyteller, not that I am, but if I were… I might send you back to the castle with some kind of protection. But then again, it might also be opportune to get you out of Tordre altogether.'

My heart sank at the thought of going back to the castle, but it also sang at the prospect of freeing this country from the grip of tyranny. What was Abiel Morda hoping to gain from this? And if by some miracle we brought an end to his games in Tordre, what is to stop him moving on to somewhere else?

Carentan even. That was how he worked, spreading his subtle conversion so entire communities depend on his leadership.

The rest of the night slipped away in fitful spurts of dreamless sleep. We were undisturbed until the murmur of morning and its shining light crept across our hiding place, revealing the true squalor of our existence. I had a moment of confusion when I lifted my eyelids to the dawn of market day in T'sar, before being doused with ice cold water, and prodded by a dour and resolved man with a besom broom.

'C'mon. Time to move yerselves.'

I gasped, coughed, and wiped the water from my face with a grubby sleeve that spread more filth across my cheeks. 'How dare you? Do you know…'

'Let's go, Lilly,' Dorshan barrelled into me, scooped me up along with an armful of bedding, and ushered me on. I looked back at the vendor, who set up his barrow and shook his head with disgust.

'What…? That's not my name,' I said, and spluttered to rid myself of dirty cold water that had run into my mouth.

'The moment anyone mentions the sight of you, word will get back to those who were searching for you yesterday and they'll turn this city inside out until they find you.'

My head reawakened to where we were and how I got there, and I had an irrepressible urge to run out into the square and have the first official I saw bundle me onto the back of a horse and take me back to the castle. At least there I would have food, water, and a clean bed.

My throat ached, my stomach stabbed me from the inside, and my arms and legs felt like they had sandbags attached to them. Not to mention the itch on my skin from sleeping on those bug-infested straw mats.

'Where do we go now?' I was weary and tired of being pushed around, dancing to everyone else's melody. I needed a safe place to hide and work out what to do next. The city was not a safe place.

'They'll be back to find you before long. If you want to stay out of enemy hands, you need to get out of here. Head back towards the marshes and follow the Caren as far as the estuary. You may not get out of Tordre, but you can hide in the marshes.'

'What about going back to the castle? If I run away, how will this story end?'

Dorshan looked at me with soulful eyes. 'I fear it will not end well for you if you stay. We may have more of a chance if you can get out of here and bring back an army.' I stumbled, and would have fallen if Dorshan had not held me up. The burden of that responsibility bore down on me.

'What if I let myself be caught?'

'Then they will keep you prisoner in Castle Ryemont, and you may never see your family again.'

'But you said only yesterday that you would send me back to the castle with protection...'

'Clarity in the light of day is a wondrous thing, my queen. I wish I could go with you for protection, but I am being watched myself. I am suspected of being in the resistance that the true king has formed, they would throw me into their dungeons without a second thought.'

We half-walked, half-stumbled across town as market stalls popped up, and horses' hooves clopped about their daily business down cobbled streets. Cartwheels clattered, and vendors shouted out their wares as the town woke up to a new day.

Apart from the odd glance of disgust and sniff of disapproval, no one gave us much attention as we hobbled around corners and lingered in doorways. We stopped by a well and slaked our thirst, before being shooed on by a group of women filling their buckets. I tried to wipe away some of the dirt on my face, but Dorshan held my hands away.

'Don't give anyone help in recognising you.' He released my hand, and I let it slump back to my side. I ruffled my hands through my hair, giving it a matted and tangled feel. Dorshan smiled. 'Better.'

The crowds thinned out the further we retreated from the city centre until we reached the outer walls. Sentry guards patrolled the gates with swords attached to their belts, and bowmen lined the walls, dotted at intervals and visible for all to see.

We stood and watched, hiding within the crowd to wait for an opportune moment.

'If I cause a distraction, do you think you can get out of the gate and over to that thicket over there?' Dorshan said.

I glanced out beyond the gates and along the track that led back to the castle. There was ample forest land to get lost in.

'Not in plain sight, they will register someone running. It always looks suspicious.' I looked around for any kind of cover.

We had almost exceeded the reasonable amount of time for a couple of beggars to be wandering near to the gate when I spied my possible salvation. A cart, loaded with grain sacks, creaked its way towards the gate. I ambled forwards with cupped hands and muttered words that made no sense, regardless of whether or not you could hear them.

The cart driver had to stop to avoid me and tried to shoo me away. He looked up when the noise of a drunken commotion nearby caught his attention. It was enough for me to slip onto the back, and slide a few empty sacks over the top of me. The driver looked back to where I had stood, shook his head, and cracked his whip to move his horses forward.

The sackcloth was musty and stank of mouldy oats, and all I saw were shadows, beside and above me, as we passed through the gates.

'Goodman.' The rough voice came from above. 'Stop your cart for a moment.'

My heart galloped. This was it. After all I had been through. It was back to the castle for me, where I was to be kept under lock and key. I held my breath.

'What wares do you carry?'

'Ah, grain for farmer's stock, sire. Meagre provisions.'

Silence. Shadows loomed above the grain sacks. A blade stabbed down beside me, and spilled oats rushed onto the cart's wooden pallet. I was about to throw off my cover, preferring that to being stabbed by a guard who knew no better, when I heard them say, 'We're looking for a young woman. Dark hair, dishevelled, possibly lost. Seen anyone of the like?'

The cart driver paused, and I prayed that my old beggar woman disguise allayed any suspicions.

'Nope,' the driver said. 'Wait.' My chest tightened. 'There was something…'

'Yes?'

'But no. This was back near the town hall some hours ago. Probably nothing. I passed some street people being ushered on. One of them had dark hair, like you say.'

'Thank you, Goodman.'

The shadows moved, and I heard feet hit the ground and stride away. I shuddered as the cart pulled into motion and the horses clip-clopped through the gate. A sudden wave of sickness overcame me, and I took some deep breaths.

To while away some time, I scooped a handful of scattered oats that had crept under my sackcloth with the jolting of the cart. I popped a couple into my mouth, and chewed laboriously as my stomach both grumbled and roiled in discontent.

After what seemed an age, I dared to peek from out of my hiding place and leapt back as two green eyes stared back at me, blinking in the shadow of my makeshift hidey-hole. I recognised the two owlish tufts in its ears and the mottled tabby fur. I leaned back as far as was humanly possible when crouched into the corner of a moving cart, as the cat reached out a tentative paw and patted first my forehead, then my nose.

Even as I closed my eyes and held my breath, the pain of my expected lacerations-by-claw didn't materialise. Releasing a long exhalation, I pulled the sackcloth over my face, and the cat settled its weight on my chest on the outside of the sack, pinning me to the cart. A loud rattle emanated from the animal and vibrated through my bones. It was purring.

I considered running the risk of discovery by making a bolt for the trees. By the time the driver would have plucked up the energy to run after me, if indeed he had any inclination to do so, I could have disappeared from sight. On reflection, this seemed like a bad idea, as all he had to do was raise the alarm in the next town, and the guards would be out scouring the undergrowth for me before I had gotten far enough. The cat apparently wasn't of the opinion that I needed to go anywhere soon.

The cart slowed down and the distant hum of people and markets grew louder as we came to a stop. There was a muffled clump as the driver dismounted from his box seat, followed by rummaging in the back of the cart, dangerously close to where I hid. I felt the cat instinctively lift its head.

'Damn soldiers, that's another bag ruined… no respect for an honest man's trade. Oh, hello Cara, didn't see you there.'

The cat made an odd mewl, as though greeting the driver, then put its head back down on top of my sack. The driver moved a little closer to stroke the cat, and I could distinguish the outline of his face. He looked around, checking the immediate area, and then inclined his head as though in curiosity. 'If I were you, I would stay still and not make a sound. I only have a quick delivery and then we'll be on our way,' he said in a low voice.

To any nearby observers, it might have looked as though he were talking to Cara, as the cat allowed him to stroke her head and continued to purr in response. Only I could see, through the thin webbing of the sackcloth, that his eyes were fixed on me. 'I can get you safe passage to the resistance. Tristan will brief them as we speak. He is a good man. You can trust in him.' Then he was gone.

What had I done? This man would trundle his cart right back to Tristan's doorstep if I stayed hidden under his grain sacks. I had to get off and away before the driver returned.

# CHAPTER SIXTEEN

## *A Timely Encounter*

I heard the cart driver stomp away, and as he left, Cara shifted her weight and stepped off my sackcloth covering. I hadn't realised how heavy the cat was until I could breathe again. It was like a medium-sized kennel hound. I had a moment of empathy for whichever of Tristan's guards had fallen foul of those claws. Cara pawed at the sackcloth, and the bustling marketplace came into view. I blinked in the daylight hitting the cobbled square and rows of winding streets. It was a smaller town, a suburb of T'sar.

'Oi, oi.' A man wheeling a barrow piled high with cabbages and carrots winked at me as he rolled past. 'Old man Grahl selling a new type of grain now, is he? You'll be wanting the bordello at the end of the street.' He laughed at his own jest and pointed towards a row of ramshackle houses that lined the street.

*Great.* Now I could add "lady of the night" to my list of disguises. If I wasn't so tired and hungry I might have been outraged. Cara pawed insistently at the sackcloth, so I stretched and rolled in a most unladylike way off the back of the cart, landing in a dusty heap. People walked on by, going about their business, hardly batting an eyelid.

I got up and stumbled, adding to the authenticity of the beggar-woman look.

'Spare any wares for a poor, hungry girl?' I said, wandering past various stalls. The scent of freshly baked bread stirred my stomach and steered me towards a friendly looking seller at the end of the row. Most that I passed shouted at me or threw rotten veg that was no good for even a street urchin. It took only minutes to reach the end of the street, and only minutes more to feel the humiliation that must be everyday life for people like Lyza and Dorshan.

Cara had followed me from the cart, but when I looked over my shoulder, all I saw was the tip of her tabby tail disappearing between stalls. The yeasty, sweet scent of fresh bread drew me forward, though I knew the response by now.

'Be on with ya, girl. No spare wares here,' the bread seller said.

'Please,' I said. 'Perhaps you have a spoiled cob you can't sell?'

'I said no. Now get!' The seller picked up a round object and made to throw it. I needed no further encouragement and turned on my heel and ran. A few yards on, the object hit me hard between the shoulder blades and dropped to the ground. It didn't hurt so much as it surprised me. I ducked down, picked it up and ran on.

The cobbled streets were unforgiving beneath my slipper-covered feet, and several times I had to slow down for fear of slipping or puncturing my foot. I reached the end of a quiet street a couple of blocks from the hustle of the marketplace.

I reached a fork in the road. Left would take me back towards the relative safety of the cart, and the unknown kindness of a stranger, but almost certainly back to Tristan. I turned right and ran headlong towards a thicket of trees that I hoped would take me off the castle track and back towards the river, then eventually out of Tordre.

Only someone looking for an escaped princess might have chanced to see the bedraggled woman hobble off into the forest. Once under cover of the trees, I stopped to catch my breath, and plopped down in a patch of bracken beneath a looming beech tree. It was the most comfortable seat I'd had in a long while.

Cara trotted out from between the bushes with a large fish hanging from her mouth, and blinked at me in the sunlight.

'Yes, all right,' I said. 'You win. All I got was a stale cob.' I lifted my prize to take a closer look. It had a hard crust, but when I took a sniff, oh... my stomach flipped over with joy. I broke open the crust and savoured its yeasty scent, then chewed on the loaf. It was so fresh it almost melted in my mouth. Not everyone hated the street folk, despite appearances.

I offered Cara a piece of bread, which she sniffed with disdain, but licked and then chewed all the same. She crouched down beside me, one paw laid possessively across her fish.

'We'll build a fire and share it later. Tonight, my queen of cats, we shall dine like royalty.'

'And where did a Princess of Carentan learn to build a fire?' Idris stepped out from between the trees and watched me. I leapt

97

up and looked around for some kind of weapon, a branch, spear, stick… anything, but the forest floor yielded no such treasure. Cara sprang to her feet, and without a by-your-leave, trotted over to Idris and rubbed her head up against his shins.

*Treacherous cat.*

'How did you…? Ah, Dorshan. That weasel. Is there no one around here you can trust?'

'There is no one who isn't being bribed or coerced by somebody else.' He reached down and rubbed the cat's tufted ears. Evidently, not all of Tristan's friends were equal. Idris looked somewhat forlorn in his long pale robes, and fair hair placed just right so that it covered the almighty bruise across the side of his face. His lip was swollen, and made his words come out with a rasping lisp. *Oh gods, was that… did I…?*

'Where are the rest of them?' Experience told me that Tristan and his merry band of queen thieves would not be far behind. 'Does he always send you in to do his dirty work?'

'Where did you find this cat, and how did you get it to attack one of us?' Idris looked at Cara.

'I have no more control over her than you. She followed me.'

He wrinkled his forehead. 'Lucky you, I wish I could pick up followers like that.' Idris looked at the surrounding space, kicked a few leaves around, then sunk down to a seated position, like some sage of ancient gods about to meditate on the path to divinity. Cara trotted over to him and, after a few sniffs, flopped down and rolled over onto her back for a belly rub. 'The others are back at the tavern. It is just me and some attendants, who are back in the village watering the horses. I saw you run and followed.'

I lowered myself back down and sat with my feet tucked beneath my skirts, ready at a moment's notice to spring up. With one eye on Idris and another on Cara, I broke off a chunk of bread and offered it to him. He shook his head.

'You look a state,' I said.

He gave me a lopsided smile. 'Have you looked in a mirror recently?'

The heat rushed up my chest and my cheeks burned. I had always been so careful about my appearance and now there I was sat on the forest floor with bird nest hair, a dirty smelly gown, and grubby hands and face. It was shameful. The exhaustion caught up with me, and all I wanted right then was to close my eyes and sleep, but I needed my wits about me. It was not safe.

'Have you come to take me back?'

Idris looked around him. 'I don't see how I'm going to do that. I'm not inclined towards conflict if I can avoid it. Besides,' he ran a hand down his face, 'you fight dirty.'

'I'm so sorry-' before I realised what I was doing, I had shuffled across the few yards between us, and reached out to touch his face. Idris kept still, but I could see in his face the effort it took not to turn away. I brushed my fingers across the bruising with a gentle, child-like curiosity, then traced my hand over the back of his head and gasped. There was a knotted lump of flesh the size of a large chestnut. He must have noted the look of alarm on my face.

'It's all right, the medic has seen me. I am to make a full recovery with no lasting damage. It looks much worse than it feels right now.'

'I could have killed you.'

He took my hand away from his injuries and held it for a brief instant before returning it to my lap. 'You were frightened for your life.' He peered around at Cara, who tore out chunks of raw fish with her teeth. 'Much like your cat would not hesitate to lash out with its claws at any threat to its life. It's instinct, and it is my own fault. I should have known better. I don't know what possessed me to agree to such a crazy plan in the first place.' He steepled his fingers on his forehead. 'I have not felt like myself at all lately.'

'That'll be down to the priests,' I said.

'Yes,' he frowned at me, 'what do you know about that?'

'Just what the priest-king told me and what I learned from some of Dorshan's stories.'

'Stories, yes. He would argue that he writes the truth, but who is left to argue what is truth and what is myth? I need to get you out of here.'

That was as far as I was willing to cooperate. I stood, scooped up my cob of bread, and walked off between the trees with Cara in tow, mutilated fish flapping between her jaws. So much for a fire and a nice cooked meal. My stomach groaned with lost desire.

# CHAPTER SEVENTEEN

## *A Safe Haven*

I didn't bother to check whether he was following me, as I knew that he was. So, there I was once again, tramping through the forest without a proper plan. But one thing I knew for sure, I was not going back to that tavern to be humiliated by the true King of Tordre.

'Stop, please... for one moment.' Idris's voice trailed behind me. 'I can keep this up for hours, you know.' The sound of his feet keeping pace through the bracken gave me a fair indication of how far away he was. He could have jumped me, applied a wad of Devil's Breath, and dragged me back to T'sar. If he managed to get past Cara, that is. I wasn't quite sure why the cat had taken up with me, but I was certainly glad she had. 'I'm an accomplished rider, you know, and a swordsman, although they haven't let me near a sword for quite some time. It comes to me in dreams sometimes. I see myself fighting on a battlefield.'

'I thought you were not inclined towards conflict?' I stopped and turned. He stopped at the same instant, and the cat manoeuvred herself between us.

He glanced nervously at her. 'I can see I'm going to have competition every time I want to speak to you,' he said. I wondered for a moment if it were not me who would have competition, as Cara sidled up to him and rubbed herself against his legs.

'And why do you need to speak to me? I'm not going back there, so if you want to follow me to the border and into Carentan, then please feel free. When I finally get to my family they will be furious. My mother arranged this marriage in good faith, when she finds out I was married to a false king, it could start a war.'

'You'll never make it past the border. They have check points set up all around the perimeter, which are constantly monitored by the priesthood to ensure no-one gets past.'

Perhaps that was why the priest-king couldn't get any further on our supposed trip back to Carentan. But he must have known. It had all been a ruse, a play for my benefit. Well, if playing court politics was what they wanted, I was the queen of that game.

'Well then. Seeing as I can't go back to Carentan and I'm not going back to the tavern in T'sar, that leaves only one other option.'

Idris looked at me wide-eyed. 'You mean to go back to Castle Ryemont?'

'Don't look so surprised. Isn't that what you and your true king wanted in the first place? A loyal insider who has the false-king's ear?'

'Yes, but-'

'You forget. I grew up in a castle around kings and queens and courtiers. I know how to play that game better than an army of priest-kings.'

'Come back to T'sar and we can help you prepare properly.' Idris looked torn. I thought he might have made a grab for me if he could restrain me.

'Why do you do what Tristan tells you?'

'He is my king,' Idris said, with a perplexed look on his face.

'You said yourself; there's no one who is not being bribed or coerced by someone else. So then who's left to tell what's truth and what's myth?'

A small smile curled at the corner of his mouth.

'You have a fine memory, my queen.' Confusion washed over his smile. 'At least let me help you.'

I suppose it was the better of two evils. In many ways, Idris was as much a victim of this situation as I was; displaced from his normal life as a courtier, only to find himself tramping around the forest at someone else's bidding, searching for a road back to his previous life.

'All right,' I said, 'But I go back on my own terms and not those of Tristan Bacha. And you don't need to call me queen. I married a false king, so I'm not a queen. Nerys will do fine.'

He looked at me with wary, round eyes and, for a moment, I thought he might ignore me and launch another attack. I was loathe to further spoil his statuesque beauty, so was relieved that he did not.

'I know a safe place in the village where we can get you cleaned up and fit to be a queen.' He paused, waiting for my reaction. 'Despite your reluctance, it may be our only hope of returning to any modicum of normality.'

'Right then.' I marched off in a direction that would take us back where we came.

'I dare say you'll appreciate a bath.'

There was laughter in his eyes as I glared at him. It was hard to stay cross with this man. 'And a proper meal, I expect,' he said.

I walked away, not letting him see the smile on my face. 'Here, I can recommend the local bakery.' I chucked the fresh cob of bread over my shoulder and waited for the thump when it hit the ground.

Silence.

Seconds later, he marched alongside me, chewing thoughtfully. Cara had disappeared, no doubt in disgust that I sided with the enemy. I suppose it was just as well. Not sure how the priest-king's court would react to having a wildcat in the castle.

By the time we got back to the village it was crawling with men in armour. Somehow the castle must have gotten wind of the appearance of a beggar woman that looked like a dishevelled queen. Black-cloaked men hid in shadows, ready to spring an attack at any given moment. Idris bundled me into a carriage and wrapped a cloak over me.

'Keep still and quiet,' he said under his breath. In the blackness of my hiding place, I felt the carriage moving us at a quick pace to a distance I hoped would be far enough from prying eyes. I closed my eyes and let the rhythmic rocking lull me into a false sense of security.

I drifted into sleep, and after what seemed only moments, woke up to voices. Idris's soft commanding tone, and the voice of a woman, both speaking in Langan. I could only catch a few muffled words here and there through the cocoon of the cloak: cloth, haste and the Langan word for dignitary, though it could have been royalty. I shouldn't have trusted him. Trust no one, he said it himself.

My chest tightened and my blood pumped. I was ready to burst out of the carriage and make a run for it, when powerful arms hauled me up and bundled me like a sack of laundry, my weight seemingly nothing to them. The same arms gave me an almost imperceptible squeeze, as Idris's confident voice chattered away in Langan to the woman, who appeared to be leading us into a building. The scent of freshly laundered clothes filled my nostrils, and it was then I realised I was meant to be a sack of laundry.

Idris took me to a small attic with a tiny square window that looked out over the town. 'I will be back,' he said and turned to leave. I watched from the window as he appeared out in the street, climbed back into the carriage and left. Moments later, a young woman came in bearing food and drink, followed by two more with a bathtub and a pile of clean clothes.

The first woman had dark hair in a long plait down her back, and a dusty apron that covered a plain calico tunic. 'Don't fret, Ma'am,' she said. 'He is a good man and true to his word.'

Had I walked from one prison into another? I would give him the benefit of the doubt, at least for the time it would take me to get cleaned up and out of there. Then, I would my next move, whether or not he came back.

The women gave me watered ale and set a platter of bread and cheese in front of me, which I devoured as though it were my last meal. Then, burying my dignity, I allowed myself to be bundled into the tub and the women to pour hot, steaming water over me. They chatted away in Langan, perhaps not realising that I understood most of what they said. They didn't know who I was, but appeared to hold Idris in such high esteem that they were willing to do his bidding with very little question. I would have to ask him his secret. The water turned a muddy grey, and when I raised my clean hands I marvelled at being able to see my fingers again.

The women helped to dry me, and then dressed me in a long pale green robe with side-ties and wide sleeves. A robe fit for a queen.

'We used to get a lot of business from the castle, Ma'am, and then one day, it all stopped. But master Idris has been kind to us. If not for him, we would surely be on the streets right now.'

Satisfied that I looked and smelt like a decent person and not some street urchin, the women left me to my own thoughts.

Idris returned some time later, when the sun was on its descent towards the sea, and most sensible folk were packing up their wares for the day and heading to the comfort of their hearth.

His eyes widened when he entered and shut the door behind him.

'What is it?' I moved away from the window. Had someone seen me looking out across the village?

'Nothing, I… never mind,' he said with an embarrassed shake of his head. 'You look… different, that's all.'

I realised that the only time he had seen me when not covered in forest detritus it had been dark, and he had been fending off my attempts to escape him. Not successfully, for that matter. The guilt returned, and this time it was me who looked away in embarrassment.

'Before we do this, I need to be sure you know what you are agreeing to,' he said.

I snapped my head back to hold his gaze, and let his words hang for a moment. 'You told them, didn't you?'

'I had to. They sent me after you.'

A courtier and a diplomat too. It occurred to me that if Tristan Bacha really was the true king, then my cooperation might be the only solution to keeping critical relations between our two countries. 'What do you want me to do?'

'We have an insider at the castle-'

'Bax, yes I know.'

'-he knows the castle inside-out, and will help Kerrin get inside to find the focal point; the key to the Priesthood's power.'

'What does it look like, this focal point?' I had a creeping sense of unease beneath my skin.

'We don't know. It could be anything from a single object to a place of worship. But we suspect it is how the priesthood retains their hold over those nearest to them. We mean to destroy it.'

An image of the faceless king standing in front of the chapel altar flashed across my mind.

'What happens once it is destroyed?'

'We don't exactly know, but Kerrin is a High Priestess of the many gods. She will restore the balance.' I gave him a blank expression, and he wrinkled his brow. 'And, of course… restore the rightful king to the throne.'

'How do you know that Tristan is the rightful king?'

'It is… I…'

'This power they have can steal your memories. I've seen it on the faces of the castle staff. They don't remember things and look confused if I try to push them to remember things about the Blue King.'

He flinched when I said Blue King.

'How do I know that I'm not replacing one false king for another?' I thought it was a fair point, but Idris shook his head in dismissal. 'Are we planning to replace the fear of the one god with the wrath of the many?'

He looked thoughtful, and I thought maybe I had got through to him, but then he held up his hands as though to ward off an attack on his thought processes.

'The many are just and forgiving,' he said, with a finality that ended the discussion.

We said very little in the carriage on the way back to Ryemont. Idris gave me minimal instructions, the main one being to trust no one other than Bax. Unfortunately, I didn't even trust Bax. The resistance had planned an attack on the castle that coincided with Kerrin's covert destruction of the focal point. All I had to do was keep quiet, pretend to agree with the false-king, and feed information to Bax. That much I was more than capable of doing. But the closer we got to the castle, the more I wanted to jump out and run for the border.

# CHAPTER EIGHTEEN

## *Return to Ryemont*

The carriage stopped outside the inner gate to Castle Ryemont.

'This is as far as I will go,' Idris said. I scrutinised his face for signs of deceit, but his brow just wrinkled and made him look worried.

'Your face looks much better,' I said, not knowing what else to say. His smile was nervous, but not as lopsided as before.

'Kerrin's special salve,' he said, as though adding the name 'Kerrin' explained everything.

'She knows a lot, this Kerrin,' I said.

'The priestesses of the many train with the apothecaries.'

*Of course. How else would she have access to the Devil's Breath?* I opened the carriage door. 'How can I contact you again?' I said, 'if I need to, of course.'

He smiled faintly. 'Bax will know. He can get a message to me, if you need to.'

I stepped down, but before I had a chance to shut the carriage door, a loud voice barked from behind the walls.

'Open the gate!'

The bolts slammed back and the heavy oak gates creaked open. A dozen guards on horseback thundered towards the carriage. Idris's driver cracked his whip, but the horses reared and bucked, causing the carriage to rock from side to side. I leapt out of the way but was not fast enough to avoid being surrounded by a circle of riders, which held the carriage in place. A single rider trotted towards me, a king's guard who I thought I recognised. One of those who had been assigned to following me around all day, no doubt. He leaned out of his saddle, and held a hand towards me through stiffened armour.

'Your Majesty, quick.' He beckoned, but I stood immobile. One way or another, I was going back to the castle, whether a captive of the guards or by my own means. Another guard swept forward, dismounted, and lifted me by the waist onto the back of the horse as though I weighed nothing. *I suppose that was it then.*

The horse broke rank from the circle and cantered through the gate towards the inner keep. I chanced a look over my shoulder, and caught a glimpse of the guards closing in on the carriage with their swords drawn.

They had known I was coming. The guard walked the horse down the centre of the court, lined on either side by attendants from the royal household, waiting in line to greet me. At the end were my own attendants, including Lana, who greeted me as though I had just come back from a ride in the country. I dismounted and entered the inner keep.

'Your Majesty.' Lana fell in behind me alongside a standard retinue of guards. 'Your lord husband awaits your company.' It was almost as if the last few days had never happened.

They accompanied me to my chambers, which looked exactly the way I had left them not seven days prior. All of my gowns and trinkets we had brought on the trip had been returned to their rightful places. Lana bustled in behind me, and the guards settled behind the door to take up their constant vigil. There was no hope now that I would ever shake off their presence.

'Your Majesty, please let me tidy you up before you meet the king. He is most eager to see you.'

*Yes, I imagine he is.*

Lana hustled me into a chair before the looking glass and brushed my hair. 'We have missed you so, but I understand you had a successful trip. You must be so relieved to have spent some time with your family.'

*So that was the story. Interesting. I'll take that one. It was infinitely better that trying to explain what had really happened.*

'Though I have to say that they didn't feed you up as well as I might have hoped. You look half-starved, if you don't mind me saying.' Lana parted my long dark hair and plaited it into winding loops.

'Lana... how is the king?' I said. She looked up at me in the glass and smiled.

'Oh, he missed you terribly, your Majesty. He hardly came out of his rooms, and when he did it was only to take himself to the chapel, to pray for your safe return.' She wound the plaited loops up and pinned them to the side of my head, then scooped the rest of my hair into a net, securing it in place. 'There, now, that's much better. Let's see if we can find you a better gown.'

'No,' I said, holding a hand to my chest. 'I like this one.' It was comfortable and regal enough, and Idris had given it to me.

'Well, then, let's brighten it up with some jewels,' Lana said, and I let her choose a few gaudy pieces to hang about my neck.

There was a light knock at the door, and some attendants brought in a platter of dried meats and sweet cakes, alongside a carafe of wine. I let them pour but insisted on diluting my drink, wondering as I put the cup to my mouth if there was something in the wine. A strong buzz in my head took up residence the moment I set foot in the castle, reminiscent of those early days when I could feel the very walls humming. It's curious how you get used to such a sinister thing when it is with you every day. It was only then, upon my return, that I noticed it once more. I looked into my cup, then took a sip. It made no difference to the noise in my head.

I don't know what I expected. Perhaps I thought he would look like the dusty priest with the ragged face who collapsed at the border, but when I entered the king's private rooms, my breath caught in my chest. The priest-king looked every bit as regal and in control as the day I first met him. Silvery-fair hair was swept over his shoulder with aching familiarity, and steely grey eyes peered at me from a thin, pale face, with hollowed cheekbones. It felt like heresy to even think that he might not be the true king.

As I stood there in front of him, my mind fogged over so much that it felt easier to believe what I saw. So much easier to have faith. I clenched my fist, and dug my fingernails into my palm to remind myself it was not real. Settling on the image of the priest in my mind's eye, I projected it over what I saw in front of me. For an instant the king's face rippled, before the priest peered at me from behind brown eyes. It took huge concentration, I couldn't hold onto it for long. Realising that I was holding my breath, I let out what I hoped sounded like a long sigh, and the Blue King's face re-emerged, the illusion as strong as ever.

He smiled. Something about the way he looked at me reminded me of Idris outside the castle gate, surrounded by guardsmen, and I snapped back to myself with a sharp intake of breath.

'Your Majesty, may I speak with you alone?'

He waved at the guards and attendants, who melted away into the background. Some of my anger returned to bubble away beneath the surface of my skin. It helped to keep me in the present. To keep things real. I must be careful to have him believe that I am once again under his influence, otherwise it will all be for naught.

'My queen, Nerys.' He moved into my space and ran a long white finger down the side of my face. I shuddered, and hoped he would assume it was from excitement, not fear of the tingling sensation of his skin's touch. 'Please, let us talk and walk, I have something to show you.' We left the chambers, and he held onto my arm as though going for an amble through the castle. I could feel the pressure of his force, keeping me close and steering my direction.

We reached the end of the corridor. I had to take pigeon steps at double time to keep up with his long stride, and all the time he pulled me forward like a wilful child.

'Your Majesty... the man outside... who brought me here, I-'

'It is all right now Nerys, you are safe. He will be brought to justice for what he has done, rest assured my queen.'

'No, I mean-'

'Hush now, I won't hear another word.' The priest-king led me down the eastern stair. The upper stairwell had window slits that allowed natural light, but as we reached further they disappeared, to be replaced by wall sconces, which became fewer and fewer, until we were plunged into near darkness. This was the stair that led to the castle dungeons.

A moment of blind panic ripped through me. I pulled away from the priest-king and took the steps back up two at a time. Two guards blocked my way. Every possibility of how to escape ran through my mind; dodge them and run, knock their big clumsy legs away, pull out a hairpin and go for their eyes. What was wrong with me? They were only men following orders.

'Hey, hey...' the priest-king held me around the shoulders. 'You don't have to worry; I will not leave you down here.' He swung me around to face him. 'It wasn't your fault; I know that.

109

You were captured and taken away from me. We awoke that morning to chaos. There were several guards unconscious and more wandering about, still drugged.'

He looked earnest and I believed him.

'The perpetrators left evidence of their crime littered across the camp,' he said. 'You have been a victim in all of this, and that is something I intend to put right. I want to show you what we do with those who plot against the crown.' There was no hint of irony in his voice. It was a story that was convenient to believe. He turned me around and ushered me down the steps.

Two guards stood either side of a large dank archway with fitted iron gates criss-crossing the entrance to the dungeons. Beyond was pitch black, and as silent as midnight but for the occasional groan. They rattled the keys and slid the gates open, allowing us to pass through into the gloom.

For a moment, I could see nothing. Then a guard handed the king a flaming torch, and the corridor lit up in all its grim glory. A large rodent scuttled across the floor in front of us at an impossible speed, and I jerked back, finding myself enclosed in the priest-king's arms.

'Don't worry, Nerys, I will protect you from all that seeks to harm you. You will be safe as long as I am king.'

For a moment, I relaxed into his arms with relief. Yes, I was home at last with the king, where I belonged. Soft moans emanated from several cells, but the priest-king took me to a quiet one at the end of the corridor, insisting that I look through the barred window and into the cell, where an indistinct bundle sat in the corner.

It was hard to tell in that gloom whether it was a male or female. They wore robes of nobility, now torn and besmirched with what could have been dirt or blood. They sat with legs drawn in, head resting upon their knees, long hair swept around like a curtain, hiding their truth. Perhaps they had given up. I turned to the priest-king.

'Why-'

'Shhh...' He swept up his torch, and illuminated the cell in all its squalid authenticity. The occupier slowly lifted their head. One eye was swollen shut, and the rest of the face mottled with bruising. I recoiled, and the priest-king tried to catch me, but this time I couldn't stand to have him touch me. 'You see... this is what happens to anyone who tries to harm you or take you away from me.' I stared back at the priest-king, not wanting to look into the cell. 'Oh, don't worry. He won't stay like this for long. It is high time the people of Tordre understood what happens to traitors.'

Idris stared at the cell wall in front of him, as though the priest-king and I did not exist. He turned his head towards me. Though unable to smile through his swollen lips, his eyes sparkled with recognition. I turned, and had to stop myself from hitting the priest-king. I took a breath to calm my voice.

'But...'

'You are safe now,' he said. 'As long as you stick with me.'

*Was there ever an alternative?*

'No.'

'No?'

'You have to let him go. He was the one who brought me back here. He is no traitor to the crown,' I said. The priest-king hung his head and smiled, and I knew then that his actions were beyond reason. I pushed him.

'No!'

He stumbled back, then grabbed my wrists as one of the guards wrapped their muscular arms around my torso, trapping my arms by sides, then dragged me kicking and screaming from the dungeons.

# CHAPTER NINETEEN

## *Escape and Rescue*

I stayed in my room for as long as would be deemed reasonable to get over my pique of dissident behaviour. Then I took to the castle battlements, and walked the circuit of the inner keep with several guards clattering along behind me. Archers and watchmen, who looked out over the city of T'sar and beyond, were placed at regular intervals along the walls. The soldiers were on edge, and had their bows raised and arrows nocked, though none were fired.

I peered through the thin slits around the battlement walls and saw in the distance a commotion at the castle gates. A group of people had gathered and begun throwing things and waving their fists. At that distance, all I could hear were raised voices on the wind.

Idris's carriage was still there, and the group had climbed on top of it to make a show of their protest. A posse of guards rode out to engage the group, who had unhinged the carriage from the horses and were proceeding to swing the sides of the carriage to topple it in place. The carriage fell with a crash, and the group took the horses and rode off at speed as the guards flooded out of the gates.

They left the carriage lying on its side, perhaps as a symbol of their discontent at losing its owner. A few arrows were loosed at the group, but fell wide of their target. I realised I had been holding my breath and let it out in a rush of relief that they had neither hurt nor captured anyone else.

I tried to talk to the priest-king later about Idris, but he would not let me speak, and repeatedly changed the subject of conversation until I became so frustrated with him I spoke over the top of his constant diatribe about justice.

'This man that you want to hang in public helped me to escape my captors.'

He stared at me from across the dinner table, and let his fork fall to his plate with a clatter. 'This man is a threat to the peace of Tordre.'

'You call this peace?' I knew it was a mistake the minute I opened my mouth. My instructions were simple, stay in accord with the priest-king and feed information to Bax. His face clouded over and wavered, which initially made me think that he might change back to his drab priest-face. But no, his deception held true, and his eyes hardened in their righteousness.

I lowered my head and picked at the food on my plate, but could feel his gaze burning into me. I needed to be more careful. I would not win by antagonising the priesthood's puppet. Idris was a target, a man to be made an example of for the people of Tordre. Appealing to the better nature of this monster that sat in parody of the Blue King would only expedite his execution. I needed to concentrate and focus on how to get him out.

'Perhaps a visit to the royal chapel would help,' he said in that soft, threatening tone. I looked up, and he narrowed his eyes at me. Eyes that did not belong to him. Eyes that deceived the entire nation. My heart thudded in my chest, and my throat constricted at the thought of that chapel, the place where I had first glimpsed the faceless priest mid-way through his transformation. I must have paled in response, because he had a self-righteous look on his face. 'Thought not. We understand each other?'

I looked back at my plate, pushing the food around with my fork.

As I lay awake in my bed that night, the image of Idris's swollen face and resolute expression stared back at me every time I closed my eyes. Thankfully, the priest-king left me alone. I think he knew not to push me too far. I would behave myself and act like the queen that I wasn't as long as he left me in peace, we had that much of an understanding. At least I had escaped the threat of re-visiting the chapel. He knew that had been the root cause of my fear in the early days, and now he had that as a weapon to hold over me.

The chapel.

I sat bolt upright in my bed. It was the seat of their power, the place that the priest-king prayed to the one god and became

113

the Blue King. If I could find it again, perhaps there was something I could do to stop them and dispel their power over the people. Once the people were released, the priesthood no longer held sway over them, and Tristan could return to his rightful place.

And me, I could go home to my family.

Disgraced and humiliated by not really being married to the King of Tordre.

Damn.

Whatever happened, I was going to have to eat some humble pie with the true king and see if I could put things right. The thought of spending a lifetime with Tristan Bacha was almost as disagreeable as remaining there with the priest-king and doing nothing.

Gods, why did life have to be so confusing? I thought about Tristan. At least he was an honest man. Well, most of the time; he did steal my letter home. But he seemed to care about the people and the future of Tordre. That is important for a king. Didn't Ailsa, the cook, say that Bacha was a strong Tordrean name with history? It was simply that the people had forgotten.

There was only one thing that did not confuse me, and that was that I must help Idris to get out of the castle and safely back to T'sar. If that required finding the chapel and a way to reverse the priesthood's hold, then that was what I was going to do.

I swung my legs over the side of the bed and rummaged around for some leggings and a tunic. After dressing in dark clothing, I tied my hair in a loose bun on top of my head, and opted for a pair of soft slippers to mask my footfall. I crept out of the door of my chamber and past my sleeping maids. There would be guards outside the door in the antechamber, but I would not opt for that route.

The antechamber window faced towards the inner keep gardens and had a walkway that encircled the rooms clustered around the royal chambers. Although not guarded, you had to be careful, as you could be seen walking through from any room within the cluster. There was only one room, to my knowledge, that wasn't guarded, that being the chambers of the old king and queen, which, according to Ailsa, had remained unchanged.

The Blue King had moved to a larger space further down the cluster in order to be closer to his new queen. I suppose it must

114

have suited the priest-king to have separate rooms, given his lack of interest in producing a royal heir. It also enabled him to hide his real identity.

I crept out onto the walkway. The gardens were pitch-black, and I ducked down below the parapet to a height where no one would see me moving past. What if someone caught me crawling along the path and creeping about the castle in the dead of night, wearing boy's clothing? How was I going to explain that?

I thought I heard a scratching noise behind me, but when I turned my head, there was nothing there. Down below, one or two lamps flickered on and off. I held my breath, then let it out slowly, but couldn't shake the creepy feeling of something watching me. If I was sure to get caught, I might as well see how far I could get.

I shuffled along, lying as flat as possible to avoid being seen, and using my elbows and knees to drag myself along. Fortunately, the old king and queen's rooms were in the opposite direction from mine than the priest-king's, which meant I didn't have to crawl past his rooms. It meant, however, that to get to the third window along, I had to crawl past the nosiest inhabitant of the castle, and the one most likely to be burning the midnight oil on the castle expenses; Seneschal Milo Dorsa.

It was unusual for a king to have his seneschal so close, but I had no doubts about the importance of Milo Dorsa to the priest-king, with his ability to both manage the castle coin and the entire domestic affairs of the royal household.

A light flickered in the window of the seneschal's antechamber. If he was working late he would be seated at his desk, which looked out onto the gardens. It was possible to crawl beneath his view, but if I made a sound which caused him to lean out, he would surely see me. Milo Dorsa was very much in the priests' pockets, that much was clear from the quick view I had of the accounts, not that long ago. Maybe he thought me too stupid to notice the indiscretions, but he would certainly sound the alarm if he found me creeping about at this hour.

I shuffled up, moving so slowly you could have heard a fly buzz above my movement. I had to assume that he was at his desk, and sure enough, as I got closer I could make out his silhouette against the darkness of his room from the flickering light of the candle at his desk. I heard him get up, so I hugged myself closer to the wall beneath the window. He moved away from his desk and I sped up my crawl, but in my haste kicked out against a loose cobblestone, which rattled across the walkway.

My heart stopped for a beat.

The silhouette moved closer to the window's edge. I held my breath. I saw Milo Dorsa's head loom above me, eyes squinting out into the darkness.

He concentrated his gaze above the window where I squeezed myself against the wall. I took deep slow breaths, and willed myself to be invisible to night eyes. A scratch-scratch noise, like nails sliding across stone, focused Milo's attention on two mirror-like eyes that hovered on the castle wall, reflecting the light back into the room. My sleep-deprived mind laboured to reach a solution to being stuck in between two monsters – a corrupt seneschal and a demon that had come to my aid in this hour of need.

I was surely damned by all the gods, the one and the many.

# CHAPTER TWENTY

### *Demons and Demagogues*

'Shoo… get away. Damn thing. Is this what you want?' Milo Dorsa launched a scrap of ham out of the window, which the demon snatched out of the air with a snap of its fangs.

I pressed my back against the wall beneath the window and watched in disbelief as Cara settled onto the parapet with a purr of contentment, devouring the peace offering from Milo. 'Hmm, thought so,' Milo said, and returned to his work with a grunt.

I laid a hand on my chest, willing my beating heart to slow, and continued past his window, taking care not to scatter any more loose cobblestones.

I stood out of my crouch and slithered in through the window of the old king and queen's room, landing in a heap on the floor and lying still for a moment to catch my breath and allow my sight to adjust to the darkness of the room. A purposeful mewl shortly followed my entrance, and I heard the tap-tap of claws on stone, as Cara followed me in.

'You wily creature… scared me half to death,' I said in a whisper. Cara bumped the top of her head on my arm and I scratched behind her tuft-covered ears. Her head was nearly the size of a small dinner plate, and I soothed myself with the knowledge that she wasn't trying to eat me with her protruding fangs, that glistened with the gristle of Milo's ham. I didn't like Milo, but he had gone up a notch in my estimation. 'How in the world did you find me?'

Cara purred and stretched out on the cold floor, then rolled over to show off her white under-belly. She was almost the length of a small child when stretched out like that. I rubbed her stomach, and she purred louder. If she continued like that, the maids would have no need to dust the floors. Cara rolled again and sprang to her feet. Far from being covered in the dust of years gone by, she appeared quite clean. I took another look at the floor, wiped my hand across the stones, and lifted my dust-free palm to my face. Perhaps they kept it clean to honour their memory.

As my eyes adjusted to the darkness, I noticed other things in the room that seemed out of keeping with the belief that this was the old king and queen's quarters, as I had been told. The walls of the antechamber held an assortment of swords and long sticks, making the space look very much like an armoury room.

I crept around the edges of the wall, taking care not to touch the weapons, and found what I was looking for. In the far wall there was an opening that led into a small dressing room with shelves piled high with leather armour, belts, buckles, and sheaths. Whoever dressed in there meant serious business when they went out into the world. This was the dressing room of a warrior, not one of an old king and queen. I ran a hand across a leather breastplate and my palm came away clean with the faint smell of oil and sweat.

Cara leapt up onto the shelves and hopped from one level to another. She sniffed and mewled, as though searching for something, and every so often stared back at me in expectation. There were folded piles of tunics and trews alongside a row of hanging robes, obviously designed for formal occasions. I ran a hand down the fabric of a light green garment with tiny jewels sewn into the collar, that sparkled despite the poor light in there.

I shuddered. Perhaps this was Tristan Bacha's room. I went back out into the antechamber and gazed at the displayed weapons, not quite able to imagine him wielding one of those. I was by no means a weapons expert, but I had watched the knights practicing in the castle yard. Amongst the array of sticks, swords, hammers, and throwing weapons, I found a sturdy knife with an intricate engraving on the hilt. I lifted it up, wondering if anyone would miss it for a while, then returned to the dressing room to find a suitable sheath. I found one and belted it around my waist.

*Just in case,* I told myself.

The room was locked from the inside, so I lifted the catch and peered out into the corridor. With no one in sight, I slipped out and gently shut the door behind me. It wasn't until I was halfway down the corridor that I realised I had left Cara behind. No matter. She was probably safer in that room, anyway.

If my memory was serving me correctly, somewhere along that stretch of corridor was a spiral staircase that led down into the depths of the castle, which is where I last found the chapel.

I knew they conducted their ceremonies past the midnight hour, which I supposed saved them from interruptions from nosy queens, but how did I stumble upon them before? There was nothing but solid rock walls along that stretch of the corridor. I stood still and listened.

Nothing.

About to turn back and admit defeat, I caught a faint hum. I crossed the corridor and placed a palm on the wall. It vibrated under my touch. As I trailed my fingertips along the wall, the vibration lessened, and when I moved back towards the chambers it intensified.

I kept moving down the corridor with my palm pressed to the wall. The vibration pulsed, sending a tingling wave down my arm and into my chest. I had the sudden urge to go back to my room and hide beneath the blankets, as the image of the faceless king sprang to mind as though it were only yesterday when I had first seen him. My heart hammered and my palms became slippery and clammy against the wall.

Then the vibration trailed off, and I stopped. I moved a step back, and it grew stronger. This was it. I knew the opening to the stairwell must be there, but all I could see was a flat, stone wall. The vibration filled my head and made it hard to think, hard to find the motivation to carry on.

Then I thought of Idris sitting in that dank cell, knees drawn to his chest like a child, his face battered and cut, his elegant robe in tatters around him, and his eyes staring at the wall in front of him as though no one else was there. The image strengthened me, and I pushed back at the fear that paralysed me, taking back control of myself. I had to stay strong for Idris to get him out of there.

When I stepped away from the wall, the vibration in my palm stayed with me, travelling not just down my arm, but through me, like I was being lit up from the inside. Instead of fearing it, I embraced it, and before my eyes the outline of an entry door etched itself into the wall in front of me. It was all a matter of belief. The priesthood predicated their entire control system on faith. If you could break the faith, you could break the hold.

I ducked into the entry door and sure enough found the spiral stairway that I had happened upon on my first night in the castle. As I made my way down, the humming increased with every step. I knew what would come at the bottom of the winding stair and steeled myself as I peered through the open door into the chapel.

But it wasn't the priest-king who stood at the altar of the one god. It wasn't the face of my Blue King who turned in profile to utter the words of faith that gripped a nation. It was the objectionable priest who followed his brethren around, and frequently appeared waving his fingers and getting all and sundry to do his bidding.

His face turned back to the altar. Just when I thought I knew who stood in front of me, his features wavered and flattened out, and a new face appeared. His body shimmered into a shorter, stockier weight, his nose became more of a snub, and his hair sprouted in places not uncommon in older people. I knew that face, having seen him so many times at court in Carentan.

His head twitched in my direction as I gasped. It was Abiel Morda, the Archbishop of the church of the one god, here in Castle Ryemont, posing as a dusty old priest. I wanted to step into that holy space and challenge him; demand to know what he was doing to the people of Tordre, but before my anger took away all reason a small pebble hit me on the top of the arm.

I turned, expecting to see an avalanche of stones and the walls falling in on me. Instead, I saw Bax standing on the steps behind me with a finger to his mouth, urging me back from the chapel.

I scrambled back into the relative safety of the stairwell and followed him, though I couldn't resist a curious glance over my shoulder at the chapel. The low hum became an agitated chant, and I was satisfied that he hadn't seen me. We tumbled out into the corridor as the doorway closed up behind us. Bax grabbed my arm and pulled me back towards the sleeping quarters.

'What do you think you are doing?' I pulled my arm out of his grip and he held his hands up.

'Your Majesty, I'm sorry. Please forgive me…'

'Don't call me that,' I said, although in my heart I knew this wasn't the time or the place to get huffy like a princess. 'You know I'm not really a queen. This whole thing is a charade and you know it. You even stole my letters home.' At least he had the good grace to look embarrassed. 'Wait. How come this hold doesn't affect you?'

'It does, but every day I fight it, and every day a small piece of my memory returns. Kerrin has helped us all to remember the past. Whatever your faith, hold on to it, because that will help you fight. They can only turn you if you believe in them.'

'Who really is Kerrin?'

Bax looked at me askance. 'She's the king's sister. I thought you knew. She can use the power of the many gods to defeat the one. She's coming here to save us all. To rescue Idris.' He looked so earnest and young with all his heart and faith put into this one redeeming truth; Kerrin was coming to save them all.

I remembered the image of the redheaded woman in a long burgundy cloak who accompanied Tristan and Idris in their quest to steal a queen. She was with them again in the tavern. If she was indeed the king's sister, then all her efforts would focus on restoring the true king to the throne and she may well indeed save us. It gave me hope.

As we neared the door to the old king and queen's apartments, I slowed down, and Bax looked over his shoulder.

'You must return to your chambers before the night is out. I have my instructions to meet Kerrin and bring her into the castle. I'm to act as her guide. You must act as though nothing is out of the ordinary.' He lifted his chin, pleased with this new sense of importance.

I was confused. If she was the king's sister, then why did she need a guide in her own home? I kept my query to myself; it wasn't the time to question help when it was all we had to rely on.

'I can't get back into the room without being seen,' I said. Bax frowned at me. 'I slipped out of the window and came out through one of the other rooms.' Best not to disclose that I had been defiling the true king's apartments.

Bax seemed to get it, though as I waved him away he looked over his shoulder, doubt creasing his brow. I waited for him to get out of sight before slipping back into the king's vestibule, locking it once again from the inside. My guess was that locking it from the inside prevented nosy people like me from encroaching on the truth, but they hadn't bargained on my resourcefulness. No matter, it served my own purposes and ensured no one would disturb me.

It was dark and quiet, but I no longer felt afraid. The humming in the walls had disappeared when I entered, as though this room had some kind of protection of its own. I stood for a moment, allowed my eyes to adjust, and took a deep breath. I hadn't noticed it before, but the air had a strangely familiar scent to it. Familiar, and yet I couldn't quite place it.

There was a door to the left, which I hadn't noticed when I came through before. It was ajar now, but perhaps I hadn't noticed it before as it had been closed. The thought struck me: it was open, someone had been in there. I crept towards the door and peered through the thin slit of the opening. Ornate curtains in green and blue were drawn back, revealing a bed that took up most of the room, unmade and messy, with only one long pillow in the centre. Definitely not the sleeping quarters of an old couple. In the centre of the bed lay the probable reason for the open door.

Cara lifted her head and blinked lazily at me, and her tail lashed, warning me not to disturb her peace. She seemed at home in there. Perhaps this was where she spent most of her days. It seemed as good a place as any to get away from the madness of the castle. With that thought in mind, I crept up to the bed. It looked so inviting, and the fatigue of having stayed awake half the night threatened to overwhelm me.

I sat down on the bed and ruffled Cara's fur, making her purr almost as loudly as the vibrating walls. Then, thinking I would lie down for just a moment, I kicked off my slippers and stretched out alongside the cat. It may have been the bed of a king, but there was more than enough room for two.

As I lay my head on the pillow, the faint residue of scent from the room came back to me. I found it comforting, and when I closed my eyes the darkness of sleep drew a curtain around me.

# CHAPTER TWENTY-ONE

## *An Unlikely Ally*

In my dreams the castle was falling down around me. It wasn't a fast destruction, like an explosion during a war when an entire wing might be destroyed by a single, carefully aimed ballista. It was more like a long, drawn-out disintegration of its very fabric.

A steady crumble of masonry replaced the usual humming of the walls. Every so often, a chunk of stone hit my shoulder or my back. All around me, people shouted and footsteps crashed up and down corridors, but I could see no one. It was as though I was stuck in my own secret part of the castle, that no one else knew about and where no one could find me.

There were voices calling my name. *Was that Lana?* I knew I had to get out and find them before the walls fell in on themselves and buried me alive, but it was one of those dreams where every step forward meant two steps back. What was it I had to do before I could leave? There was someone I had to save. The thoughts plagued me, and all the while, the clatter of stones falling surrounded me.

My eyes shot open.

I was on the bed in the old king and queen's room. The chamber door was ajar and Cara stalked up and down, her claws click-clacking on the stone floor. There was a commotion going on outside the main door, and several times someone pulled and rattled the door.

My head was fuzzy from sleep and I couldn't think straight. I had meant to get back to my room before morning, but the bed had been so comfortable and inviting with Cara purring next to me that it had been hard to hold back the sweeping fatigue. And now I was in trouble. The door rattled again, and I heard the voice of the priest-king.

'Where is the damn key, then? Get it, now.'

Boots stomped off amidst a clash of armour. Gods, did it take an army to capture one stray queen?

Choices. I could stay there and let them catch me, though I would be sent back to my room, never to see the light of day again, and they would certainly step up my personal guard, preventing me from ever helping Idris. But then… Kerrin was coming.

Or…

I slipped out of the window, and took great care to stay below the balustrade that looked out onto the castle gardens. I crouched on all fours and listened to the sounds from the rooms up ahead. Cara scooted past me and leapt onto the windowsill of Milo Dorsa's room. She looked at me, expectation in her eyes. I couldn't go back to my own room, but they would never think to look in the seneschal's quarters.

I slid through the window and had to tiptoe around the desk, trying not to knock anything out of place. On the dusty surface, a large slipper-print declared my guilt to anyone who cared to look. I dusted it off with my sleeve, but only made a bigger dust-free patch on the desk.

'Well, well.'

I whipped around. Milo Dorsa stood in the doorway. He slammed the door shut as a troop clattered past in the corridor outside. 'You've certainly caused a commotion this morning.' He took in my appearance and ran his eyes up and down my boyish attire, finally settling on the knife belted to my waist. 'And what do you think you're going to do with that?'

Annoyingly, Cara sidled up to him and rubbed her back up against his leg, as though she had known him for years. He gave her a little shove. Not enough to hurt or distract her, but she got the message, and moved away to sniff around in the corners of the room.

'Are you going to let them hang that poor man in the dungeons, who has done nothing except help me get back here to my precious king?' I put a little too much emphasis on the word king, and Milo Dorsa raised an eyebrow.

'Well now, let's see.' His tone dripped with sarcasm. 'That man in the dungeon who was so helpful to return you to your keepers…' My hand wavered close to the knife. '… happens to be one of the ring-leaders in a plot to overthrow the crown.'

'A crown that certainly doesn't belong to the priesthood,' I said.

Milo Dorsa gave me a thin smile. 'My dear, whatever are you saying?'

'That I am not a queen. That the crown is a lie, and the king is a usurper. If I really were a queen, I don't doubt that you would accord me with due respect.' Did he know what was going on here, or was he as much under the control of the priesthood as the rest of the castle?

He must know. I saw the accounts and the money being bled out to the church myself.

He let out a long and dramatic exhalation.

'You would do well to return to your room and let events take their course. There is nothing you can do. The man in the dungeon will hang for his treason, the king will face his protesters before long, and the true king will return to the throne.'

Well, I wasn't expecting that.

'And trying to run away and send letters home will only make things worse for you. Be a good little queen and play your part. Then, perhaps the true king will find a place for you in the future of this good nation.'

I stared at him, silently appraising his words. I didn't trust him. 'And whose side are you on?' I said.

He smiled, as though I had told an amusing tale. 'Why, the winning side, of course.'

Milo Dorsa had a dangerous glint in his eye.

'The man in the dungeon below is part of the effort to return the true king to the throne,' I said, 'and you are prepared to let him hang for your own cause?' It was all I could do to hold my anger in check as I thought of Idris and the mess they had made of him.

'There are casualties in every war. I'm sure being a princess of Carentan and daughter to Reiner Andolin, may the gods rest his soul, that you would understand that.'

He had an answer for every question, every accusation, and they always served his own purposes. There was no point in standing there battling with words, I needed to get myself and Cara out of there and figure out how to rescue Idris.

*Cara.* Where was that cat? I looked around, and wondered how she had got past me and out of the window without me noticing. Then I saw it, a gaping hole in the wall that connected this room to the one next door. I walked over and rapped on the wooden panels with my fist. It made a hollow sound back at me. Dorsa watched me with dispassionate interest.

'The castle is riddled with secret passages inside the walls.'

'Do the priests know about them?'

'I doubt it, but once they discover their queen has disappeared into thin air, they are going to wonder.'

Cara popped her head back out and meowed at me impatiently. I looked back at Milo Dorsa.

'How else do you think we are going to get the red priestess into the castle without being seen?'

'The red priestess?'

'Kerrin Wanda, high priestess of the many gods, sister to the true king, and probably the only one who can save us from this quagmire of mental torture.'

So, he was affected. 'How? How will she save us?'

'Look, I will not stop you,' he gestured to the open passageway, 'but the best thing that you can do now for yourself, and for the future, is to go back to your room and do what you do best, play at being queen.'

It was tempting, I'll admit, but all I could see was Idris's face, and all I could think of was the betrayal of his compatriots: Kerrin, Tristan, and now Milo Dorsa. They wanted the same outcome as me, to return Tordre to its rightful ruler. There was only one difference.

My future held a place for Idris.

I stepped through the panel opening into a dark tunnel. Cara's eyes flashed up ahead, illuminated by the light from Milo Dorsa's room. The light was extinguished as Dorsa slid the panel back into place, and I was alone with my thoughts, my cat, and a more than shaky plan of action.

My timing was impeccable. As I sat behind the walls, I heard the priest-king's guards crash into the room and start questioning Dorsa. I'll give him his dues, he denied all knowledge of seeing me, and pontificated about the noise and the mess they made searching the room. I crawled along on my hands and knees, hoping to get as far away as possible, then leapt back against the far side of the tunnel as something smashed into the panelling in front of me.

I held my breath. My chest pounded and my ears ached. I must have crawled behind a dressing room, as someone large and clumsy was thumping walls and pulling things about. No wonder Milo Dorsa was shouting at them. When the noise eventually died down and the entourage tramped back out, I continued my crawl. If this was how they planned to get Kerrin in and out of the castle, then she was in for an unpleasant surprise. I would love to see the expression on her face, with her perfectly curled red hair, after a few days in here.

The darkness became a dull grey, and I could just about see the outline of Cara's movement up ahead. *Well, at least one of us knows where they are going.* Startled by a faint glow beside me, I looked down, and was in awe at the knife belted to my waist. As I moved, it emitted a soft grey shimmer. I lifted it out of the sheath and held it in front of me. My hand curled around the hilt as though it moulded itself to me.

I'd never liked weapons much. That was always the preoccupation of Gereinte, who said that his biggest ambition in life was to own a sword made of Damascene steel because it glowed in the dark. As I moved it from side to side, a grey-silver sparkle rippled through the air in front of me, giving me enough light to see Cara's eyes flash at me from up ahead. I sheathed the weapon and continued crawling at a faster pace.

Someone had set up these secret passages to move undetected throughout the castle. Of course Milo Dorsa would have knowledge of them, as he controlled the spy network on behalf of the king, but how much had he shared with the priesthood? The rooms had tiny passages that fit behind wooden panelling, and when we passed through a room it was on all fours and as quiet as was humanly possible under the circumstances.

The sounds of people moving about and the murmuring of voices made the rooms easier to identify. The passages by the rooms were often interconnected with steps leading up and down, followed by long dark stretches of dank brickwork and dripping water that reminded me of the dungeons. But at least I could stretch my legs and ease the cricks out of my neck.

The passage looped around and back into a small crawlspace. I stopped for a moment, thinking to at least to stretch out my legs before we went back into the walls. Cara sat patiently waiting for me. I did not know what time of day it was, but my stomach told me I had missed several meals.

127

My body ached all over, and I was starting to thirst like I hadn't had a drink for a week. If I could somehow find my way to the kitchens, I could remedy that, but I daren't show myself whilst the castle was in an uproar with my disappearance. If I showed up now, they would lock me up for good, and then I would be no use to anyone, least of all Idris.

I took a deep breath and got down into a crawling position to follow Cara. She seemed to know where she was going, but I still wished for a map of those damn walls. As we moved on, I had the awful thought that we had been past this section before, but travelling in the opposite direction.

The sounds of voices pealed into earshot: one male, one female. As we moved closer into the room, I recognised Milo Dorsa and my heart sank. We had taken an entire circuit back around to where we had started.

# CHAPTER TWENTY-TWO

## *Walls Have Ears*

'How could you be so stupid to let her go?' A woman's voice. Kerrin.

'Your pardon, Highness. She was armed, and as said, has struck out before. It was... an unpredictable situation.'

'Well. She could be anywhere by now.'

'Nothing changes. All it means is that the priests will be distracted, which can only benefit us.'

I shuffled closer to the crack in the panelling that outlined the entrance to the secret passages. I could see a thin sliver of the room, and Milo Dorsa pacing up and down. My hunger and thirst were enough on their own to drive me into that room, but Kerrin's tone held me back.

'With any luck,' she said, 'they'll catch her before sundown and hang her along with that miserable sop in the dungeons.'

I gasped and slapped a hand over my mouth hoping it hadn't been too loud. I thought they were supposed to be friends. Hadn't they all grown up together here in the castle?

'All he had to do was bring her back to the tavern, but no. He had to bring her here. It could jeopardise everything we have worked towards.' It seemed that Idris was always at the wrong end of Kerrin and Tristan's plan to save the people of Tordre.

'I could always send Bax into the walls to find her.' Milo Dorsa's head turned towards where I sat watching.

'No, no. I need Bax to help me find the focal point. I don't have time to concern myself with the wretched girl, she's merely an inconvenience. I mean, how long can you run around the castle without getting caught, even when the staff aren't on full alert?'

*How dare she?* I'd show her how much of an inconvenience I could be as soon as I found a path to the dungeons and a means to free Idris. They could have their little resistance and play their game of kings and priests, but by the time Tristan showed up to reclaim his throne, Idris and I would be long gone.

'Yes, quite.' Milo Dorsa said. 'May I interest you in some refreshments, your Highness?' He turned to one side and

129

revealed a trestle table, laden with fresh fruits, cheeses, and bread, alongside a flagon of drink. My stomach threatened to betray me and my mouth watered.

'No, Bax was kind enough to procure me some food from the kitchens, and I need to get to work whilst the rest of the castle staff are running ragged after the girl.'

I couldn't see Kerrin, but the sound of her voice made the hairs stand up on the back of my neck. She may be the true king's sister, but whatever future lay in store for either of us, I knew she would not be an ally of mine. I heard the main door of the room open. Milo Dorsa reached out and picked up a chunk of bread.

'I will need you to cover me if they stop us,' she said, with an edge to her voice.

'I see,' he said, and dropped the bread to the table. 'Shame that all of this will go to waste then.' He glanced towards me, then strode out and slammed the door shut behind him.

I sat in the crevice behind the wall and seethed for as long as possible before I began feeling faint from fatigue and hunger. I pressed the secret panel free from its frame and slipped into the room. Cara shot past me, leapt onto the table, and snaffled a block of cheese between her teeth, before hunkering down in a corner to consume her prize. I nibbled at some bread and fruit, and took a cup of heavily watered ale to slake my thirst.

I couldn't keep this circling inside the castle walls up for long. We would never find Idris at that rate. Why had Cara brought me back here?

My stomach settled, but I continued to stuff as much as possible into my mouth, worried that this would be my last meal for a long time, and that at any moment someone might come back. I threw several pieces of ham down to Cara, who wolfed them down as though it were her last meal too. I lifted the ale jug, and a piece of parchment that had stuck to the bottom came away and dropped to the table. It was soggy, but in one piece as I peeled it open and stared at the strange script inked across the page. Written in faltering Etanese, someone clearly directed it at me.

'Follow the walls to the left and only take downward steps. The knife will be your guide.'

I stared at the words. Milo Dorsa must have known it was there and meant for me to find it. I looked down at Cara, who picked at crumbs underneath the table.

'A lot of use you are. I thought you were supposed to be guiding me?' She looked up at me, licked her paws, and purred.

Clearly Milo Dorsa felt he must spread his loyalty across the many options, waiting to see who came out on top. Though I didn't trust him, in the absence of any other plan or a map of the castle, what alternative was there?

I could stay inside the walls and move around freely, albeit with the danger of going around in circles and not getting anywhere, or I could stay within the rooms and move in the shadows, hoping that they wouldn't find me. Given that the entire household was on high alert looking for me, I didn't rate my chances of lasting the day. And I had only a day to find Idris and get out of there.

After making swift use of the privy, I splashed a jug of water over my face and hands, stuffed my pockets with the leftover food, and stowed the message away. I crept back into the walls, followed by Cara, and slid the secret panel back into place.

I followed the instructions and crawled to the end of the wall space in Milo Dorsa's rooms, then turned left. There was a slope downwards towards a further tunnel and steps up. I took the slope down until I found another crawl space and edged myself along. The space got smaller and smaller, and a couple of times I knocked an elbow on the panelling and stopped, held my breath, and listened for sounds. Twice I heard shuffling on the other side, but nothing to indicate that anyone had noticed a strange knocking sound inside the walls.

How many times had I heard weird noises in the walls and put it down to creaky old castle structures? I wondered how many times they had listened to my own conversations during the times I had spent in my rooms.

The space was almost too small to move in, but I could see up ahead where the room's walls ended and a new tunnel began. Cara was up there somewhere, staking out our escape route. As my movement became more and more restricted, my breath shortened, and I felt at once hot and then cold. What if I crawled so far in that I couldn't get out? My breath sped up and my heart hammered.

Then I heard voices. Two males, distinct. I inched a little further and my limbs became so squashed up I wanted to cry out. My knee slipped and knocked into the wooden panelling.

Then I recognised the voices.

'… take care of the problem in your dungeons, before… wait. What was that?'

I let my body go limp, my breath still.

'Your Excellency, this castle is old. It makes many strange noises. Some days you can hear the chapel's song in its walls.'

Through a tiny crack in the panel, I saw a sliver of the priest-king holding his palm out to the wall and inspecting it with reverence. He had his back to the Archbishop, Abiel Morda, whose brow was creased with a tiny frown. He was close. So close I could almost hear his breath.

A tiny scritch-scratch noise drew his attention to the other end of the wall. My eyes darted to the left, where Cara made little furrows in the dust with her claws.

*No.* I wanted to cry out, throw something at her to make her stop.

But then the priest-king looked away, and the Archbishop strode over to inspect the wall. The two of them had dropped all pretence of being the King of Tordre and his priest adviser, and wore their own faces.

Seeing the priest-king up close again, with his dusty-brown hair curled around his face, made me want to put my fist through the panelling. But I held myself in check. The Archbishop, Abiel Morda, looked exactly as I remembered him when I was a child, like a weathered old uncle with a grudge to bear.

'Rats,' Morda said. 'You have rats in the walls.' He dismissed the scratching with a wave of his hand and turned back to the table, where he poured himself a cup of wine. 'Now, where were we?'

The priest-king looked back to where I was hiding behind the panelling and narrowed his eyes. It appeared he was looking right at me.

I held my breath.

Then, with a tiny shake of his head, he turned away and walked back towards Morda.

'The power base in Tordre, your Excellency.'

'With Tordre under our control, it will be easier to gain a foothold in Vermondie. Once we have secured the South, it will open up conversations with the church leaders further north in Sarlat and Malvas. Once surrounded, Carentan will have no option but to bow to a unified Holy Church Authority.'

My cheeks burned, and the urge to shout was almost overwhelming.

'We first need to crush this resistance, your Excellency.'

'Quite so,' Abiel Morda said. 'Which is why you cannot wait a moment longer.'

'Let's put the messages out, then. Tomorrow, when the sun is at its height,' the priest-king said, then took a cup and filled it. 'We'll make it a public event; set the gallows up in the town square. That should keep the resistance in line for a while, at least.'

My throat constricted, and a dull ache in my chest left me breathless for air. I had to get out of there and reach Idris. I was compelled to move fast but paralysed by my own stupid curiosity.

Abiel Morda scowled, though come to think of it, he had a permanent scowl on his face. I always wondered how someone so pious could look so tainted. 'You forget, my son, that such power we wield is only transitory. The power lies in the true conversion of this land. In time, they will forget the face of their old king.'

'But for now,' the priest-king's face shimmered for a moment, and I had to shake my head as my ears began to buzz. His hair lengthened and lightened, his bone structure sharpened, and the Blue King emerged.

I swallowed, but my throat was dry from the dust and the musty air. I needed to cough, and held my hand over my throat and rubbed it to ease the discomfort.

'And the other little problem?' Abiel Morda said.

I felt the pressure building in my nose and throat, a tickle that grew into an irritation, and when I couldn't help myself but draw breath, I was beyond the point of return. I turned to glare at Cara, as if it were all her fault for stirring up the dust. I put both hands over my nose and mouth to stifle the sneeze as much as I could, but all I succeeded in doing was to limit it to a strangled grunt.

The priest-king's head lifted in response, and he stared back at the wall. A tiny smile curled around his mouth. 'Oh, I think the other problem will take care of itself.'

# CHAPTER TWENTY-THREE

## *How to Spring a Trap*

I sat there for some time with my hand over my nose and mouth, willing the tingle to dissipate. By the time the priest-king and the Archbishop had left the room, my nose streamed and my eyes watered. I wiped the sleeve of my jerkin across my face, and shuffled to the end of the crawl space, looking for the next passage down that would take me along the quickest route towards the dungeons.

The priest-king had suspected something and that meant I had to move fast. Cara was nowhere to be seen. She must have been ahead, scouting for the way down, because down was the only way to go now. We had to get to Idris before evening. It would be another long night ahead, and a quick road to oblivion tomorrow if we didn't find a way of getting out of the castle.

My whole body relaxed in relief as I reached the end of that tiny crawl space and I could move my limbs again. One thing was sure given my current record; I was not suitable material for a spy. There was enough light from the cracks in the walls to give me a fair impression of where I was heading, which enabled me to follow the trail of paw prints that led further down the narrow stone corridors carved into the walls of the castle.

The knife belted to my side gave me a modicum of confidence that I could protect myself if caught, but that would mean the end of my attempts at freedom. That would mean I had nothing left to lose. My only hope lay somehow with the words on the crumpled piece of parchment I had tucked inside my jerkin, which gave me a degree of comfort that I was not all alone in my quest.

The tunnels became easier to navigate as we moved beyond the thin spaces behind the walls of the rooms and into the labyrinth of the castle. The smell got mustier, the walls wetter with a constant drip-drip, and the light became non-existent. It was only the soft glow from the knife and the responding flash of Cara's eyes up ahead that kept me moving in the right direction. Down and to the left. I stumbled over loose stones and put my hand out against the wall to steady myself. My hand met with the spongy wet moss on the wall and I snatched it back in disgust.

My resolve kept me moving; that and the thought that Idris was rotting in worse conditions than I was in. When I finally reached the end of the tunnel, my hunger and thirst had returned to ravage me anew. My pockets were stuffed with leftovers, but I needed those to give some strength to Idris when I got to him.

If I got to him.

I looked up at the iron gate that separated me from the other side of the castle. The side where people could move freely and didn't have to hide in the shadows. Light flicked in the corridor outside, from a sconce in which the candle had burnt almost to the bottom of its wick. It was enough to see that I was facing a wall in a little alcove, from where I could see the staircase that the priest-king had led me down to visit the dungeon only days before.

I heard voices. Laughter, banter. It grew louder, then dissipated as someone moved past. Was that up or down they were going? I pressed myself to the wall, kept to the shadows, and listened. The sound travelled upward, then disappeared.

Silence again.

I tried the gate. It was locked, of course, and rattled when I shook it. Cara slipped easily through the bars, and stared at me as though I was some kind of freak to not be able to squish my clumsy human body through the iron barrier. On further inspection, the gate was fixed with a chain and padlock.

*Keys.* Why had I not thought to bring some kind of key or instrument to force a lock? Milo Dorsa would have known what waited for me at the end of this breadcrumb trail. I pulled out the parchment from my jerkin and looked at the words that now laughed at me. Perhaps he was sending a troop of guards to meet me even now. I should never have trusted those words. In a pique of anger, I screwed up the paper and was about to toss it away when I had an idea.

I flattened out the thick, waxy, paper and folded it once, twice, three times, then rolled it into a tube. It held its shape for a second, then sprang back into a coil. I let out a groan and looked longingly at Cara. She sat on the other side of the gate licking her paws. I tried again, but this time twisted the paper after rolling it so that it made a thin, wiry rod. This time, when I let go, it held its shape.

Maybe… if it fit into the keyhole on the padlock.

I had to put both hands out of the gate to turn the padlock towards me. The light was not good enough to see the mechanism inside the lock, but I managed to get the rod into the keyhole to fiddle about. Having a brother had proven useful, especially one who spent the best part of his youth with the spymaster's son. I hadn't a clue about half of the things they used to get up to, but I remembered this.

Twisting the parchment back and forth, I listened for the little click that would unlock the gate, but all I felt in my hands was the inadequate give of the tool, which crumpled back into being a piece of parchment paper.

I sat down with a slump on the ground and leaned my head back against the wall, not caring about the wet, slimy surface that would make my hair sticky and dank. A lump formed in my throat. This was all going wrong. What was I thinking?

Something hard dug into my side. I fished around in my pocket and pulled out a lump of bread. *Oh well.* If I was going to get caught, I might as well do it with some food in my belly. I tore a bite and chewed, but my thoughts kept returning to Idris. I might as well have been eating the parchment paper.

Wait. There was still something digging into my side.

The knife.

Of course.

I dropped the bread and knelt up against the gate, then drew the knife from its sheath. It shimmered grey in my hands and I thought maybe, just maybe, the tip was thin enough.

With both hands poking out of the bars to reach the padlock, I tried the tip in the keyhole.

No, it was too big, too clumsy, and I couldn't see what I was doing. I pulled the knife in and sat back against the wall. It was no good. Even if it could work, I couldn't get at the padlock from the right angle.

'Meow.' Cara told me to hurry. Hurry and get this problem solved like only a human can. She stalked back and forth outside the gate, lashing her tail. At any moment, she was likely to give up on me. Perhaps her loyalties lay elsewhere.

I got up again on my knees with both arms outside the bars of the gate and turned the padlock upside down to face me. The knife went in. It was tight, but the mechanism only needed a tiny point of pressure in the right direction and...

Click.

The shackle sprung free, and I carefully lifted it from the gate. With a creaky squeak that made me wince, I pushed open the gate and stepped out. Cara wrapped herself around my legs once, then darted off around the corner. I pushed the gate back, and put the lock in place so that it looked as though it had been left undisturbed. I was about to turn the corner when I heard a deep voice.

'Hello puss, where did you come from?'

I slipped back into the alcove and pressed myself against the wall to hide my presence, but anyone passing need only take a cursory look into the shadows to see there was someone hiding there. The disembodied voice faded into the distance alongside a meek little meow; that cat had everyone under its influence.

I followed the fading sounds, keeping enough distance to remain hidden but close enough to discern their direction. I knew enough of the layout to know that we were approaching the dungeons from the opposite side to the main staircase, where the priest-king had brought me down before.

*Good.* That would mean fewer guards patrolling, and my plan to get us out unseen began looking more like a real possibility, instead of some crazy idea that my brother might have come up with.

The sounds of movement ahead stopped. I crept forward enough to see two more guards at the entrance to the dungeon squatting down to pet Cara. She dutifully rolled over to bathe in the dust on the ground and purr with all the human attention. Well they were certainly distracted, but there was no way I was going to be able to creep past them.

I picked up a loose stone from the ground and hurled it as far as I could into the distance beyond the dungeons, hoping they were distracted enough not to see it flying over their heads. It made a tiny clunk as it landed and one of them looked up. He shook his head and resumed his attention on the cat.

I spotted a larger stone, then, thinking that I might as well give it my best shot, scooped a small handful. Too many would likely scatter and land short of the target, so I chose reasonable-sized rocks and launched them underhand, the way that Gereinte had taught me to skim stones across Lake Mariac.

There was a moment's silence, and then a small patter of sound, far enough into the shadows not to be seen, but close enough to make them look up and at each other in question. They stood up slowly, hands resting on their weapons. They were no doubt on full alert anyway, but I needed them to go in the opposite direction so I could slip through the entrance unseen. I picked up a smaller stone and launched it high above their heads. It made a decisive clunk, and they instantly followed the direction of the sound.

Cara sprang to her feet and darted through the archway gates into the dungeons, and I flitted in past her, clinging to the shadows and willing myself not to make a sound. The dungeon area was a long corridor with barred doors, behind some of which you could see piles of wretched rags slumped in corners. Some heads turned, but most sat and stared at unseen ghosts. The smell of dead vermin, vomit, and faeces made my throat constrict, and I had to breathe through my mouth to get through it.

I peered through the bars of a door near the far end and found Idris. He sat in exactly the same position I had seen him in when I visited with the priest-king, seated on the ground, knees bent and pulled in, eyes focused ahead. A bowl of brown lumpy muck with what could once have been bread floating in it sat on the floor near the door.

The light was so faint I wasn't sure he would see me, but he turned his head, sensing my movement, and looked right at me. I suppose his eyes had gotten used to seeing in that gloom. He smiled in expectation. His swollen eye had gotten worse and seeped blood and pus. The bruising around his face had turned darker and mottled, like the skin of a lizard. I wondered if he had moved at all since the last time I had visited.

The priest-king's words floated back into my mind; 'I want to show you what we do with those who plot against the crown.'

This wasn't the time to test his resolve. I grabbed the knife from my belt and got to work on the lock. It proved not be as easy as the padlock on the gates, and I cursed to myself as I fumbled at the door. Cara stretched up on her hind legs, front paws almost reaching the lock, and I shooed her away with impatience.

The sound of metal scraping on metal echoed down the corridor, but I didn't have time to worry about it. I hadn't enough time to concern myself with where those two guards had gone. Not enough time to acknowledge the absurdity of what I was trying to do. There wasn't enough light to see, so the knife kept slipping, though it wasn't small enough to get into the locking mechanism anyway. I kept listening, hoping to hear that telltale click that would give us freedom, but it never came.

'Allow me.'

I swung around towards the voice and saw the priest-king stride down the corridor, a flaming torch in one hand and two men flanking him on either side. For one crazy moment, I thought he had come to help, but then I saw the look on his face and my heart sank.

One of the guards grabbed my arms and relieved me of the knife, while the other unlocked the door with his set of keys. I hardly had time to acknowledge their presence before the priest-king gave me a rough shove and I stumbled into the cell.

The door slammed shut behind me, and the lock clicked back into place.

# CHAPTER TWENTY-FOUR

## *Best Laid Plans*

I stumbled and dropped to my hands and knees. The light of the priest-king's torch filled the cell, and I could see the pain in Idris's eyes. I leapt up and slammed myself against the door, grabbing the bars and shaking it for all it was worth. It didn't budge, of course. The priest-king's face peered back at me.

'Please... you don't understand. How can this ever be right? You will start a war.'

The priest-king said nothing. All I saw was pity on his face, and then he was gone. I shook the bars one last time and one of the guards turned to look back at me. He wavered for a brief instant, then he too was gone.

'Nerys.'

I turned and looked at Idris. We had come so close and now it was all lost. With my back against the door, I slid down. His stoic expression compelled me to crawl over to him. I took his face in my hands, and he winced as I gently used my sleeve to wipe away the blood and tears that had pooled around his eyes. I remembered the remains of the food I had stuffed into my pockets and pulled out my last lump of bread feeding it to him in tiny little chunks. He rolled it around his parched mouth, searching for saliva to help him swallow.

'I'm sorry,' I said.

He shook his head, then winced. 'Kerrin will come.'

I sat back and looked away. *How do I tell him? No, she won't come. She is already here and she will let the both of us hang. What does that say about your precious true king?*

'Kerrin... is not who you think she is.'

He gazed at me without blinking, and I expected him to dispute this and argue the case for his friends, but he was silent. Looking down at his hands he flexed his fingers, as though discovering them for the first time. He had been there for nearly two days and hadn't appeared to have moved from that spot since the first time I saw him in there.

'Why are you here?' he said. The dim light from the wall sconces outside the cell cast a yellow hue across the room. He looked at me as though for the first time. 'You look... different.'

Yes, I suppose I probably did, wearing trousers, tunic and hair bundled up into a bun. He reached out a hand to my face but stopped short of touching me. His eyes trailed down my body to the belt at my waist and he flinched, then frowned and looked up at me.

'Where did you get that?'

I untied the belt and the sheath that came with it, now just an empty shell. The weight of the knife at my side had become almost a part of me over the last day or so, and now that it wasn't there, I sensed its loss.

'I found a room, near to my chambers, where the old king and queen used to reside. Except...' Idris held the belt now and ran a finger down the embossed leather pattern. He looked up, and for the first time in... well, ever, he looked animated.

'Where is the knife?' He looped the belt around his waist and fastened it.

'They took it... they would never let me bring it in here. It guided me here. Well, that and Cara. Also made a good lock pick, but...' The guards. The knife. I suppose he could have guessed that an empty sheath would be home for a knife. Though the belt had been a loose fit on me, it was snug on Idris and sat above his hips like it belonged there.

I sat back against the opposite wall, and we looked at each other for a long moment. I did not know how close we were to the break of day; how soon they might come to take us away. That might be our only hope, our only opportunity. If we didn't get away, the next stop for us both would be the gallows in the town square.

'How badly are you injured?'

He was on his feet in one fluid motion, like how a cat might spring from half asleep to stalking its prey. I had never seen him move like that before.

'My mother always said that I had strong bones.' He flexed his fingers, then made a fist. 'It is mostly surface bruising, I think.'

'You remember?'

142

'Fleeting memories. They seem to come and go in my dreams. I remember Tristan and I playing as boys.' He paced up and down, then turned on me. 'What are you doing here?'

'I...' Taken aback at his accusatory tone, my mind went blank, '... couldn't leave you here.'

'That wasn't part of the plan.'

'I suppose you being caught and thrown into the dungeons was part of the plan?'

He dismissed that with a wave of his hand.

'You look different too,' I said. Apart from the bruising on his face, there was something about the way he moved and held himself that had changed. Perhaps the isolation had brought out his anger. Or perhaps he realised the truth about his so-called friends. He circled the small cell now, like a trapped mountain cat.

Cara. Where was that cat?

'Sit down, please. It's making me dizzy to watch you.'

He stopped and looked at me, eyes searching like a little boy lost.

'Kerrin's not coming, is she?'

I shook my head, and he looked crestfallen. 'Damn it, everything I've done for Tris. Why would he do this?' The one solid foundation he had in his memory blew away like autumn leaves on the wind. It made my heart ache once again for my family, the rock at my centre that kept me together.

I grabbed his arm and pulled him down to sit opposite me. 'We have little time to work out how to do this. They are going to come for us both in the morning and take us to the town square to hang. They intend to make a public example of how they deal with traitors,' I said.

He looked horrified.

'How well do you know the castle?'

'Well enough. Like I said, I grew up here,' he said.

'Good. Because I have an escape route through the hidden tunnels inside the walls.'

'I know those tunnels.' Idris's eyes lit up. 'I used to hide in there as a boy. I had forgotten all about them.' He frowned, then shook his head as though to dislodge an errant thought.

I wanted to reach out and hold him. He had just found out that his best friend had betrayed him. Instead, I took his hand and he let me hold it in my palm for a moment.

'Was he a good king?' I said.

Idris's head lifted to look at me, and his eyes reflected his hurt. 'I wish I could remember, but it all seems like fog in my mind. How do you fight it?'

That was interesting. I hadn't given it much thought until then. The objectionable priest, who I now know to be Abiel Morda himself, had tried to sway my mind a couple of times and failed. Had I known at the time who he really was, I might have obeyed his wishes with no hesitation. It was all to do with perception. How laughable.

'When I first came here, I was terribly homesick. It confounded me, because I had been so excited at the prospect of meeting and marrying the King of Tordre. It was like a dream come true for me.' A flicker of a smile played on Idris's lips. 'Yes, well, I suppose it was naïve. Reality can never match what we dream up in our heads. Anyway, it felt like I had lost something fundamental to my existence and I didn't understand why. There was this empty hole inside me. So maybe I was too preoccupied with feeling lonely and lost to pay much attention to what was going on around me. But something that Bax told me rings true,' I said.

'Bax?'

'Assistant to the seneschal. You know... Bax.'

'Seneschal Dorsa.' Idris had a contemplative look on his face.

'You remember him?'

'He's been around for years. I never trusted him.'

'He helped me get here. I mean... kind of. He let me go. I suppose it is helping in a subtle way. But he wanted me to go back to my room, to let Kerrin come and put things right.'

'You told me she's not coming,' he said.

'She is coming. Just not for us,' I said.

Idris had a faraway look in his eye. He turned his gaze back to me.

'What did you learn?'

'Oh yes, Bax. He told me to hold on to my faith, because they can only turn you if you believe in them. It makes sense when I think back; I was too focused on my family and getting home, or at least getting a message home. That and the faceless king, of course.'

Idris frowned, but I could see the effect of my revelation whirring away behind his eyes. Faith, what did that mean? Religion was one thing, but a deep, unshakeable belief in something was altogether different. He looked down at the belt and sheath around his waist and made a show of adjusting it, but left his hands in place, thumbs hooked underneath the belt.

There was a light scratch at the door and a soft mewling. Idris looked up.

'How long do you think we've got?' he said.

'I don't know. Maybe a few hours. It was late already by the time I made it through the tunnels, then it took a while to get the damn gates open and coax the guards away,' I said.

'How in the world did you do that?'

'A bit of misdirection and a distraction from Cara; that cat has friends all over this castle.'

His face had that faraway look again. 'Tristan always talked about the cat. How she had helped him out of numerous scrapes over the years.'

'If you grew up here with him, you would have been there too.'

He looked thoughtful. 'Yes, I remember the cat.' The mewling outside the door picked up again. 'The cat! Were the men distracted by the cat?'

'Yes. I can't quite believe it worked, but they were.'

'Maybe that's it then,' he said. 'Familiarity. Faith. An unshakeable belief in something you know to be true. The cat is familiar and friendly. Any ordinary cat would not have been able to attach itself so readily to everyone it comes across, but she has infiltrated castle life to the extent that people expect to see her. She is truth. How can a cat be lying to you? She just is.'

'If that's so, then why can't people see through the priest-king's lies?'

'Because he is enough like the true king to fool everyone,' Idris said.

I thought about the way he changed his face from the rugged brown-haired priest to the sleek and chiselled features of the king. 'But I'd only ever seen portraits of the king before. How

145

would I know what I was seeing?' I said. Maybe it had to do with demeanour. Tristan was imperious enough to be convincing as a king. And the priest-king in his Morra Dreiden guise scared the daylight out of me. 'Are kings supposed to be terrifying?' It seemed like a stupid question for a princess of the court of Carentan, but I was in a foreign land, with foreign rules and foreign traditions.

Idris thought about it for a moment. 'No, I don't think so. The old king wasn't terrifying. In fact, the people loved him. He was a national hero, so it was only natural that his son would succeed him at the acclamation.'

'You remember the old king?'

'I remember... some of it. I remember feeling devastated when he died. The entire country went into mourning. It took an age before we could take the public acclamation to determine who would succeed.' He tilted his head to one side as though trying to tip the memories back into his mind. 'I was there with Tristan... at the acclamation. Tris was playing the fool, as ever, but I remember being there, and the crowds erupting with exultation at the decision. I remember thinking that the old king would rest assured in his grave.'

I stared at him for a moment and watched his memories sink in. There was silence all around us. Even the low-level groans from the other cells had ceased. Then Cara started up her insistent scratching at the door and I sprung up.

'We have to get out of here. Out of here and out of Tordre.'

# CHAPTER TWENTY-FIVE

## *To Storm a Castle*

'Hello?' I banged on the cell door and was rewarded with a hollow thunk. I stood up on tiptoes so my nose reached the bars. On the opposite side of the door, Cara scratched and heaved herself half-way up in an attempt to reach me.

'If we get out of here, where would we go?' Idris said.

'Back home… Carentan. I know it's not home for you, but why stay in this gods-forsaken place when everyone you know has-'

'Betrayed us?' he said. I couldn't bear to look at the hurt in his eyes, so I resumed banging on the door. He stood up with a relaxed ease. 'They won't come with you making all that noise. Here.' He stepped up to the metal bars, which framed his face, and made a soft clicking noise with his tongue. A second later, a paw appeared between the bars as Cara hoisted her body weight up, hanging on by the strength of her claws. Idris reached a hand through the bars and took some of the weight off her body. He leaned in close and whispered to the cat before releasing her back down to the ground. Then silence. No more scratching at the door.

'What did you do?'

'Let's see how much the castle guards remember.' Idris sat cross-legged, as though he had all the time in the world to wait. I slumped down with my back against the door and looked at him. He watched me with cool, appraising eyes. 'You would take me back with you to Carentan?'

'Of course. You're more of a king than any of these idiots in charge around here,' I said. He dropped his gaze to the knife belt around his waist.

'I can't leave my country to be torn apart by this false truth. I will see you to the border, though.' Footsteps echoed down the corridor outside, and his head jerked up.

'Let's get out of this cell first.' I sprang to my feet, then jumped back as a large gruff face filled the small square of bars. The edges around the man's face softened when he saw who

147

occupied the cell, though he didn't look too disposed toward opening the door.

'I recognise you,' I said. 'Didn't you accompany me a few times?' I hung my head and tried to extract a modicum of empathy, but he was ready and steeled his expression.

'What's all this noise? You won't have to wait long. It'll soon be time to go,' he said with a whisper of apology in his tone.

'I'm so desperately hungry and thirsty. Won't you please get me something? I don't know why I'm in here. I got scared, so I ran and I hid, and then the king locked me up in here. At least tell me what I've done so that I can make amends.' I hung my head and let tears leak down my cheeks. It wasn't hard to let the lump in my throat take over and the emotion to spill into my words.

'Colluding with that... traitor?' he said, with a confused glance at Idris. He shook his head to dislodge an uncomfortable thought, then turned to leave.

'Wait. Where is the cat? Please, let me see the cat one more time,' I said. He turned around, his grim, knobbly face smoothed into a familiar smile when I mentioned Cara.

'You mean this little devil?' And he lifted her up to the bars. Cara stuck a paw through the bars and patted my nose. 'She likes you. Look, your Maj... look, I don't like what has happened to you, but it's the king's orders,' he said.

'I understand.' I leaned in closer to Cara. 'Why do you suppose she likes me? I mean, she should rip me to shreds if I were a traitor to the king.' The guard looked thoughtful.

'It is true, she is the king's cat. She has lived here as long as I can remember and served the crown as much as any of us.'

'So why do you suppose she is not ripping me apart as a traitor?' I pressed the point with him, and he frowned, then, in a moment of distraction, disappeared from sight, taking Cara with him. I turned and looked back at Idris, who watched me with interest.

'I tried, but we need more time,' I said. 'The threads of his memories are unravelling with Cara's presence. Maybe Kerrin has already sabotaged the focal point...'

There was a commotion going on in the corridor – raised voices. Then the clash of steel on steel. Moments later, the guard reappeared.

148

'Look… I can't let you out. There's a siege at the castle gates and we're all summoned. But here,' and just like that, he handed me the knife.

Idris was on his feet in an instant.

'What is it?' I said. He reached out, then retracted his hand as though touching the knife might burn his skin. 'You know this knife?' I grabbed his wrist with my free hand and slapped the hilt of the knife into his open palm. His fingers curled around it and I swear that the dimness of the room illuminated a little, enough to see the look of curiosity on his face as he moved the blade experimentally back and forth. He looked up at me, sheathed it and settled the belt at his waist, then drew the knife back out. 'You remember, don't you?'

'I remember how to get out of these bloody cells,' he said, and set to work on the lock. After a few seconds of intricate twists, the lock released with a solid click and the door eased back on its hinges. We stared at each other, not quite believing our luck. I was about to bolt out of the door, when he held me back with a hand pressed against my shoulder. 'We have to move carefully. If Kerrin has breached the focal point and Tristan has launched an attack at the gates, it will be chaos in the castle. We won't know who's the enemy and who is not.'

'Well, I'll make that easy for you then. Trust no-one, not castle guards, priests, nor rebels,' I said. He edged in front of me and peered cat-like around the cell door. He leapt back, and my heart jumped into my throat, but it was only Cara. She sprang playfully towards us, then turned on her tail and raised her nose, chiding us for our stupidity. Darkness, I felt like chiding us for our stupidity.

'Clear,' Idris said, then moved out into the corridor. He checked over his shoulder to make sure I was following, but there was no way I was going to let him out of my sight now. Now that he was the only ally I had in this place.

The corridor leading to the staircase where I had come out of the wall tunnels was empty, but in the distance we could hear fighting and shouting. As we were about to go around the corner, a booming voice reverberated down the corridor.

'Wait.'

149

# CHAPTER TWENTY-SIX

## *Partners in Crime*

Idris and I stopped and looked at each other, then over our shoulders. The voice had come from one of the cells.

'We can't-'

'-leave them.' I finished his sentence, and we turned back to the cells. Idris headed straight for the cell where the voice had come from, but I lingered on the ones in between. At first glance they looked empty, but then a steady row of heads began appearing at the barred windows. The first one I looked into held a young woman, not far off my own age, dirty and bruised with sallow cheeks and sad eyes. She looked as though she hadn't eaten in days.

'Y… your Majesty,' she said in a faltering voice. 'Please tell him I didn't mean it… they wanted to hear the story of the rebel king, the song from the taverns. I didn't know they were going to lock me up for singing it.'

'We'll get you out of here, don't worry,' I said. 'Are you castle staff?'

'From the kitchens, your Majesty.' She took a low curtsy and nearly fell over. My stomach recoiled in disgust. These dungeons were meant for dangerous criminals, not ordinary staff who sang controversial songs. The taverns were full of minstrels who sang songs to make a living, casting aspersions and making a parody of royalty. It had been like that for centuries. They did it in Carentan as well. If we locked up every minstrel, there would be no room for any real criminals.

I looked up, and Idris made his way down the line of doors using his knife to unlock each cell as he went. Familiar faces edged their way out of the doors, people who, in normal times, would hold this place together.

There was indeed one of the castle minstrels who I assumed had been singing the wrong songs. Then a giant of a man who I am certain once accompanied me on a walk of the coastal road. He bowed low to me as Idris released him from his incarceration.

There was a scribe who was teaching letters to children when I had looked for Bax, then... oh my word, Lana. My former maid looked at me as though she wanted to throw her arms around me, but sank into a curtsy that took her to the floor, sobbing in a heap. My throat constricted. What could I say? It was my fault she was in there. She wouldn't have been culpable if I had not run off.

The last cell door creaked open. Arvind, the king's former trusted adviser, staggered out and shielded his eyes from the bright torchlight of the corridor. Dressed in tattered and grimy robes, someone had truly knocked his customary cheery positivity out of him. His nose sloped to one side, and his eyes were blackened with purple trails running down his cheeks. He took measured steps with one leg dipping to the side as he limped to join the waiting assortment of prisoners, who all looked up at me as though I were their salvation.

I looked at Idris, who stood at the back of the group. I wanted to hit something; preferably something in priest's robes.

'You are not traitors. We are not traitors,' I said. 'We have all been misled, and now the time has come to release the nation. The rebels are inside the castle. Stay hidden, arm yourselves for protection, but find somewhere safe to hide. And don't trust anyone. Even your closest friends may be compromised. Let's go.' I turned to leave, but no-one followed. They huddled together in a group and stared at me.

'The hell we're going to sit here and hide,' the giant stepped forward and stood to attention, waiting for orders. The others rallied behind him with noises of affirmation, and the group appeared to swell as though they had grown in numbers. I looked over at Idris, who shrugged. *Bloody great.* I had a small mutinous army, which was starved, thirsty and injured, with no weapons, and no way out.

I had an idea.

'Okay then, follow me.' I turned as two men with swords appeared in the archway leading out of the dungeons. In seconds, the confidence in the room dropped and everyone scattered back into their cells. I chanced a glance over my shoulder. Only Idris and the giant remained. The two in front of me grinned when they realised how easy it had been to round up their prisoners and circled their swords in a leisurely fashion.

151

'I think we know where this is going,' one of them said. Behind him, Cara slipped into view.

'Nerys. To Cara,' Idris said. I glanced at the cat, who hunkered down as though to pounce, and I dropped to the floor in a crouch. A flying object whistled over the top of my head and the guard nearest to me fell back, the knife protruding from his neck. Blood spurted out and ran down his armour to pool on the floor.

Moments later, the giant skidded past me, slid on the wet red of blood on the floor and slammed into the second man, who toppled to the ground. The two men wrestled and slipped around on the ground. At first I thought our man might not be in any fit state to win the advantage, but the guard, encumbered with sword and armour, could not get enough purchase on the enormous man to defend himself.

It was over in seconds. His sword spun away on the floor and, with a sickening crunch, the giant twisted his neck at an impossible angle. He slumped into a heap and the giant sprang up, growling and looking for someone else to fight.

I had seen all this before, having grown up amongst knights who practised their skill daily in the yards, but up close and so real... I shuddered. *Pull yourself together, Nerys, or you might be next.*

I jumped up.

'Let's go,' I said. Idris retrieved his knife, barely batting an eyelid, and I wondered at that. Strange behaviour for a man who said he preferred to avoid conflict. He noticed me watching him and did that shrug-thing as if to say it wasn't his preferred outcome but needs must. I could only agree with that sentiment.

The giant was busy relieving one of the dead of his armour and sword. He picked up the second sword and gave it to a reluctant court adviser who had crept out of one cell. A few other faces appeared in doorways. I strode towards the archway, Idris and the giant flanked on either side and Cara up ahead. I stopped to check they were all following me, but they stood outside the cell doors staring at the dead bodies. 'Well, come on then,' I said, and they shuffled along behind us.

We made it to the small iron gate that was the entrance to the catacomb of tunnels that resided inside the walls of the castle. I had left the lock loosely in place, and it took only a quick twist to release it and open the way into the tunnels. One by one, Idris and I ushered them inside. Some of them took off, while others lingered with uncertainty, waiting for further instruction.

As the giant approached the entrance, my heart dropped into my stomach. Idris and I glanced at each other, then back at him. He would never make it through the smaller sections of the walls without getting stuck.

'What is your name, my friend?' Idris said. The giant looked confused for a moment before responding.

'Koeda, your... Sire.' There was a flicker of recognition in his eyes.

'Koeda, do you remember this man?' I said. Koeda looked down at his feet.

'He is... a courtier, but one of the good ones,' he said. I had to wonder what constituted good and bad in this place. The politics of court wasn't so different in Carentan, although at that moment in time, I was satisfied with anyone in priestly robes being the bad ones.

'The hold is shifting, there will be confusion for some time,' Idris said. 'Koeda, I need you to stand firm against the priests. There are rebels outside laying siege to the castle. They are on our side and mean to take back control.' With the dead guard's armour and weapons, Koeda could easily pass for one of the priests' men. 'If you encounter anyone from the resistance, we have a code signal shared with those within the castle who are friends to our cause.' I looked up at Idris. He might have thought to tell me some of these plans before he sent me back into the castle unawares. He looked at me and dipped his head. We would talk about it later, but I had an uneasy feeling about all of this. Idris made a singular gesture of solidarity with his right fist across his chest to his left shoulder.

'Koeda, make your way to the old king and queen's rooms, we will meet you there. I could use a man like you to help me get out of the castle,' I said.

'You are leaving us?' Koeda looked crestfallen, and I felt a twinge of guilt in my gut, but all I wanted was to escape this chaos and return to my family. Koeda repeated the gesture Idris has shown him, turned on his heels and disappeared up the stairs.

I turned to enter the tunnels, and Idris placed a hand over mine as I reached for the gate. It felt comforting, and sent a tingle up my arm that made me turn to look at him. For the first time since I had entered the dungeons, I could see the intensity of his grey gaze. His stoic expression and pale face reminded me a little of the priest-king, which unnerved me, and I jerked my hand away.

'You don't have to leave, you know.'

'What would you have me do?' I said. 'Sit as queen beside Tristan's side after he left us to die in this place? He may attack the castle with his army of rebels, but if they lose, we stand to be taken to the gallows in a matter of hours if we are caught.'

'I will never let them take you,' he said. 'They will have to kill me first.'

A vision came back to me of that knife as it whistled over my head. A split-second sooner and it would have been my neck that blossomed with a crimson blood fountain. I shuddered, and he reached out and trailed a fingertip down the side of my cheek. It was such a tender gesture that I was taken aback, and stood there staring at him when we should have been running.

'I don't know how, but I have influence in this castle. Perhaps the priests' hold is weakening. Perhaps Kerrin has already breached the focal point. I don't know, but something is changing,' Idris said.

I shook myself, trying for some composure. 'How did you know I would duck in time?' *More to the point, how did the cat know what to do?*

He smiled. 'No one can resist Cara's charms.'

'But in the forest, you didn't know her,' I said.

'Be wary of the wild. A lesson to all those who happen to cross her path,' he said. The way he looked at me, I wasn't sure if he was referring to me or the cat. He patted the sheath at his side where the knife nestled with its own sense of belonging.

'I have to go back. You know that, don't you?' I said.

He looked thoughtful for a moment. 'And when you return, what then?'

I tried to imagine the reaction of my family, but it wasn't pretty. 'My mother will find some other insipid prince or king to marry me off to as soon as she learns this one is null and void.' At that, I turned and entered the darkness of the hidden tunnels.

# CHAPTER TWENTY-SEVEN

## *Resistance from Within*

It was as well that Idris had started to remember things, as I realised my sense of direction had clearly been compromised when I attempted to lead the small party back through the catacombs of the walls. He redirected our journey so that we didn't end up bursting into the throne room or the great hall in the middle of a skirmish.

We heard the sounds of fighting going on inside the castle, but I managed to sneak out into an empty chamber and filch a few bread rolls, some cheese, and watered ale. With that, the group grew a little more human and replenished some of the damage done to them, although it would take a lot longer for most of them to fully recover.

Lana was my shadow; I couldn't shake her presence, even if I wanted to. Because of whatever strange hold the priests had over her, she had been broken quite decisively when they had branded her a traitor. It wasn't her fault, I realised that now. In times of strife, we all try to survive.

In the tight crawlspace of the walls, I glanced behind me. She struggled to keep up, so I slowed enough to allow her to catch up and held out my hand. Together we made slower progress, but the faint smile on her lips and the glow of hope in her cheeks made it worth my while.

Arvind kept close to Idris, as though he had chosen his new subject for leadership and was intent on making his mark. It was almost comical to see him, robes in tatters, face bruised but bright with a new hope. His whispered voice reached us down the length of the tunnel. 'Sire… once we reach our destination, how will we defeat the usurper and his minions? If you share the plan, I will do my utmost to advise at the best of my capacity. I know this castle like the back of my hand.'

'As do I, my friend,' Idris said, with constrained patience in his voice. 'But for now, we must aim to get to the old king and queen's rooms. There, I am told, we will find fresh clothing and weapons. I fear the castle has fallen. There is no telling what we may find on the other side of these walls.'

It was true enough that we heard the cries of unprepared staff and the clash of blades as people were set upon. By whom, it was hard to tell. Had the priesthood turned against the staff, or were Tristan's rebels slaying anyone who got in the way? It made me push forward harder, before I realised poor Lana was struggling along on her knees.

'Sorry,' I whispered, and slowed my pace. She looked as though she would have curtsied if she could, but continued without complaint. I suppose it was preferable to being locked in a cell with no hope at all.

The going was slow as a result, and it must have been well past the midday hour when we reached the gap in the wall that led out into the seneschal's chambers. Thankfully the room was empty, and we managed to all squeeze out one-by-one, then climb out of the window onto the ledge that led us to the old king and queen's rooms.

I looked back and winced at the dusty footprints across Milo Dorsa's floor, and the wreck we had made of climbing onto his desk to reach the window. But it wasn't a time to worry about etiquette. I could only hope he had decided on which side he belonged to, and he had not chosen the side of the priests.

We kept below the parapet, low enough to not be seen by anyone looking out of windows on the other side of the keep. We could hear the cries clearer, and a fire had sprung up and licked its way up the gates.

Inside the safety of the room, the castle staff were quick to find the dressing room and change into fresh clothes that vaguely resembled what would pass for normal in this place. We availed ourselves of what little water we could find in a long-abandoned jug, using it to clean our faces as much as possible.

Idris walked around the room in a daze, looking at everything with careful attention. He disappeared several times into an annex room, reappearing moments later swinging a weapon and trying its weight for size. He still had the knife belted to his waist, but now he had a sword and a baldric, with an array of strange-shaped knives.

Cara had joined us and sat on the window ledge, watching us with blinking eyes. Now and then, she turned her head and stared into thin air, as though she sensed something we were too blind to see.

Arvind had rallied the staff into some kind of train of servants, who looked as though they were going about their daily business. The kitchen maid carried the now empty water jug, the minstrel dressed as a kitchen apprentice and carried a stack of empty bowls, and the scribe had found a wad of loose-leaf parchment from somewhere and was rolling them into scrolls. Lana helped me to dust down my tunic and found me a small cloak.

'Your Majesty,' she said, then stopped when I gave her a measured look. 'I will keep calling you that until someone tells me otherwise.'

*Really unnecessary, but who am I to argue if it makes her feel somewhat closer to normal?*

'We should try to get back to your rooms and get you properly changed into something more fitting,' she said, with a distasteful look at my tattered tunic and trews.

'Oh, I don't know. I could pass for a stable boy if I bundle my hair up into a hat,' I said. She looked me up and down, and her eyes started to tear up again. I placed my hand across hers. 'We can get through this, Lana, you have to believe. Believe in the real king, who is even now making his way back into the castle. Normal life will be resumed.'

'I don't remember the real king. I only have his face in my memory; the face of the usurper.' Lana shuddered. I looked over to Arvind, who had readied his troops for their exit into the castle.

'Arvind, what does the real king look like?'

He looked up. 'Your Majesty, he looks a lot like the false-king, of course. How else could they make everyone believe?'

I saw the image of the priest-king in my mind, looking up at me through dazed eyes, dusty, brown, and priest-like. The image was replaced by the chiselled features of the Blue King. I blinked the image away, my attention drawn once more to our escape from that gods-forsaken place.

There was a loud rap on the door, and we all looked up in unison. A sudden silence cast across the space. Seconds later, Idris marched across the room and flicked the lock with habitual ease. Koeda peered around the door and made the solidarity sign.

'All clear, your Majesty.'

157

I was about to protest about the royal address, but then realised that he was not looking at me. I looked at Idris, who waved it away as though inconsequential.

'Take them back through the castle as quickly as possible to the safety of the servant's wing. There is a room that Arvind has access to where you can all hide.' Idris glanced at Arvind, who looked confused.

'I do? Oh, yes… I do. It is starting to come back.'

I could only hope that Kerrin, whatever her motive, had indeed breached the focal point. The validity of the priesthood in the castle would soon be thrown into question once people started to remember. Koeda led the little group of disenchanted followers out of the room, checking the corridors before leading them with sword drawn. Arvind followed behind, and I had to all but push Lana out of the door.

'But, your Maj- my queen,' she protested.

'Lana, go. I have Idris to watch my back, and many leagues to travel back to my home where I belong.'

Tears rolled down her cheeks, already flush with the trauma. 'You belong here and you are still my queen.'

'I will return. I promise.'

She seemed to accept my words, and, with a final furtive glance over her shoulder, slipped out of the room and shut the door behind her. I let out a long breath, and hoped that Koeda would indeed get them all to safety. Now all I had to worry about was how to get myself and Idris out of the castle without being seen. I looked around. He was nowhere in the main anteroom, but I could hear steel ringing clearly from a scabbard.

'We have to get out of here, and there is no way you'll be able to carry all of these weapons into the walls,' I said.

'You need something to protect yourself.' He carried a short sword, and scabbard that looked like it was designed more for a child than soldier. He raised an eyebrow at the look of disbelief on my face. 'I had one of these when I was a boy.' As if that explained everything, he moved into a fighting stance and drew the weapon in an arc across his body, disembowelling an invisible opponent.

'That's all very well,' I said, 'but I am not a boy and I didn't learn these skills when I was growing up. I only know how to be a queen.'

He frowned at me and sheathed the sword. 'I think you do yourself a disservice, Princess, and I have the wound to prove it.' He touched the back of his head and I looked away, full of shame. I lifted my arms and he wrapped the sword belt around my waist. 'All you have to do is sweep across like you did with the skillet, only it will be much easier and do much more damage.'

I'm not sure if I felt relieved or terrified that it fit perfectly. His hands brushed against my hips and he shied away from my gaze. His scent filled my nostrils, earthy with faint undertones of the forest. He didn't move back out of my personal space.

It happened so fast I wasn't sure if it was real or not. Our gaze met, eyes locked so steady and close, I could see amber flecks in the grey of his gaze. His lips brushed mine and he was gone. *Wait. Did he just kiss me?*

'Wait, did you…?' But he had ducked into the dressing room. I stood and looked at the empty space in front of me, as a tingle raced over my lips and rippled across my cheeks in a flush. A warm sensation stirred inside me and made my stomach flutter. *What just happened? This was not supposed to happen.* 'Hey…,' I said to an empty doorway. 'That's not supposed to happen. I'm supposed to be the Queen of Tordre.'

I threw my hands up in frustration as his head popped around the doorway. His chest was bare, and he waved a blue tunic in one hand. There was some mottled bruising around his ribs, but apart from that, his skin was flawless and chiselled, with toned muscles from years of training. It felt like the air was sucked out of the room as I took a breath. I was desperate to look away, but unable to wrench my eyes from his body. His expression danced with mischief.

'If you are the Queen of Tordre, then I must be the Blue King,' he said with irony, then ducked back inside. I let out a slow breath and gathered my wits. What the darkness had I done? If I didn't die before I made it back home, my mother was sure to finish me off.

*Wait. Did he just say?* I couldn't help smiling to myself.

'Idris. I've had an idea.'

# CHAPTER TWENTY-EIGHT

## *Aiding the Rebellion*

I stood behind Idris, who sat in front of the looking glass in the old king and queen's bedroom. He looked bemused as I rummaged around in drawers to find a container of face colours.

'There, I knew it. Every king and queen have a supply of face paint.' I pulled the lid off the box.

'You mean to make me up to look like the Blue King?' I put my hands on my hips.

'Or am I to be paraded around the castle like a court jester?' He patted his tunic, beneath which lay the baldric of knives. 'I'd much rather resolve this the traditional way.'

'I thought you didn't like fighting,' I said, and picked out a pot of pale skin powder and a brush.

'This situation has progressed well beyond the point of no conflict. Do you think if I kindly approached the priest-king and asked for the castle back, he would acquiesce?'

'We just need to buy enough time to get us out of here, no more.' I swirled the brush in the powder. 'And I may have found a way for you to move around in plain sight without causing too much of a stir.'

With a few sweeping strokes across his face, cheekbones, forehead, and chin, his skin took on a paleness that resembled the priest-king's alter ego. I applied a few dabs of skin-coloured cream over his bruises, then a little colour to his lips with the tip of my finger, which trembled a little. I hoped he didn't notice, but the corners of his mouth twitched as though he held back a smile.

'There.' I stood back to view my handiwork. 'I just need to do something with your hair,' I said, and searched for a comb. I found a wooden wide-tooth comb and drew it through his fair hair, which was matted with dirt and spatters of blood. He winced a little when the comb caught in some areas, so I was careful with the back of his head. In the end, I abandoned the comb and used my fingers to smooth his hair back from his face and drape it into a silver-blond train across his shoulder. I found a small piece of linen to tie it into place. He didn't seem interested in his own reflection and kept his eyes fixed on me all the while, watching as I transformed his likeness to that of the Blue King.

'What do you think?' I said.

'I think you'd make a very good maid,' he said. I slapped his shoulder and he laughed. 'See, you're a natural fighter. Put a skillet in that hand and the priests won't stand a chance.'

'We need to get out of here.'

He turned to look at me. 'I don't know if I can come with you. This is my home and whatever Tristan has said and done, he is my king and I live to serve.'

'And who do you serve? A king who would sell your soul to the enemy, or the people who need a strong and loyal leader?'

'It's not as simple as that,' he said.

'Seemed simple enough to me when I sat on the streets of T'sar with people who have nothing. For some, the only pressing thought is where their next meal is coming from.'

He gave me a measured look. 'I understand something about that. Things have not been easy.'

'I've lived this lie for the best part of a year and now…'

'And now you're just going to run out on Tordre? Where is your duty and your loyalty to those people on the streets who need a strong leader?'

I turned away, trying to hide my discomfort, and brushed some of the dust from my tunic. When he put it like that, I was a coward. I glanced back at the looking glass, and my heart caught in my throat. He looked so much like the Blue King; it was distracting. All the looks with none of the cruelty and lies.

'If… if I were to stay, and if Tristan were to take back the throne, would he accept me as his queen?'

An angry grimace passed across Idris's face.

'I think that is rather up to you, but you may have to use your charms on him. He didn't take too well to your first encounter.'

'He kidnapped me… you kidnapped me; how did you think I was going to react?'

'I know, I know,' he said, rubbing the back of his head. 'I'm just saying that it is something we may need to work on. For now, we must aid in the rebellion to rid this castle of the priests and their poisonous lies.'

He had a point. I could hardly go back to Carentan to my mother with such a fantastical story, the outcome of which was that I ran away and left the country to sort itself out. Perhaps if Tristan didn't want me I could persuade Idris to come back to Carentan. At least a Tordrean nobleman was an improvement on a false king.

'Right. Let's go then,' I said. But he shook his head. 'What now?'

'You look like a street urchin. No one will believe I am the Blue King if I'm being trailed by a street urchin.' He stood and took off my hat, let my hair tumble down around my shoulders and looked me up and down with silent appraisal. 'Well, it's a start. Sit.'

I sat down with a humph. 'Such a bossy-boots,' I muttered, understanding now what it felt like to be on the other end of my own ministrations. When I looked at my reflection, I didn't recognise myself with all the cuts and bruises. I had a thin, sallow look, as though I hadn't eaten for days.

'Comb, make-up. I might have just the dress for you,' he said, and disappeared into the anteroom. I shook my head at my reflection. It was me who was the bossy one in Carentan, especially when it came to boys and men, but now here was a man who was as comfortable giving it as receiving it. It felt both strange and oddly liberating. I picked up the comb and ran it through my tangled locks, wincing as it snagged on the knots. By the time Idris returned, I had smoothed my hair and applied enough make-up to dispel the beggar woman aesthetic.

'Much better,' he said and held up a dress. It was a beautiful gold and green design, with a practical split skirt to allow for riding a horse, and a close-fitting bodice. 'Look,' he unfurled a shoulder cloak, 'designed for hiding a small short sword.' He laid it over the back of the chair. 'Don't be too long, we must be quick.' And then I was alone again, with only my reflection for company.

I stripped down and stepped into the dress, afraid more by the prospect of Idris walking in on me than the thought of stepping out of the comfort and privacy of those rooms. No one apart from those we had rescued from the dungeons knew we were there. We could sit out the whole siege waiting for Tristan to come in and claim his rights to the royal suites. I shook my head at the folly. There were only two choices, run back to Carentan or stay and fight for the people of Tordre.

I pulled the dress up and gathered it around me, then realised that I would not be able to tighten and tie off the criss-cross ribbons that ran down the back and held it in place. I was about to scream my frustration when Idris popped his head around the door.

'Allow me,' he said. 'I thought you might need a hand.' He pulled the ties, and I gasped as the air was forced out of me when the bodice tightened around my midriff. His touch was purposeful and swift.

'You, on the other hand, would not make a very good maid,' I said between gasps, as he manhandled me into the dress. He turned me to face the looking glass and picked up the sword from the seat, belting it around my waist and laying the cloak over my shoulder. Then, with a gentle touch, he swept my hair over one shoulder and placed his hands on the tops of my arms, his face beside mine as we looked at each other in the looking glass. His breath was warm on my cheek.

'Now we both look the part. Let's go help with this rebellion,' he said.

Outside in the corridor there were shouts coming from both directions, the ringing chime of swords being drawn, and the clash of metal-on-metal. I took a decisive step toward where I remembered the spiral stair was located, which led down to the chapel. If there was any way out of this, it was by destroying whatever witchcraft the priests had enacted at that focal point. Idris put a hand on my arm. 'Be careful. We don't yet know who we can trust.'

I nodded and led the way, but no sooner had we rounded the corner than we were met with a skirmish between two castle guards and five priests. I had barely got my hand to the hilt of my sword when a sleek, feline shape shot past me and leapt onto the face of a priest, who dropped his sword and reached for the fur ball in his face. His badly injured opponent dropped back but was attacked by another priest.

Cara leapt off the priest's face dropping to the floor in a crouch. I followed suit, then drew my blade and swept it across the floor in front of me. Several missiles of sharpened metal whizzed over my head and thudded into two priests.

163

A spray of blood decorated the melee, and my sword caught the feet of an advancing priest, who dropped to the floor in front of me. I was so surprised that I froze temporarily, but when I stepped over him, he leapt up with a knife in his hand. I hadn't had the time to master the dexterity needed to bring my short sword up to block. All I could see was the knife cutting a path in the air towards me.

*Damn this,* I thought. I took a step back, gripped the sword with both hands, and lifted it above my head. I brought it down like I was beating the dust out of an old rug. The priest stopped in his tracks and looked at me in disbelief, then looked at the end of his arm where his hand used to be. He stared back at me, then his eyes rolled up into the back of his head and he fell backwards. The bloody, severed hand still gripped its knife as it fell harmlessly to the ground.

I felt a gorge rise to my throat and gulped it back. This was not the time to feel sick over hurting a few renegade priests who had ruined our lives and our country. When I looked up, Idris and the remaining guards were locked in combat with the priests. Two of them lay immobile on the ground, and the other three, one of whom still wrestled with Cara, lay down their weapons and put up their hands.

'Your Majesty, please. We didn't sign up for this. Please… how may we serve?' All three dropped to their knees in front of Idris. We exchanged a glance. The disguise had worked better than expected.

'Take them to the dungeons,' he said, and the castle guards marched the priests away with their arms twisted behind their backs. He looked back at me. 'It is going to take a good many more skirmishes to clear the castle. Are you okay?'

'Yes, but perhaps we should split up.'

'No.'

'I won't be seen as a threat on my own. Besides,' I sheathed the sword. 'I'm getting the hang of this.'

We followed the corridor until I was sure we had missed the entrance. 'It's hidden here, I know it.' I closed my eyes and willed the door to appear.

Nothing.

I placed my hand on the wall and felt the hum of power vibrating in the walls. 'Do you feel that?' I said.

Idris put his hand to the wall. 'Whatever is happening down there, we need to put a stop to it for good.'

'I have to find the entrance.' I stalked up and down, certain it was there but unable to make it appear like I had before. 'Perhaps it is further down here.' We were about to follow the hum down the hall when a shout rang out from behind us. Idris turned, and I saw a mob of angry fighters chasing several priests down the corridor towards us. They wielded all manner of weapons cobbled together from farming implements.

Idris stepped out in front of the group. 'Stop, in the name of the king.'

'No,' I shrieked, but my voice was lost in the cacophony of battle cries. The priests thought he was their king and rallied around him, and the mob stopped a few paces in front of him, unsure what to do next. Then out of the crowd stepped the true king, Tristan, wielding a long sword and looking for all intents and purposes like he was spoiling for a fight.

# CHAPTER TWENTY-NINE

## Kings, Courtiers and Priests

Idris spoke to Tristan. I saw him make the solidarity sign, and Tristan listened for a while. He said something in return, then all of a sudden they were surrounded. Idris disappeared in the middle of a vicious group that waved weapons about and shouted threats.

At first I thought the priests were protecting him, but it looked like he was being jostled on all sides. As Idris receded from view, I caught the flick of an amber tail as Cara launched from the shadows. I wasn't surprised. She was always there when Idris was around, and when he was not she nudged me towards him at every opportunity.

I slipped back into the shadows and leant against the wall. With my eyes closed, I took a few deep breaths and willed my imagination to see him victorious and escaping this confrontation, but all I could see was his face slip away from me into a brawling mass. I choked back a sob.

There was only one way to resolve this; I had to find the entrance to the chapel. It took every fibre of my strength to walk away. The sounds of fighting receded as the corridor curved around, and I saw in the distance the entrance to the spiral staircase. It opened up in the wall before me, but as I was about to disappear into the door, the priest-king knocked me to the ground as he ran away from the chapel.

'What? You can't be here. Didn't I lock you up?' His face was shifting already, losing its disguise as the Blue King. A hand reached out from behind him, and Abiel Morda stepped into view with a disgusting grin on his face. I ignored his offer of help and pushed myself back up.

'You were going to let me die. After all we've been through?' I said. 'Have you never had the slightest shred of empathy for me?'

'It's not like we were really man and wife. You were too busy crying into your pillow, as I recall,' he said with a sneer, an insult far greater than anything he could ever have done as the king. Those days were long gone, but I was certain of a kindness of sorts in the way he had dealt with me during my fog of homesickness.

'Thank the gods for small mercies,' I muttered. I couldn't tell if his aggrieved expression was for himself and his own situation, or whether he felt the slightest bit of contrition.

Abiel Morda frowned at me. 'Young lady, you would do well to review your allegiances. The one god does not look favourably upon blasphemers and infidels.'

'I think you're done here,' I said. 'He doesn't look like the Blue King anymore, and the true king has stormed the castle.'

'My dear, we are far from done here.'

'I think your priests might argue to the contrary,' I said, and glanced over my shoulder. The two of them looked beyond me and stretched their necks as though they could see around corners. 'Your priests can't possibly hold the castle now that your lies are fading.'

'Is that what you seek?' Morda had an incongruent smile on his face. 'To destroy the focal point? Well, I have to say you might be a little disappointed to learn that you are too late.' He gestured towards the spiral staircase. 'The high priestess has other ideas. Now, I must leave you both. Duty calls.' With that, he disappeared back along the corridor in the opposite direction, hobbling away like an elderly gentleman. He left us standing looking at each other, mouths open.

'Wait, what?' the priest-king said.

'What?' I said at the same time. But Morda was gone. 'Did you somehow expect the Archbishop to be loyal to his brethren? My brother once told me that Abiel Morda is only loyal to one.'

The priest-king nodded as though he understood.

'No. Not the one god, himself.'

The priest-king had a brief look of abandonment, before he pulled himself together and marched off in the direction of the fighting. I watched in disbelief as he waded into the fight.

'Stop, in the name of the king.'

*Good grief.*

Keeping to the shadows and as close to the walls as possible, I sneaked closer to the group. Close enough to hear what was going on, but far enough to run if I needed to.

Both Tristan and Idris appeared out of the crowd, and turned as the dusty-looking priest, with mousy curled hair and chunky

167

cheeks in a king's robe, elbowed his way into the centre of the group. The priests surrounding Idris reluctantly made way for him.

'This man is a fake,' the priest-king said, and stabbed a finger into Idris's chest. 'And this man is a criminal.' He waved in Tristan's direction. 'Have them seized and slung in the dungeons.'

Everyone looked around at each other, frowning in disbelief.

'Poke me one more time and you'll be a dead priest, never mind locking me up again,' Idris said. The priest-king must have been wild on some kind of potion, because he seemed to think he had control of the situation and went to poke Idris again in the chest. This time, Idris grabbed his finger and bent it back at an impossible angle. The finger cracked and he wailed out in pain. The other priests surged around Idris in anger, and the mob surrounding Tristan nearly knocked him flat in their haste to get into a fight. The entire corridor descended into chaos as the priests fought for their brethren, and the mob fought to rid the castle of priests.

Tristan elbowed his way outside the circle of battle, and Idris disappeared beneath a pile of bodies, dragging the priest-king with him. As they went down together their faces appeared to merge, with the priest-king flickering in and out of Idris' likeness to a point where it was impossible to tell which was which but for their attire.

I saw a flash of swirling colours as Tristan played with his stupid banda on the outside of the scuffle and watched as Idris fought for his life. Then he wrapped it back up and hid it away inside his jerkin.

A streak of orange and fawn landed in the middle of the mayhem, and the priest-king popped up momentarily, clutching his face as blood seeped out from between his fingers.

Tristan was protected from most of the fighting by a wall of his own people, until a priest burst out from the fray and ran directly for him, screaming and bloody. Tristan thrust out his sword and, with what looked more like luck than judgement, impaled the priest on the end of it.

The priest crumpled, and Tristan placed a boot on his shoulder and wrenched his sword free. The fighting came to a close as the bodies piled up and the remaining combatants either fled or held their ground. Tristan looked around for something or someone. A few of his own people flanked him on either side as they realised a little too late that they had left their king unprotected. He walked into the centre of the mayhem, stepped over bodies, and eyed the damage.

Was he searching for Idris? Perhaps it was going to be all right after all.

I released a rush of breath that I hadn't realised I had been holding when Idris popped up behind him, a god-like look of triumph on his blood-streaked face. Idris reached out and placed his hand on Tristan's shoulder. At first Tristan flinched back, but he seemed to relax as they both looked down at the dead priest-king. Only I could see the calculating look on Tristan's face.

Idris smiled a genuine smile that made my stomach squirm. He still believed in his friend. He didn't suspect a thing.

# CHAPTER THIRTY

## *The Focal Point*

I stumbled back to the place where the priest-king and Abiel Morda had emerged from the wall, and found the spiral steps. The floor beneath my feet hummed with a power I had not felt since that first night in the castle.

Had Kerrin lost her battle to destroy the focal point? If that were so, then we were all doomed to failure. But the hold was lifting. Idris remembered more about the castle and his past every moment, and others, like the servants they had rescued, were making connections to their past. It was slow, but it was happening.

As I reached the opening to the chapel, I steeled myself for what I might see, taking a deep breath before peering into the room, conscious of keeping myself hidden. I stepped through an ornate archway with stone filigree engravings. The chapel was criss-crossed with pillars carved in stone and large enough in width to hide a slim person like me.

I slipped behind the nearest one and held my breath in anticipation. The humming continued alongside a low chant that emanated from the front of the room where the altar was. I closed my eyes. My heart thumped in my chest, and images of the faceless king from my nightmares popped up unbidden.

In the centre of the room lay a body. It looked like a bundle of priest-robes someone had piled up, but I could see the shape of a torso, arms, and legs. It wasn't moving. As my eyes adjusted to the dim light, I could see other bodies in similar dress and in a similar state.

Kerrin stood in front of the altar with her back to me. It didn't look as though she was intent on destroying anything apart from the priests on the floor who had once stood guard here. The shadows around the edges of the room shifted, as black-robed rebels kept a watchful eye on their mistress. Their faces were covered by scarves wrapped around their heads, leaving only their eyes visible. They had seen me for sure but stayed back in the shadows, humouring my presence.

Kerrin muttered and chanted, and swirled a bowl of incense, filling the room with a sickly-sweet scent. She was garbed in a flowing long robe of amber and red, her head covered in a similar fashion, and her long auburn locks flowed down her back like a river of fire. The smoke disappeared into the cracks in the walls and was replaced by fresh plumes as she fanned the burning material.

The figures around the edges of the room seemed to melt back into the shadows, as though they belonged to the walls. The smell was overpowering, and I wished I too had a shroud to tie over my nose and mouth, though I doubted even that would stop the smoke from infiltrating every part of my being.

'Come,' she said without turning her head, and beckoned to me with one raised hand. 'I know you're there, child. I can feel your presence.'

*Damn.* What was I to do? It was just me and a short sword that I didn't know how to use versus her and her army of rebel fanatics. *I don't fancy my chances,* I thought, looking at the immobile bodies littered across the room. The shadows shifted as I stepped out into view. Kerrin held one hand up and the black figures receded. She turned to look at me.

'Is it true that you are here to destroy the focal point and return the castle back to its true king?' I said, daring to hope that she was at least on the side of justice, if not that of Idris and myself.

'Oh, yes,' she said. 'You could have made it much easier for us all if you had cooperated and played your part, but I'm afraid I've lost patience with you now.'

I lifted my chin a little and straightened my back. 'Are you really the king's sister?' I had never been told about her in the briefings given to me before I left Carentan.

'Sister to the true king of Tordre and high priestess to the many gods,' she said. It was hard to tell if she spoke the truth, as everything she said was coated in a veneer of entitlement. I hadn't asked about her religious affiliation, but never mind.

'So, what exactly are you doing? I heard that your intention was to destroy the focal point and render the priesthood's hold useless.' I said, looking around the room. 'It looks like you have destroyed a few of the somewhat misguided priests, but you appear to be fanning the flames on the altar.' I peered over her shoulder. The constant hum in the walls seemed to have stopped, but there was a strange buzz in my head that made me a little light-headed. 'Is that how you do it? With your herbs and apoth… apothecary thing?' I giggled. This was nothing like what the priests had served.

'This?' She waved a hand over her shoulder towards the altar. 'This is just a little helping hand. The priesthood's methods were quite rudimentary. I prefer a more subtle approach, a few herbs, tinctures, and incense. After having been fed a lie for so long, the people of Tordre are remarkably malleable. I have my own followers at all the outposts to ensure that people are compliant when we usher in a new era.'

'New?' Now my head was full of cotton wool. I wanted to sit down, or better still, lie down. I couldn't think straight. What was I there for? 'I thought… I thought… that the idea was to restore things back to where they were?'

'Oh no, child. Things will certainly never go back to how they once were.'

'What… what is it you want?' I fought to keep my eyes focused.

Kerrin looked around her, then rolled her eyes upward before meeting my gaze. 'What does anyone ever want? Power, control.'

I could understand that view if it came from someone who had spent a lifetime being downtrodden, but from someone purporting to be the king's sister? I couldn't wrap my thoughts around it.

I had to sleep and couldn't stop myself. I laughed, despite the desire to cry. I last saw Idris disappear beneath an angry mob. For the first time in my life, I felt the insistent tug of connection pull me towards him. And now, now he was lost to me. I was too tired to contemplate the irony as my eyes slid shut and the world descended into darkness.

# CHAPTER THIRTY-ONE

## *The True King's Justice*

I woke to an insistent thumping in my head. As I moved further towards consciousness I realised it wasn't inside my head, it was my head, thumping against the side of a moving object, and I was inside that object. For a moment, I kept my eyes closed and tried to remember.

The thumping continued and my head hurt. I found that when I lifted it a fraction, the repetitive motion ceased to make contact and the pain lessened. None of that helped though to stop the nausea that rose through my chest and into my throat.

I dared to lift an eyelid. Sunlight was obscured by the sackcloth that covered me from head to foot. My companions on this journey appeared to be a pile of potato sacks jostling for position on the back of this rickety cart, which transferred every bump and hole in the track to my bruised body.

For a fleeting moment, I thought I was back in the cart during my escape from Tristan at the tavern, and I looked around to see if Cara was with me. But my incense-addled brain soon remembered that it had been a grain cart, and that these were definitely potatoes competing for my space. One sack had spilled open and my feet were being slowly buried.

My head felt like it was filled with cotton, similar to the last time that Kerrin had administered the Devil's Breath to me, only this time I awoke to significantly greater levels of discomfort. My mouth was covered with a dirty rag tied around the back of my head. I tried to sit up, and discovered my hands were secured with knotted rope around my back. That would account for the ache in my shoulders and the numb sensation in my fingers and wrists.

I had no idea how long I had been laid out, or how far we had travelled. The crashing of labouring sellers and the sweet scent of fruit buns gave me the idea that we might have been in T'sar during market day. Through the mesh of the sackcloth I could tell that the sun was high in sky.

It was midday on the day that Idris and I were scheduled to hang.

Panic overwhelmed me, and I struggled with the restraints around my wrists. I opened my mouth to shout out, but all I managed was some kind of demented grunt. I kicked out and successfully upended the leaking sack, burying myself further in potatoes. The voices of bartering stall holders and the crowds of market goers around me grew in intensity as the cart slowed its pace.

Children laughed and screamed, pots were banged to elicit attention, sellers wailed: 'Come buy!'

No one took the slightest bit of notice of a cart load of potatoes moving through the crowds, the contents of which bounced around to the demands of the cobbled streets.

I tried rolling my body left and right, forward and back, in the hope that I might fall off the back of the cart, but I ended up being rammed up against more potatoes. I lay my head back, exhausted from the exertion. Tears leaked from the corners of my eyes and I tried to calm myself with sobbing breaths through my nose.

Then the cart picked up speed again and the noises of market day faded into the distance. No sooner had I adjusted to the new speed and flatter ground when the cart came to an abrupt halt. There was a brief moment of stillness before I heard several sets of feet drop to the ground, followed by a distinct thud, perhaps from the driver, and more subdued steps.

Someone with a purposeful stride approached the back of the cart. The sackcloth was ripped away and the sun glared down, momentarily blinding me. I squinted up into the concerned face of Milo Dorsa, whose expression turned cruel as Kerrin stepped into view at his shoulder.

'Well, I suppose if she's not dead already, we will have our little spectacle yet,' she said, and leaned in towards me to gloat. I jerked forward, more out of instinctive anger than any hope of retaliation, but it had the desired effect. She jumped back with a look of surprise.

Milo frowned at me, then leaned back out of Kerrin's peripheral vision and gave a barely perceptible shake of the head.

'Ooh, feisty,' she said. 'This is going to be fun. Bring her to the platform.' She turned and strode off.

174

Milo helped me to my feet, then allowed me a moment to let the numbness from my limbs dissipate. He kept my hands tied but loosened the rag around my mouth, so at least I could breathe and speak for a moment. I took a few sweet breaths of air and filled my chest.

'What hold does she have on you?' I said, and kicked a few potatoes. Milo helped me out of the cart.

'Releasing the country from the grip of the priesthood is the least of our worries. The high priestess has the entire apothecary network in her own web of control. Her influence has risen to the import and export of food supplies, ale, and wine. The people may survive a while without their medical supplies, but they can't live without food and drink.'

'How did this happen?' Had I slept through this insidious revolution? Milo grunted, as though there was nothing to be said or done that could possibly change the situation.

'The hold of the priesthood would never have lasted; you've seen so yourself. It didn't affect you nor I in the same way as the castle folk. It is a belief system, as effective as any religion if your followers have faith. There was never much danger of Abiel Morda containing his seat of control for long. I think even he knew that. He'll no doubt take his brand of poison somewhere else. The real power centre sits with the people, and the control of goods in and out of the country. Kerrin has been clever in setting up her web. All she needed was to rid the country of the priests and restore a king to the throne.'

'A king?' I stumbled. Milo put an arm around my waist, and walked me to an area in the centre of the square cordoned off with ropes.

'A king, the king, any king. What does it matter, so long as whoever sits on the throne can gain the trust of the people and do what they are told?'

I stopped and looked down at my bare feet, all bruised and grubby, before looking up into Milo's eyes. Was there any shred of empathy there? Well, I suppose he could have let me hobble my own way up to the square, he at least had the decency to grant me the dignity of a helping hand. He shook his head, as though I were a child he was about to chastise.

175

'Why couldn't you just sit comfortably in your chamber and play at being queen? All you had to do was feign ignorance to this whole charade. Perhaps they might have spared you.'

That final declaration of allegiance made my stomach sink. I realised then that Milo's arm around my waist was less about him affording me any kind of dignity, and more to avoid the embarrassment of another attempted escape. This time, I had reached the end of my road, and Milo had run out of free passes. But I wasn't ready to give up.

'This will cause a war, you know,' I said, and he nudged me back into a slow walk.

'Don't you think she has prepared for that?' Milo smiled at me. It was a cunning smile, but there was sadness in the depth of his eyes. 'It will be worth it in the end. The true king is a good king.'

I'm not sure I agreed with that last statement. Perhaps it was just as well that I might not be around to witness the mess that Tristan might make of running the country. *But wait, it wouldn't be him at the helm. He was just the figurehead.* An involuntary shiver ran through me. Kerrin was a more chilling prospect.

As we approached the square, the cordoned-off area disappeared amidst a crowd of milling observers. Beyond the people I could see a raised platform, where two dark-robed men hoisted ropes over a large beam that was propped up by wooden posts on either side.

Two more men walked past us each heaving a sack, and I realised with horror what those potatoes were for. The sacks were tied to the ends of the two ropes, heavy enough to hold down a body. Two nooses swayed from the beam, and the bray of the crowd became amplified by my own beating heart as Milo led me through to the platform.

I had expected Kerrin and the priests to have influenced public opinion, so was fully prepared for what they might hurl at me as they marched me to the platform: insults, rotten food, spittle. What I wasn't prepared for was the level of empathy conveyed by the people. Whatever lies had been told, they still found a place in their hearts for their Carentan princess. The unrest was not for their desire to see justice done, but for the evil that was being planned on the platform.

One of the men carrying a sack had been ambushed and brought to the ground by a mob. The man had risen and run back to the cart, leaving a pile of potatoes spilling out across the square, which fast disappeared into people's pockets. Whatever happened, at least some families would not go hungry tonight.

I dropped my gaze to the ground, unable to meet the eyes of those who sought to overturn this appalling miscarriage of justice. Hands reached and touched my arms, my shoulders, and my hair, which now hung limp and lifeless down my back. A small child pulled at the hem of my skirts, and the shrill voice of a woman cried somewhere in the crowd as they led me up the steps to the platform.

The braying started up in earnest again.

Two large wooden crates sat beneath the nooses that hung from the wooden beam, in front of which were two large square holes, big enough to allow a body to sink beneath the platform without reaching the ground below.

My breath caught, and my heart thrummed in time to the rhythmic chants of the crowd.

Milo stood by my side and held my arms as though I might at any moment take off. The thought of doing so had not escaped me. If I could get into a fortuitous position, there was much I could do to stop him from forcing me to stand on that crate. But if I did manage to escape Milo, where would I run?

The cacophonous chanting abated as Kerrin stepped onto the platform, with one hand held aloft and a bright halo of golden red hair plaited around her head like a crown. She wore a scarlet robe and cloak, trimmed with ermine, and looked every bit the queen that I did not. The crowd thought so too. A sea of hushes whispered across the breeze and an awed silence fell.

'My people,' Kerrin's voice rang clear and true across the square and echoed off the town hall in the near distance. I looked out across the sea of faces. Some people lifted their chins, though I was unsure whether it was in allegiance or defiance. Others looked at their feet or away towards the market. Everyone had somewhere else they would rather be. 'Our country has suffered enough.' There were jeers and grunts of agreement. 'Today marks a new beginning.'

Silence.

'Today, we sweep away an old foe and usher in a bright future.'

There were some shouts of agreement and scattered applause, but it seemed that the people still needed something to convince them. But Kerrin hadn't finished her little speech. 'We don't need to be ruled by the one god.' There was a tumultuous cheer at that. 'The many serve our purposes well enough.'

Silence. Then a small voiced piped up from the back of the crowd.

'Why do we need a god at all, Ma'am?'

I was close enough to see the flash of anger across Kerrin's face, which she hid with a strained smile.

'Quite right,' she said, though I was certain that was not what she was thinking. 'No god is enough for the people of Tordre. You need a leader. Someone with truth in their heart. Someone who holds dear this country and its people, who has lived among you and suffered your strife. Someone who understands what it means to be Tordrean. People of T'sar, I give you back your true king.'

Then onto the stage stepped Tristan, dressed in splendour with a what seemed like a sash across his chest. After a moment I realised this was not a sash, it was Idris's baldric with its cache of weapons on display. He looked like a true king and warrior. His silken shirt and golden tunic looked very much like the ones that Idris wore when I saw him earlier.

Tristan had affected a haughty lift of the chin that made him look every bit the courtier who had been bred and raised in the castle. True to form, an attendant trailed in his wake, bowing and scraping to his needs. Dusty and battle-worn, his attendant looked up and my heart dropped to the bottom of my stomach.

Idris stared back at me.

# CHAPTER THIRTY-TWO

## *The Deconstruction of Truth*

So, Idris was serving Tristan now. *But why is Tristan wearing Idris's fine clothes and Idris… are those priest's robes? Surely not.*

I tried to catch his eye, but he wouldn't look at me. Had Kerrin worked her magic on him again and returned him back to the servile courtier he once was? Maybe it wasn't him after all. On further scrutiny, it was uncanny how he resembled the priest-king, but I had seen the priest-king killed. I was sickened by betrayal on every front, and made an involuntary move towards Idris, only to have Milo tighten his hold on me.

Idris glanced at me and made an infinitesimally small shake of his head. What was he trying to say… don't try, don't approach, don't worry? His obeisance said it all; he was backing Tristan. My blood boiled and I pulled at Milo's restraints, but he wrapped an arm around me in a bear hug and I couldn't move at all.

Kerrin had stepped back to allow Tristan the stage; she looked pleased with herself. She caught my eye and moved her cloak to one side, revealing a small sword buckled to her waist.

It was my sword; the one Idris had given to me. I wanted to run it through her and wipe that self-satisfied smile off her face. Gods, what had I become?

A few deep breaths brought me back to the moment, the crowd, the crate of doom in front of me, and the noose hanging down, waiting for its turn to be useful. I looked to my left where an empty place stood with another crate, and a noose that didn't yet have a name to it.

As Tristan stepped forward there was a scattering of whoops from the crowd, some disgruntled braying, but in general a quiet reception.

'People of Tordre.' His voice echoed. 'For too long now we have been under the influence of the one god and its brethren. For too long, a false king has ruled your lives. A king who serves only his own purpose and that of the one god. A king who has misled you into believing he is true by taking the form of

179

another. Today, we strip away those lies and turn back the clock to a time when our country was true only to herself, and our people were free to move across borders and trade with our neighbours.'

A few cheers from the crowd, clearly the merchants were there today. Of course, it was market day. I couldn't help feeling that Tristan was trying too hard to prove a point. Kerrin looked worried and signalled her supporters. A bit of scurrying behind the platform, and the air held a spicy fresh scent that lingered for a moment, and then dissipated on the breeze. A few onlookers nudged each other. She would have to do more than that to hold the people in her favour.

'As we speak, trade routes are being opened up. The border controls have been destroyed and replaced with new check points. We will put a levy on the price of grain that shall bring back wealth to an ailing nation.'

The crowd looked a little confused at the mention of a levy, but then perked up when Tristan talked about wealth. Perhaps Kerrin had the right idea to control the nation through trade routes, but it was too soon to cast that die. I could visualise the steam coming out of the ears of the grain merchants. The fishermen stood on the periphery of the crowd, waiting to see what would come next.

'The ports will reopen for business, allowing foreign trade to once again reach our shores, but there will be prices to pay for the freedom of movement this great nation once enjoyed.'

Tristan was getting carried away with his dream, and Kerrin was restless. It was too much too soon, even I could see that. A voice shouted out above the growing cacophony.

'We're starving now, what you gonna do about that?'

They were not that impressed with their new king.

'And why are you starving? I ask you that,' Tristan said. 'You are starving because of this man,' he turned and pointed to Idris, whose head snapped up, 'this man betrayed you as a false king.'

'No.' Idris held a hand towards to Tristan, and his eyes reflected hurt and betrayal.

'This man took my true place as king and fed you all a pack of lies to cover his duplicitous treason. And this foreign woman,' he turned to point at me, 'assisted him in his subterfuge. Well, I'll say no more. In this country, we hang traitors.'

There was a loud cheer from the crowd, who at that point probably didn't care who was hanging as long as they got the promise of a better life and more food on their tables. I stifled a sob, and they hauled Idris over to the second crate and the noose next to me.

'People of Tordre, I give you Idris Morra Dreiden, the false King. May his soul rest in eternal damnation for what he has done to his country.'

My heart stammered, and I glanced sideways at Idris. A little smile played on his lips. I had never known his full name. Was it true? Was he the Morra Dreiden that my mother had intended me to marry instead of the dusty priest that pretended to be someone else, or the jumped-up courtier pretending to be the true king? Was it all for naught, as we stood side-by-side as king and queen for our first and last time? I looked at Tristan, who smiled as though he had told a good joke. I wanted to wipe that smile from his self-satisfied patrician face.

The crowd had fallen silent as they watched this unusual turn of events play out. They knew something was not right, I could see it on their faces. Memories were seeping back into the here and now, bringing with them a combination of confusion and longing. They had loved their king and were torn now between the reality of food on their tables, albeit at a price, the prospect of a good hanging, and the memories of Morra Dreiden held dear, a fair and just leader who held the promise of a better life with long-term stability.

Idris looked calm. How could he just stand there? Was he going to let us hang? We had to get out of there, and quick. Someone gave me a gentle push forward to step up onto the crate. Idris did likewise.

We stood side-by-side.

They lowered the ropes over our heads.

Out of the midst of bodies that grunted, shouted, and jeered, an object sailed above the sea of heads that gathered around the platform. Directed like a projectile weapon onto the stage, it moved as though the world had slowed down time. I watched it arc over the crowd, and a multitude of faces turn upward to watch. At first, I thought it was aimed at me or Idris, but it missed us by several spans and landed on Tristan's chest, then dropped with a thud to the wooden platform.

It was a potato.

He looked at the object, his face a picture of rage and disbelief. 'Who threw that?'

The silence of the crowd was uncanny.

Tristan paced up and down and fumed. Kerrin came up to him and whispered in his ear, but he shoved her away and pointed an accusing finger at the crowd. Trying to contain his rage, he reached into his tunic and pulled out that damned banda, then started the wheel whirling up and down its string. Kerrin had a smug look of satisfaction, and the front row of the crowd moved their heads up and down in time with the rhythm of the banda.

Another potato whizzed through the air and landed at Tristan's feet. He swung around and pointed at Idris and me without taking his eyes from the crowd, 'Let them hang!'

The rope tightened around my neck, and in a panic I looked over at Idris. He had both hands underneath the rope and kicked his legs out at the black-clad figure behind him, who was trying to push him off his crate.

The force of a blow buckled my legs at the knee and I fell on top of the crate, the rope tightening enough to force my breath to ragged gasps. The kick must have been aimed at the crate, but missed and took me down instead.

A knife sliced quick and true through the rope holding my wrists and my arms sprung free. Milo tipped his head as though to say, "you're welcome" then disappeared beneath a brute of a fellow who wrestled him to the floor and kicked the knife away. I hung on to the rope, trying to stop myself falling into the abyss beneath the crate.

Idris had swung himself clear, freed his head from the noose, and was using the thrust from the crate to launch himself at the executioner. He landed cat-like on all fours, stood up, then punched him square across the jaw. The man looked confused for a moment, before his eyes rolled back and he slumped onto the platform. A cheer rose from the crowd. 'Look to the queen,' they shouted.

With no hesitation, he drew a sword from the executioner's scabbard and, with one swift move, sliced the rope holding my throat. The release of pressure was instant, and I pulled the damned noose from around my neck. The sack of potatoes used to weigh down the rope dropped at speed, and landed on top of the man that Milo wrestled with. It hit his head with incredible force and he disappeared underneath a pile of dirty potatoes and lay still. Milo stood up and brushed down his robes.

'Your Majesty… about time,' he said through wracked breath.

The crowd was going wild. More potatoes rained down on the platform, forcing Tristan and Kerrin to weave back and forth to avoid being pelted.

A streak of golden fur shot out from the crowd and pounced on the string of the banda as Tristan unfurled it, who was trying without success to keep his dream alive. Every time he pulled it one way, Cara countered the force. He tried to draw the string back up, but she had her claws out and pinned it to the platform.

The anger and pain that had built up in Tristan unleashed itself on Cara and her game of cat and mouse. He pulled his sword out and was about to strike her when Idris flew into him, blocking his blow and knocking the sword out of his hand.

I looked at Kerrin, who had a horrified expression on her face as though her whole life was being held in the balance. It hit me in a moment of clarity how Kerrin maintained her control over Tristan. Whilst Idris wrestled Tristan's sword away from him, I barged my way to where the banda lay and stomped on it with my heel, then picked up a potato and smashed it again for good measure. It cracked and splintered, bits flying across the platform every which way.

'Noooo…' Kerrin shrieked.

Everything around me faded into the background and I fixed my gaze on Tristan. His expression went from abject fury, to astonishment, through grief and longing, then settled on sad remorse. His grip on Idris loosened, and all the fight went out of him. He buried his head into Idris's shoulder and wept.

# CHAPTER THIRTY-THREE

## *Truth, Lies and Betrayal*

Idris appeared magnanimous in Tristan's defeat. I had to remind myself that they had been friends at one point, though how far back that went and how deep it ran was their truth alone to disclose.

I looked up to see Kerrin, who watched us all with a calculated look. She glanced towards the steps, where Cara sat and licked her paws pretending for all the world that this was another day at the market. Kerrin's black-clad supporters amassed around the steps and waited for her. I sprang into her path, fury driving me.

'What did you do to him? What did you do to them both?' I said.

She laughed, a high-pitched tinkling sound that grated on my nerves. 'It's an age-old trick of the mind. Faith is a remarkable thing, don't you think?'

'Well, I hope so, because it is all you'll have to keep you company in the castle dungeons,' I said.

'Step aside, child, I have work to do.'

She stepped forward and I reached for her robe, snatching up the hilt of the sword she had taken from me. I weighed it in my hand and was surprised at how light and manoeuvrable it was. She gasped, taking a step back when I held the point to her throat.

'Perhaps you didn't quite hear what I said.'

'Your Majesty,' Milo stepped in. He was not quite foolish enough to stand between us, but he seemed concerned enough not to let his queen do anything that might compromise her position. There was a skirmish at the foot of the steps between Kerrin's supporters and a band of castle guards who had popped up from amid the crowd.

For a brief moment, I wondered who Milo was talking to. I had every confidence in his ability to control a situation, regardless of whoever's side he took. Kerrin and I stood toe to toe, my sword levelled at her throat. Her expression was a mixture of resignation and smug justice.

Milo reached out and placed two fingers on my sword hand, applying enough pressure to embed the message into my mind. I glanced at him and he raised an eyebrow. He appeared to have indeed picked a side, and I was relieved that his queen was me.

I lowered the sword, and the guards took Kerrin away. In exasperation, I dropped the blade to the platform with a clatter, and gave Milo a measured look. *Ah well. Better the demon you know.*

The people were getting impatient. They had come to see a hanging, after all, and there was little else that matched that level of public interest, save perhaps a coronation. Although they had stopped throwing potatoes, some had taken up a chant and were stomping their feet in time to "hang him, hang him, hang him". I could only hope they were not still referring to Idris. Milo strode up to the front of the platform.

'Go home. There will be no hanging today,' he said. 'Your king has returned.'

'Sire,' a meek voice pitched up from the front row, 'Does that mean we don't have to attend prayer on the seventh day?'

Milo looked exasperated. 'Pray, sing, sleep… whatever you wish and wherever you fancy,' he said. There was a loud cheer from the crowd and they dispersed at their leisure, going about their business as though nothing of importance had happened at all.

A young man raised a little girl onto the platform. She ran towards me, then stopped and dropped into a deep curtsy. Her little green cap and matching apron marked her out as a blacksmith's daughter. She lifted her eyes and peered at me through a fringe of mousy curls.

Reaching forwards with cupped hands, she laid at my feet a flower crown of yarrow threaded with daisies. She was up and gone before I uttered a word. I waved at the young man, who bowed his head in return, and they left.

There was a smattering of cheers when I lifted the crown and settled it on my head, and I heard the words, "our Lady of Carentan" muttered several times. My throat closed and my eyes welled. For the first time since I had ridden into T'sar as Morra Dreiden's betrothed, I felt a sense of belonging that tugged at my insides.

The guards had to prise Tristan away from Idris, who gave them instructions to treat him with the utmost respect. He looked around for me and, as soon as he found me, stopped to stare as I stood there with a crown of flowers on my head, which must have looked comical in stark contrast to my dishevelled clothes.

The true king is a good king.

Despite my ability to see the priest-king for what he was, I had been blind to what was right under my nose. Idris looked every bit the king, more so than the priest or Tristan could ever have. But he was still Idris. He smiled.

'Very fitting,' he said, looking at my crown.

I gave him a modest smile and went into a deep curtsy. 'Your Majesty,' I said.

His gaze softened. 'What was it you said earlier? I'm supposed to be the Queen of Tordre...'

'... and if I'm the Queen of Tordre, then you must be the Blue King.'

'Not very blue,' he said. 'Especially now that I've found my queen.' He held out his hands, and I stepped forward. 'Are you still intent on returning to Carentan?'

His hands felt warm and the touch of him sent my stomach into turmoil. My cheeks burned. He released one of my hands and traced a finger down the side of my face. I shuddered.

'I don't think I could ever find a woman who blushes so well at my words,' he said. I released his hand and gave him a light punch on the shoulder. 'Ow, ow... such a cruel mistress.' He took my face in both hands and lowered his lips to mine.

I closed my eyes in anticipation, but before we had a chance to kiss, the retreating crowd cheered and whooped, and all of a sudden the platform erupted with people around us. I opened my eyes and there was Milo, directing attendants and guardsmen. There was a carriage waiting at the foot of the platform to take us back to the castle.

'Your Majesties, I'm sure you will appreciate the delicate nature of this situation,' Milo said. Both Idris and I looked quizzically at him. He huffed and grunted in his usual fashion, as though he was having to explain duties to a young page boy. 'Princess Nerys married a false king.'

We looked at each other, then back out at the departing crowds, then back at each other. We weren't married. The ceremony with the priest-king had to be annulled, and we would have to go through all that pomp and circumstance again.

'I'm sure they don't know or care,' Idris said.

'Yes, but still. We must adhere to protocol. There are many things that need to be set straight considering... recent events,' Milo said.

He was right, of course. The eyes of the entire country were upon us now; we had to be honest with the people of Tordre. Otherwise, how could we learn from this and move on with reassurance that it would never happen again? Idris and I bowed our heads graciously to one another, then allowed Milo and the attendants to accompany us to the carriage.

I was grateful, at least, that Milo had seen fit to give us a carriage to ourselves, though there was little privacy with the crowds running alongside us, peering through the windows to catch a rare glimpse of their king and queen who had been absent from public life since their royal marriage. That would somehow have to be justified, but I knew Milo was most skilful at diverting public attention from one thing to another with just a few careful words and misdirection. That was a useful skill for a seneschal, and Milo had exceeded all expectations in that respect.

Frankly, I felt more like a kitchen maid than a queen in my ragged dress. The beauty of its gold and green fabric had been destroyed by potato mud and being hurled around in the back of a cart. A warm glow spread through me at the memory of Idris's firm touch when lacing the bodice, and our faces side-by-side in the looking glass. For now, though, my hair looked like a mess, and I would have some ugly trailing purple welts running down my neck from where the rope had dug into me.

Idris fared little better, though he seemed to bear it more like a royal than I could muster. He looked battle weary, but determined and full of hope. I hadn't noticed before how the muscle in his cheek twitched when he set his jaw with that look of gritty single-mindedness.

He caught me looking and I turned my head, filled with shyness as though this was the first time I had met him. Well, I suppose it was in a way. We were betrothed to one another without having seen each other, without knowing each other, and then led astray by circumstances out of our control. It was the first time we were seeing each other for what we really were. This was the man my mother had meant me to marry. Gods... if only she knew.

And would he still want me when he could have any bride in the entire Western Isles?

'We shall have the ceremony we should have had the first time,' he said, reading my thoughts. 'We'll declare it a public holiday and pave the streets with as much joy as the royal coffers can spare.'

'Which may not be much, since Abiel Morda has been siphoning off funds to the church while you have been otherwise indisposed,' I said with a snort. He had a calculating look in his eye. This was a side to Idris I had not before seen.

'I think we may look to the seneschal to set us straight on that one.'

*Interesting.* Milo had played his part well. So well that I had never been quite sure where his loyalties lay. I was still not sure I could entirely trust myself to his care, although, to my knowledge, he had never once compromised my position. He had also never once taken me into his confidence.

I looked out of the window at the buoyant people, trying to keep up with the carriage but falling slowly behind, and eventually left waving in our wake. Looking back at Idris, I realised I was always the last person to know what the demon had been going on in Tordre.

'How long have you known?' I said.

That measured look again.

He paused for a long while and watched me, before looking out of the window, his thoughts distant. 'It was necessary,' he said. 'Necessary to ensure that everyone played their part, which allowed us to take control once and for all and put our enemies down for good. The people won't be so quick to judge in the future.'

A dawning realisation crept over me. *How long had he known?* The question was redundant.

I looked out of the window again at the disappearing people, as the track unfolded onto the country road and the trees of the forest flew past, replacing the unequivocal reverence of our public entourage. I could envisage the trees bowing towards us as the wind carried us back to Castle Ryemont.

A sick sense of betrayal stirred in the pit of my stomach. Perhaps he had always known.

# CHAPTER THIRTY-FOUR

## Accusations and Recriminations

I returned to my suite of rooms in a daze. Lack of sleep, food, and want of a good bath could be the cause of my ill feeling, but after all those needs had been met, and I stood in my antechamber while Lana fussed around me, I was left with a sour taste in my mouth.

With access now to all the gowns and accoutrements that accompany being a queen, I wore a red and gold dress with wide sweeping sleeves and a train that followed me around the room with my every step. Lana had threaded my hair with glistening gems that sparkled in the setting sun.

'Your Majesty.' Lana's head moved from side to side as she watched me pace up and down in front of the window. Cara sat on the windowsill, watching me with feline curiosity. 'You look so beautiful. Do not fret that the king is so delayed, he must surely have his own needs to attend to.'

I looked up at her face. I had no doubt now about Lana. Since we had rescued her from the dungeons, she had a renewed loyalty about her. Right then, she had a pleading expression.

'Thank you, Lana. You always say the right thing,' I said, and reached out for her hands to give them a reassuring squeeze. 'Please let the king know I await his presence.' Lana gave me a nervous smile, curtsied, and left. There were two castle guards outside my door. Had I replaced one cage for another?

I went over every encounter with Idris leading up to today and could not find a crack in his story, apart from the moment in the carriage when he had all but admitted he knew all along what had been going on. Would a king switch themselves with a fake to show his people how good he could be in comparison? It was a long stretch of the imagination, and a whole crazy length to go to in order to prove a point. Surely the better course of action was to prove to your people through your own actions. None of it made sense to me, but I had to know. I turned and strode towards the door, and threw it open to find myself nose-to-nose with Idris.

He looked strained, worry creasing his brow. His hair was brushed out and flicked over his shoulder to frame his face in the same way that the priest-king had favoured. He wore a green and gold doublet with a white silken shirt underneath, and green hose that flattered his legs. He wore the baldric and a sword and belt as though he were ready to deal with any latent skirmishes in the castle.

Perhaps he was on his way out to somewhere else, to deal with whatever affairs the king needed to deal with in this hour of restoration. He hadn't really come to see his queen at all. I was probably a second thought, if I was his queen at all. I determined by the look on his face that he had something important to tell me, so I stepped back into the antechamber and allowed him in. I might as well get it over with.

'So… '

'Nerys,' he reached for my hand, but I snatched it away. It hurt too much to see him like this, so beautiful and regal. Close enough to be within reach, and yet so far from what I had expected.

'You lied to me.'

'It's not what you think-'

'Wait,' I held up my hand. I had to think this through and get it right in my head. 'You agreed to this marriage?'

He dropped his head. Was that shame? Was he ashamed to admit he wanted to marry me? He lifted his chin and settled his gaze on me. Yes, he knew what he was entering into. He was party to the original conversations between our families.

'Was it you at the betrothal ceremony?'

He smiled at me the same way he did the day I first arrived in Tordre, when our paths had crossed for the first time. We were not meant to see each other before the ceremony, but our attendants had misjudged their timing, and as we passed each other our eyes met and something had sparked inside me, a little beacon of hope. It had all been dashed when we were married. 'But we weren't married, were we? Because it wasn't you taking the marriage vows.'

He took a step back, and wiped a hand across his face as though to pull away the mask of deceit. I should have realised this and understood it better right from the start. I had undergone weeks of study about Tordre, on the political system, the royal

191

family, customs and festivities, religion. I should have known. The country was struggling after the passing of the old king and queen. It struggled to hold on to its identity, or to build a new identity with a king thrown into office in the thick of mourning. Amid a nation mourning, the Blue King was crowned.

'So you agreed to a pact with Abiel Morda?' I turned my back on him, it pained me too much to see his expression. 'A pact to instate a false king, to bring the people to heel, to create a false sense of security, and then to dash it all with a new constitution. Just in time to bring you back to save the day. How very clever.' I snapped around to catch his look of surprise. Yes, surprise. Surprise that I had uncovered the truth.

'Nerys, please...' he reached for me again, but I spun away and paced the room, my skirts trailing in my wake.

'Only you couldn't save the day how you had planned, because Kerrin came along and reset the entire focus. Suddenly it became a people's revolution, and you had no choice but to play her game until the time was right.' My anger was boiling now that I'd put all the pieces together and spoken aloud what I dared not suspect until that moment. I couldn't look at him, it was too much. I even felt a shred of empathy for Kerrin and Tristan, who sat alone in the dungeons awaiting an uncertain fate.

'And I fell for it,' I said to myself with renewed clarity. It explained the money going out to the church of the one god. It wasn't Abiel Morda siphoning money at all, it was payment for a service; a service to king and country. 'Tell me, was I just a tool to you? Something to use and discard once I had played my part?' I stopped pacing and looked up.

'No, Nerys... please, let me explain.' He looked forlorn, his expression pained, but I wasn't about to fall for that again. He reached for my hands but I pulled away, and his arms dropped to his side.

'Think about what you are saying... can you just-'

'Don't. I don't want to hear any more of your lies.' I folded my arms across my chest. His eyes seemed to cloud over, and he shook his head with a small smile. Was that a smile of resignation, or of triumph? Well, the only thing he had triumphed over was securing his kingdom back. But it would be a lonely one. At least, one without this queen. 'I'll pack my trunk and expect a carriage before nightfall.' I turned away and a lump rose in my throat. He moved behind me and tried to put his hands on my shoulders, but I shrugged him off.

'As you wish,' he said in a soft voice. I heard the door shut behind him, and I dropped to my knees to sob into my lap.

My dress pooled around me like a shroud of flames. I wished it would swallow me up and take away all the awful things I had said to Idris. In the end he had not tried to deny it. He had stood there and taken the accusations.

Cara sat on the windowsill and stared at me. She turned and with a flick of the tail, leapt out of the window and onto the parapet outside, disappearing. *Great, even the cat hates me.*

For some time, I sat on the floor trying to get my thoughts together and motivate myself to prepare for the journey. This time they would not stop me at the borders. I would seek Bax and send a letter home, and this time my letter would reach my family. They might not like what I had to say, but I could not marry a man who lied and manoeuvred his way into the public grace in the way that he had.

Lana returned to my rooms with a look of misery on her face. I wanted to reassure her, make her feel better, but there was nothing I could say.

'Please pack a light trunk for two day's travel and... whatever you think I might need,' I said, moving to the door. She curtsied, but there were tears in her eyes. 'The king?'

She shook her head. 'He has taken to his rooms and will see no one, your Majesty,' she said, her voice cracking.

'I see. Perhaps that is best.' At least I wouldn't bump into him whilst I sought Bax. I left the room and the guard outside made to follow me, but I turned around quick sharp.

'Don't. Just... don't,' I said.

'But, the king said... until we are quite sure all is safe in the castle,' the guard said.

'I don't care what his Majesty said.' My voice was bitter. 'I discharge you from your duty.' And at that, I stalked off down the corridor. He didn't follow me.

I made my way down the eastern staircase and took a right turn that led to the tutorial rooms, hoping that I might find Bax and that he had survived the castle siege with enough sensibility to meet my immediate needs.

As I swept along the corridors, staff stopped at regular intervals to offer a deep curtsy to me. I bowed my head in response. In normal times I would have stopped to talk to them, but I had only one thought in mind and that was to get out of that place before my heart broke.

The great hall was silent but for a few maids and kitchen folk who scurried around, setting places at the table. I passed the king's solar, an annex of the hall where he entertained private guests. Outside the small room, the soft strum of a lute filled the air with its sweet melody and I stopped in my tracks, doubling back out of curiosity.

Perhaps the king's bard had survived the mayhem and was practising for the next grand feast. The notes had a sad, lilting quality, with a familiarity that made my stomach flutter. I stood by the door to the solar and looked through the tiniest crack, which transported me back to the tavern in T'sar, when I looked into a very different room. What I saw, however, was very familiar. I saw the same effortless touch on the instrument, fingers strumming across the strings, eyes closed, head leaning just so, and silent words whispered across open lips.

He looked up and stared straight at me. I gasped and stepped back, about to run, but Tristan called out to me with a voice so small and broken it made all my own concerns fade into the background.

'Please…' he gestured for me to enter and I hesitated. Was it a trap? Had he somehow escaped the dungeons and was planning a coup from the inside? I inched the door open further and looked around, half expecting Kerrin to pop up from somewhere.

His lips curled up in a smile to himself, but it was a genuine smile. This was a different man, a humble man. He stood up as I took a seat, then lowered himself back down. Despite a change of clothes and a good bath, Tristan looked ragged and worn, a look that I feared might sit with him for years to come.

'I'm sorry. For what happened to you,' I said.

He shook his head. 'It is me who should apologise to you.'

'You didn't know what you were doing, it is not your fault.' I placed a hand across his. His skin felt clammy and his hand trembled. He smiled again in that sad, remote way.

'Our king is a truly magnanimous man,' he said. My back stiffened. He caught the nuance and glanced at me. 'You don't think?'

'We... I... we all had our part to play,' I said.

'I know you feel you've been played. The gods know we all have. But the king was in a dark place when this all happened. I had never known him to be so distracted. I tried every uplifting melody and humorous ditty in my repertoire, but to no avail. Nothing would lift him free of the chains of mourning. Perhaps it was a blessing that the priesthood took him and made him forget. Perhaps that is indeed the power of faith, it accepts those who need to see or feel differently.'

'But,' now I was confused, 'did he not have a hand in bringing the Archbishop to Tordre?'

Tristan jerked his head up. 'What? No. Idris despised the man. He was about to ban religious fanaticism in his new constitution.'

'But I thought...'

'What?'

'No... never mind.' What had I done? I had ruined the one chance given to me to make this whole sorry affair right. I had the memory of Idris's hurt expression imprinted on the back of my eyelids. He had looked like a little boy, lost in a sea of emotion that he did not fully understand.

I cursed my damned imagination. 'Were... are you close?'

Tristan had a faraway look in his eye. He strummed a few chords which brought him back into the room. 'That bit is at least true. We did indeed grow up together, but we were never on an equal footing. He was always going to be a king, and I was always going to be a bard. I suppose I did harbour envy, which opened the door to the likes of the high priestess who is no sister of either of us.'

'What will happen to her?'

'They will probably excommunicate her. Hanging is not the king's style.'

'And you?'

Tristan gazed at me. 'I live to serve the king, and as I said, he is a magnanimous man. What about you, my queen? How will your story end?'

I didn't know what to say. I didn't know how I felt. Perhaps it was moot anyway, as I had probably ruined any chances I had at being Idris's queen. I had hurt him when he was most vulnerable. He had escaped a dark place only to be slammed back into reality. The reality of having to deal with such profound damage to his beloved country. What he needed most was an ally, an equal to share the burden.

Tristan must have registered the look of panic and shame on my face, as a flicker of that cheeky smile peered out from beneath the cloud of remorse that enshrouded him. 'Perhaps you'd rather marry a minstrel, your Majesty?'

The moment was gone and he returned to his self-reflection, lightly plucking the strings of his lute. In my heart, I knew Tristan would be okay.

As for Idris and myself... well, that was another matter.

# CHAPTER THIRTY-FIVE

## *Nerys' Final Verse*

I ran back the way I had come, taking the castle steps two at a time. I had to hold fistfuls of fabric up to my waist to stop myself tripping over my damned skirts. After this was over, I would have the seamstresses craft me some clothing that was more practical to wear, queen or not. I put the idea of returning to Carentan on hold for the moment, and if at the end of that day I still needed to leave, then so be it. At least I had tried.

I looped around the corridors of the inner keep to approach the royal apartments from the opposite direction and came upon the old king and queen's room where Idris had taken up residence. Outside the doors were four castle guards, two on either side. I stepped up to the door, breathless and hurried. I went to push on the door but they crossed their spears in front of the entrance stopping me. *Well that was rude.*

I took a step back.

'I am your queen. Let me see the king.'

'Your Majesty,' the two guards who had stopped me could not have looked more uncomfortable. They withdrew their weapons, but stepped in front of the door. They went down on one knee to reduce their towering height and so they looked up at me. I put on my haughtiest royal face and glared at them.

'You will let me pass. I have vital information for the king. I must see him,' I said. They looked at each other, then at the floor.

'Your Majesty. The king specifically told us not to allow you passage.'

My stomach felt queasy and a lump formed in my throat. 'What do you mean, specifically? Specifically me, the queen, or specifically no person, as in anyone?'

The two guards stayed silent and looked at the floor. They resembled two small children who had got caught in between their parents fighting. They didn't need to respond for me to know the answer, it was written all over their faces. I stamped my foot and screamed my frustration at the closed door. The guards winced but held their position, so I had no option but to retreat.

For a while, I paced up and down outside the door. I figured that if I stayed there long enough, eventually he would have to come out. The guards watched me with worried expressions, probably hoping I would go away so they didn't have to deal with the explosion when the king finally stepped out of his rooms.

'Your Majesty.' One guard was trying to get my attention, but I continued to pace; pace and think. 'Your Majesty-'

'What?' I stopped and threw up my hands, instantly regretting it when I saw the look of empathy on the guard's face. 'I'm sorry... I am worried about the king.'

'He always used to have blue moods, especially after the old king and queen passed away. Sometimes he didn't come out for days, and one time he stayed in there for over a week.'

I stood agog. *A week?* But someone must go in at some time... he must eat, after all. I would wait until the servants arrived with supper and try to talk to him then, or at least let him know I was there. I continued my pacing for a while, but soon I had an idea. I turned on my heels and raced off to my rooms, leaving the king's guards to puzzle over their queen's strange behaviour.

The guards outside my door stepped to one side as I rushed past them. They knew what was good for them. Inside my vestibule, a tearful Lana loaded a handful of dresses into a trunk. She looked up, saw me, and then started sobbing.

'Y... your Majesty. You cannot mean to leave like this?'

I ran a hand along the side of the massive trunk. 'This is light?' I said. 'I would hate to see what you would pack for a long trip.' Despite her misery, Lana managed a small smile.

'You are coming back aren't you, your Majesty?'

I smiled at the question. She was not ready to let go either.

'Lana, take a moment's rest, I may not have to go at all. But first, I need your help to get out of this ridiculous dress.' She wiped her eyes and we bundled into the dressing room.

I emerged after much deliberation wearing the only pair of trews and tunic we could find, which had been rescued from my previous escapade, washed up, and placed back on my shelves by some well-meaning maid.

Lana was horrified at first but calmed down somewhat when I explained. She helped me to bundle my hair up into a net and pin it in place so that it wouldn't distract me from climbing in and out of windows. Then, before she knew it, I was up and out of the room via the vestibule window.

I landed like a cat on all fours and crouched down so as not to be seen by any nosy onlookers from the other side of the keep. This time there would be no stopping at Milo's window, and no distractions from wandering mountain cats. Cara was nowhere to be seen. Perhaps she had claimed her stake and was keeping the king all to herself. Well, we couldn't have that. Especially since she had taken such pains to connect us together in the first place.

I crawled along at a pace that seemed to take an age until I was directly below the windowsill of Idris's rooms. I don't know why I hadn't realised before that they were his rooms; he had been so at ease with them when we had escaped from the dungeons and, now that I thought on it, familiar with where to find what he had needed. The weapons, the clothes, the unmade bed, it had all screamed of the absence of one man.

And Cara. She had been sleeping on his bed.

*Oh, Lord.* I had slept in his bed. Despite it being dark and there being no one around to see, my cheeks burned with an embarrassed blush. I sat there beneath his window for as long as I dared, listening to the silence of the evening and taking long deep breaths.

The stillness of the castle and the deathly silence of the king's rooms made my back quiver. Perhaps he was sleeping. That would explain it, but the thought made me angry. How could he sleep when I was boiling over with turmoil? They said he had done this before, retreated to his rooms for days… weeks. Maybe that was how he dealt with troublesome issues, by cutting himself off from everyone. It wasn't healthy. My father always said you had to talk things through. He claimed it was the foundation of a good marriage and a strong political alliance. Forget everything that had gone before, it was my duty to make this work.

I peered up above the windowsill. The anteroom was empty but for the flickering candles in the wall sconces. Fortunately for me he had left the shutters open, allowing me to slither my

199

body over the threshold and land with a muffled thump on the floor.

I stayed in a crouched position and listened to the sounds of the room. Nothing. No sound, other than a faint cough and the shuffling of feet from outside the main door. The guards were doing their duty, oblivious to the shenanigans of their libertarian royals behind the closed doors. I stood up, keeping my ears attuned whilst my eyes adjusted to the light of the room.

He walked right in, head bowed, hypnotically pacing as though he had done nothing less for several hours. My whole body was alive with a rush of energy that creeped across my skin like a blush. I thought I would explode. I stood still and held my breath. A frown creased his brow, and he mumbled something to himself.

He was about to turn on his heel and retreat into the bedchamber when he looked up and saw me. His hair was a beautiful mess over his shoulder, as though he had been raking his hands through it for the last few hours. He had taken off the doublet, and his silk shirt was half untucked and unbuttoned, revealing the soft bare skin of his chest. My whole body burned with desire for him.

We stood looking at each other. I had gotten this far but had no notion of what to say or do next. His frown turned to surprise, then shock, then after what seemed an eternity, a soft smile played at his lips and he gently shook his head.

'They… wouldn't let me in, so I…' I waved a vague hand at the main door, then behind me at the open window. Cara trotted in and walked up to me, rubbing her head and the length of her golden body against my legs.

'Hardly fitting for the Queen of Tordre,' he said.

'Well… you know. Never let it be said that I shy away from a challenge.' I meant to sound confident, but my voice quivered. He laughed. *Was he laughing with me or at me?*

'Strange way of packing for your trip home. Did you forget something?' He was playing with me now. The indignant Carentan princess rose to the bait, but I quashed her back down by remembering all the awful things I had said to him earlier. I lowered my gaze, then looked back at the window, desperate to run but forcing myself to stand my ground.

'Yes,' I said. 'My husband.' He had no words to say to that, so we stood staring at each other. I wish I knew what was going on inside his head. Should I stay, run, hide?

'Is this how it is to be, then?' he said. 'You berate me with your words, not allowing a beaten man to get a word in edgeways, threaten to leave, then sneak into my chambers in the still of night?' His face was deadpan, his voice serious. My insides turned to a queasy mush.

'Let me explain.' I moved towards him, but he took a step back and held up his hands as though he couldn't stand to have me any closer.

'Well, that's very interesting,' he said. 'Should I let you explain, when you wouldn't let me?'

The shock of his words was tempered by a small twitch of a smile in the corner of his mouth. Oh, he was good, perhaps I had met my match after all.

'But-'

'Should I expect anything less of a woman who would beat a man senseless with a skillet?'

I threw up my hands. 'But, I was-'

He couldn't stop himself from laughing. I was half angry, half scared, and wholly confused. While his face was turned I launched myself at him, wrapping my hands around his slender neck and planted my lips onto his. He jerked back at first, perhaps out of surprise. I looked into the deep pools of his eyes and saw that his desire burned like a furnace.

If there was any doubt left in my mind, it was obliterated in that moment. He pulled away and looked down into my face, his fingers tracing a line across my cheek. He fiddled with the net in my hair and glanced down at my attire.

'You are going to be quite the trend-setter for the noble houses. Fashion is a fickle preoccupation in Tordre,' he said with a wry look. He pulled out a few pins and tossed away the hair net, letting my dark locks flow around my shoulders. 'Better,' he said, and before I could retort, he smothered me with his lips.

He hooked one arm behind my shoulders and the other underneath my legs, lifting me as though I weighed nothing, and carried me into his bedchamber. As he lay me down I had the sudden irrational thought about how this might look to those

201

who knew the truth. He leaned towards me, and I pressed a hand to his chest. His heart galloped beneath my fingertips.

'Should we?'

He gazed at me, took my hand in his, and kissed me right in the centre of my palm. It sent a rush of energy through me. He continued to plant small kisses on my cheeks and my neck.

'Technically... we... are married. The... only thing... missing... is-'

Every last barrier came tumbling down, and I sank into his embrace.

**The End**

# About the author

FG Laval is an author of fantasy fiction, who lives in London, UK and has been writing and creating stories for over thirty years. It was a love of reading fantasy fiction that sparked a desire to write and to share the joy that she has found in authors like Tamora Pierce, Sharon Shinn, Robin McKinley, Megan Whelan Turner and Martha Wells.

The first three novels in the Carentan Series were co-written with her Dad, before he passed away in 2016. She now writes under the name of FG Laval. She has been practising martial arts for as long as she has been writing, which comes in handy for those fight scenes in epic fantasy. Themes of love, loss and coming-of-age reverberate through her books and stories.

www.francesgow.co.uk

Other books by FG Laval

The Prince of Carentan (2020)
The King of Carentan (2020)
The Prince and the Assassin (2021)

I hope you enjoyed reading The Blue King as much I enjoyed writing it. Please consider leaving a review to help other readers to find it and I would love to connect with you in any of the ways below. Look forward to hearing from you.

FREE ebook and updates from me here.
Follow me on BookBub.

Social Media
Twitter
Facebook
Pinterest
Tumblr
Goodreads
Instagram

# Acknowledgements

Many thanks to Charlotte Laval, my Mum and alpha reader, for her undiminished enthusiasm for my books, her encouragement for me to get them written and her dedication to reading drafts, suggesting changes and edits.

Thanks to the Orbiter #5 of the British Science Fiction Association, who read through some early drafts of this book. Particular thanks to Pam Baddeley and Mjke Wood for beta reading the first completed draft and making invaluable observations that have shaped the final version.

For his insightful critique and editing, I thank Geoff Nelder, author of Sci-Fi novels, The ARIA trilogy, and The Flying Crooked series of novellas.

I would also like to thank Jon Palframan for his expert copy-editing and proofreading services.

Special thanks to Billy and Will for putting up with my mind being in another world for large chunks of time and to Damien for reading through final drafts.

Finally, I would like to thank you, my dear readers, for joining me on this journey into the world of Carentan. If you would like more on the background of the Western Isles, including geopolitical notes and a map, please visit: www.carentan.co.uk

Printed in Great Britain
by Amazon

80131168R00120